CW01465460

WEDDING BELLS FOR THE EAST END LIBRARY GIRLS

PATRICIA MCBRIDE

B
Boldwood

First published in Great Britain in 2025 by Boldwood Books Ltd.

Copyright © Partricia McBride, 2025

Cover Design by Colin Thomas

Cover Images: Colin Thomas

The moral right of Patricia McBride to be identified as the author of this work has been asserted in accordance with the Copyright, Designs and Patents Act 1988.

All rights reserved. No part of this book may be reproduced in any form or by any electronic or mechanical means, including information storage and retrieval systems, without written permission from the author, except for the use of brief quotations in a book review. This book is a work of fiction and, except in the case of historical fact, any resemblance to actual persons, living or dead, is purely coincidental.

Every effort has been made to obtain the necessary permissions with reference to copyright material, both illustrative and quoted. We apologise for any omissions in this respect and will be pleased to make the appropriate acknowledgements in any future edition.

A CIP catalogue record for this book is available from the British Library.

Paperback ISBN 978-1-83633-302-9

Large Print ISBN 978-1-83633-303-6

Hardback ISBN 978-1-83633-301-2

Ebook ISBN 978-1-83633-304-3

Kindle ISBN 978-1-83633-305-0

Audio CD ISBN 978-1-83633-296-1

MP3 CD ISBN 978-1-83633-297-8

Digital audio download ISBN 978-1-83633-300-5

This book is printed on certified sustainable paper. Boldwood Books is dedicated to putting sustainability at the heart of our business. For more information please visit https://www.boldwoodbooks.com/about-us/sustainability/

Boldwood Books Ltd, 23 Bowerdean Street, London, SW6 3TN

www.boldwoodbooks.com

This book is dedicated to my lovely husband, Rick Leggatt

This page is intentionally left blank.

'I now pronounce you man and wife. You may kiss the bride!'

The small congregation smiled and clapped as Reverend Kennings concluded the wedding service in St Mark's Church in Silvertown.

Joe, smart in his army uniform, didn't need telling twice to kiss his new wife, Mavis. Their kiss was long and passionate, making the congregation laugh, and Bob, Joe's best man, put his fingers to his mouth and whistled long and loud. But, like Joe and Mavis, he was hiding a secret that might change their future forever.

The couple had met some time ago, but Joe had been posted in a different part of England, so they had to rely on letters much of the time to keep their romance afloat. But despite the distance their love had grown and grown. Joe's steady and kind personality had finally overcome Mavis's distrust of men, caused by events earlier in her life. She never thought she'd find a man she could give her heart to, not after what happened. But Joe had been patient, never pushing, always listening. She remembered the first time she'd let her guard down – how he'd held her hand and simply said, 'There's no rush, love. I'm here, I'm not going anywhere.'

As the wedding kiss ended, Cordelia and Jane, two of Mavis's friends whom she worked with, looked at each other, puzzled. Was that a stifled sob they heard from her?

But the moment soon passed, and Mavis turned to her friends and family. 'Right, you lot!' she called out. 'Drinks and sandwiches at the Dog and Drake.'

Joe laughed. 'Better do what she says. Now I've got the ball and chain round my ankle I certainly wouldn't risk doing anything else.'

Smiling, the couple walked towards the big oak door. Joyce, Mavis's adopted daughter, had been one of two bridesmaids. She left Linda, the other bridesmaid, and ran to hold her mother's hand. The three of them chatted to family and friends as they walked towards the sunshine coming through the open door.

'This is tickety-boo, isn't it?' Joe said, looking to his new bride and his stepdaughter. He bent forward and straightened Joyce's flower headdress which was a little crooked.

Cordelia and Jane, sitting together, looked at each other again. 'The smile didn't reach her eyes, did it?' Jane whispered. 'I wonder what's wrong.' Mavis had said nothing in the library about any problems.

There was no need for cars, even if the congregation had had one, or the petrol to use it. The spring day was mild and balmy, and they looked forward to the short walk.

Mavis had spent ages wondering what to wear. Her son was in his twenties and a soldier based in Scotland. 'I can't wear a white dress, I'm too long in the tooth, and no one's going to believe I'm a virgin,' she moaned to Cordelia, her boss, and Jane, her colleague. 'Trouble is, even if I 'ad the money, I'd never find something suitable to wear. I don't want to look like mutton dressed as lamb, do I?'

Cordelia had waited for her to finish her worries, then offered a suggestion. 'Mavis, don't think I'm being pushy, but would you like to see if I've got anything suitable? We're about the same size.'

Mavis's eyes widened. 'Yours? Something of yours?' She paused and looked around as if the answer were somewhere in the stacks of the library. 'But all your posh dresses must be worth a fortune. I'd be worried I'd spill me beer on it.'

But she'd given in and looked wonderful in a mid-length A-line dress in a subtle shade of cream. The elegant silhouette was made special by the beading around the neckline and cuffs. She'd found a pair of shoes to match and borrowed a hat from Cordelia as well.

At the altar, when Joe turned to see her, his eyes had sparkled. 'You look like a million dollars, love,' he whispered as he kissed her cheek. And for the first time in her life, Mavis felt beautiful.

After four years of war, the Duck and Drake had struggled to decorate their back room for the reception but managed to transform it into a makeshift celebration hall. Usually drab, it now had an air of revelry. Wooden tables and chairs were crammed together to accommodate the guests. They'd been warned that although only twenty-five people were there for lunch, many more would appear throughout the rest of the day and the evening.

Bunting, made by the library's sewing circle in patriotic colours, hung around the pub walls. Part of the library had been bombed but they'd managed to rescue some books and other items, including the bunting. It had taken a battering and had been covered in dust, but nothing a good wash couldn't fix. It looked proud up there on the walls. An old upright piano stood in one corner, a pint of beer already standing on it.

Mavis and Joe had pinched pennies since choosing their wedding day, determined to treat all their family and friends to the first drink. They walked in with Joyce, a few minutes ahead of everyone else, and immediately felt the familiar warmth of the place wrap around them. The barman and barmaid cheered loudly as they entered. 'Congratulations!' they cried and offered them any drink they wanted on the house. Within minutes, the guests arrived, and the sandwiches and drinks quickly helped to make the room full of good cheer. Joe's best man, Bob, was a dab hand on the piano and soon everyone was singing all the popular songs – 'We'll Meet Again', 'Ain't She Sweet', 'Blowing Bubbles' and many more. Joe pulled Mavis up for a dance on one of the slower numbers and several people catcalled as they watched them.

More guests arrived later, and it would have been a perfect party but for the secret only three people in the room knew.

Hot from dancing, Mavis sat next to her two colleagues, glad to rest her feet and cool down. She took off her shoes and rubbed her feet. 'I 'ope everything's going to be all right,' she muttered, seemingly to herself.

But Cordelia had heard her and worried. 'What do you mean, Mavis? Everything's going swimmingly.' As Mavis's boss, she knew her very well and knew Mavis rarely hesitated to speak her mind about anything.

Mavis looked away. 'Oh, nothing. I'm not going to worry about it now.'

Jane looked at Cordelia, their communication unspoken. Should they press Mavis to find out what she was concerned about, or leave it until another day?

Their worries were interrupted when Bob clapped his hands

loudly. 'Right, you 'orrible lot!' he shouted. 'Shut your gobs! I'm the best man and I gotta make a speech.' He raised his pint. 'So I'm not going to. I'm lousy at speeches. Instead, let's all raise a glass to my best mate Joe and his lovely bride.' His voice boomed over the crowd and the hubbub from the bar at the other side of the pub. He looked over at the newly-weds who stood holding hands. 'May your days be filled with love and laughter, and your nights be blessed with peaceful sleep.'

'Not too much sleep!' someone called out, his innuendo clear.

'So raise that glass again. To Mavis and Joe.'

The crowd needed no urging to raise their glasses and drink. 'Hear! Hear!' several people called out. 'Speech, Joe!' the cry went up.

Joe squeezed Mavis's hand. 'I'm no speech-maker either,' he said. 'So I'll just say thank you to the wonderful girl who for some strange reason agreed to marry me.' He paused and looked at Joyce. 'And thank you to Joyce for very kindly putting up with me. It means the world to us that you're all here by our side. And now... it's time to cut the cake!'

The landlady, Beryl, appeared holding a modest cake. The three librarians and several of the library users had each contributed ingredients in order to make it. Jane gave some dried fruit, Cordelia the flour, Mrs O'Connor, Mavis's neighbour, gave some sugar – a change as she was usually knocking on Mavis's door for a loan of a twist of sugar for herself. Old Bert, a grumpy library user, produced a battered little statue of a bride and groom which he'd repaired and made good. And Mavis had hoarded some coupons for scarce icing sugar. It couldn't have been better – or better represented the closeness of the people she knew and loved. As they held hands holding the knife, Mavis and Joe exchanged a fleeting glance, a shadow of tension passing between them, hinting at the unspoken worry that lingered beneath their smiles. The worry they'd decided not to share so everyone could enjoy the day along with them.

In no time at all, the cake was cut and shared. 'No point saving some for the christening!' Mavis said with a laugh. 'Let's eat the blooming lot!'

Soon everyone was singing again and Mavis particularly noticed that Jane, who was standing near her, had a wonderful voice. The library was no place for singing so she'd never realised it before.

Knowing that Jane, who could be shy sometimes, would never agree, she clapped her hands for quiet. 'I've just heard my friend Jane here singing like an angel. Now she's not a show-off type so we need to give 'er some encouragement to give us a song.' She turned to Jane, who was looking at her in horror.

'Don't...' she started.

'I'm going to ask Jane to sing something. Maybe "We'll Meet Again"?'

It took several minutes to persuade Jane to sing, and she almost ran out of the door several times and had to be pulled back. Eventually, Bob pulled her over to the piano. 'We can always get this drunken mob to join in if it gets too much for you, love,' he said with a smile.

Trembling with nerves, Jane missed the first note, but no one seemed to notice, they were already singing along with her. Hearing that, she began to relax and by halfway through the number found to her surprise that she was enjoying herself.

'More! More!' people cried when she'd finished and she allowed herself to be persuaded to sing two Andrews Sisters numbers including the always popular 'Don't Sit Under the Apple Tree'.

'Wow, I didn't know you could sing,' Cordelia said when Jane rejoined her, her face flushed from success and applause.

'I can't, not really,' Jane said. 'I sing in the church choir but that's all. Now it's just around the house when no one's listening.'

Cordelia nudged her arm. 'None of your *I can't sing!* You have the most amazing voice, Jane. You could go in for competitions.'

Jane went pink and picked up their glasses. 'More shandy?' She looked around for Linda, her daughter, who was playing with Joyce. 'I'd better get off before too long or madam over there will be ratty all day tomorrow.'

'Before you go,' Cordelia said. 'Have you noticed that there's something... I don't know... not right with Mavis and Joe? Is it my imagination?'

'I saw it too,' Jane said. 'But perhaps it's just nerves.'

Cordelia laughed. 'Mavis? Nerves? That woman has nerves of steel.' She shrugged. 'Perhaps it's just the attention or perhaps my dress is a bit too tight... or her shoes hurt. We'll see on Monday.'

But the wedding reception hadn't finished yet, and something was about to disrupt it.

2

The siren sounded, its eerie wail sending a chill through the crowd.

'Damn!' Jane's voice was harsh with worry.

Her daughter Linda heard her. 'Mummy! You sweared. That's naughty!'

But there was no time to discuss it. They all needed to get to safety quickly. The nearest shelter big enough for them all was Canning Town Underground station. 'We can't talk about it now, Linda,' Jane said, reaching for her daughter's hand. 'We've got to run to the shelter.'

Behind her, the landlord was all action. 'Quick, you lot,' he shouted. 'Grab all the grub and grog!' They didn't need telling twice.

They sprinted towards the shelter, urged on by ARP wardens. Staggering under the weight of the food and drink, they were determined not to miss a good knees-up even if it was underground.

Mavis's shoes caught on a crack in the pavement, and she

stumbled. Joe managed to catch her before she fell, although she was still holding her posy of flowers.

'Give them to me, love,' her new husband said, reaching for them. He held her other hand tight.

They made a chaotic, ragtag procession, a mismatched parade of finery and fear, all dashing towards the station's entrance.

Despite their rush to get to safety, almost everyone around them looked at the wedding couple. 'Good luck, you two!' an elderly man shouted, his voice hardly heard over the din.

Soon they huddled in the depths of the station, sweat beading on their foreheads and under their arms as bodies pressed close to bodies. The dank air hung heavy with the mingled scents of so many people and anxious perspiration. Yet despite these disadvantages and the unwelcome disruption to their plans, the wedding guests were in high spirits.

Jane looked around, her mood briefly dropping. Was this how weddings should be celebrated? Should they be grateful to be alive at all? What would life be like if the German army did invade? She was smart enough to know the news they heard probably didn't tell the whole picture of what was happening to those countries that had already been invaded. But what she'd heard was terrifying. She shivered at the thought and swallowed hard to get control.

Luckily Linda distracted her. 'Look, Mum,' she said in a stage whisper that carried halfway down the platform. 'That lady's got a big spot on her nose and it's as red as Rudolph's!' Jane's face went as red as the lady's nose, and she hastily changed the subject.

There wasn't enough space for all the wedding party to stay together. But bridegroom Joe soon sorted that out.

'Ay, you lot!' he shouted over the muffled sound of the siren.

'We'd all like to be together 'cos me and the lovely bride here just got hitched. Would you all shift along a bit so we can all stay together?'

'Do I get to kiss the bride?' a man's voice piped up.

His wife's elbow connected with his ribs with a resounding thwack. 'Not on your life, sunshine. You'll be lucky if you get a cup of tea tonight!'

The landlord had taken charge of the food, somehow having organised it in some shopping bags he'd wisely snatched before leaving the pub.

'Come on then, who wants a sandwich?'

A young lad put up his hand so high it was like he was trying to reach the ceiling of the shelter. 'Me! I like sandwiches!'

The landlord passed him one. 'Don't you go dropping that, fella me lad,' he said with a smile. 'Who knew running from bombs would make everyone so hungry!'

'Do we get any wedding cake?' someone else shouted.

Mavis stood and looked at all the kind people sitting on the platform. Some of them were regulars at the library, others were just people she'd seen around Silvertown. The rest were strangers to her. It was never comfortable being down there, but Londoners had had three years to get used to it.

'Not enough cake, I'm afraid. Most of it's cardboard!' This brought howls of laughter. After years of rationing, cardboard cakes weren't unusual. 'But what I will do,' she went on, 'is throw my bouquet.'

Following a long tradition at weddings, she turned and threw her flowers over her head behind her. Whoever caught it was said to be next to get married. She turned round to see a very elderly man holding it, looking amused. 'Okay, I'm game,' he laughed. 'Anyone want an oldie? I still know a few tricks!' Then with a smile he threw the flowers again and this time a young woman caught them. She buried her face in the petals, looking thrilled.

Cordelia couldn't help but wish it had been her. Was every wedding she saw going to unsettle her? Going to trigger her fear that something terrible might happen to her boyfriend Robert before the endless war finally finished?

But the wedding party wasn't settled yet. Dressed in their Sunday best, they looked around at the grubby tiled floor. Mavis's bottom lip trembled as she imagined sitting there in the lovely dress she had borrowed from Cordelia.

Luckily a kind old man who hadn't got a hair on his head or a tooth in his mouth spoke up. "Ere, love, you can't sit down in that there posh dress. I always bring a blanket with me down 'ere. You borrow it!'

Mavis was so delighted at the stranger's generosity that she went over and kissed him. There was a glorious round of applause and much whooping as others noticed. 'You after a new bloke already, love?' someone shouted. She blew him a kiss in response and then went back to her new husband.

Within minutes, the wedding reception was underway again. Sandwiches and tarts were shared out, hands were used as plates, teeth as knives. Crumbs fell on Sunday best clothes, but no one cared.

A fair bit of alcohol had found its way underground and as the revellers drank more, the noise level increased. 'Come on, Jane, give us a song!' the best man pleaded.

'Yes, go on, Mummy,' Linda pleaded. 'I like it when you sing. I can sing with you.'

The alcohol had overcome Jane's nerves. 'Come on then, sweetheart, we'll sing together.' She pulled Linda to her feet and put her arm around her shoulders. 'Do you know "Over the Rainbow"?' she whispered.

Linda looked at her as if she was crazy. 'Of course I do, you sing it all the time, Mummy.'

Many of the people sheltering in the station were looking at them, urging them on. 'Go on, gel. Let's 'ave a good ole sing-song!'

'Right, take a deep breath, Linda,' Jane said, squeezing her shoulder. 'One, two, three...'

They sang for half an hour and most of the audience sang along with them, some with tears in their eyes. All the old favourites: 'It's a Long Way to Tipperary', 'Kiss Me Goodnight, Sergeant Major', 'Run, Rabbit, Run' and 'The Lambeth Walk' among them.

'Did you notice that bloke in the grey overcoat listening to you singing?' Mavis asked Jane when she'd finished.

Jane looked around, easily spotting the man who looked more prosperous than most East Enders. 'No, I didn't notice him. Why did you mention it?'

Mavis shook her head. 'I dunno. We all enjoyed it, but he seemed to be taking notes, not just listening.'

'That's strange, I wonder what that's all about,' Jane replied, but Linda wanting her attention soon made her forget all about it.

It didn't take long before the food and drink supplies began to run out and there was no way to replace them. As people reached for a sandwich or broke off a piece of pie and stuffed it in their mouth, or grabbed one of the few bottles of beer, tempers began to fray. The stuffy atmosphere and endless mosquitoes didn't help.

Mavis clapped her hands. 'Oy, you lot, no rows at my wedding...' She might spend her days in the quiet library but she still knew how to shout loudly if she needed to.

'It wouldn't be an East End wedding without a punch-up!' someone called out.

'Well, not at my wedding. Slow down, the lot of you! No one gets anything to eat or drink for another fifteen minutes. If we're lucky the all-clear will sound by then.'

'Fifteen minutes!' one man shouted. 'I'll die of thirst by then.'

'No, you won't, and this is my wedding. Our wedding, our rules, so just behave yourselves.'

Mavis's new husband watched her with admiration as she handled the situation. There was plenty of moaning, but it soon subsided, especially when people looked around and saw those who weren't part of the wedding party had a lot less.

'It's not the celebration they wanted, but it's going well, isn't it?' Cordelia said, sitting near Jane. Even though Jane and Mavis worked for her, they were close friends after years of working together.

As the laughter and singing continued, Jane's attention was once again caught by the man in the grey overcoat. He was still writing, his face unreadable. She felt a flicker of unease as he looked up, caught her eye and quickly looked back at his note-book again. But she pushed the thought aside, her daughter's enjoyment of the occasion was all that mattered.

3

Sunday mornings in Silvertown were quieter than other days but never completely peaceful. As her heels clicked on the pock-marked pavements, Cordelia could hear familiar sounds from the Thames, the clanging and groaning of dock machinery, the calls of men shouting instructions to each other, all piercing the relative Sunday quiet. Even in wartime, some work never ceased.

'Hello, library lady,' a ginger-haired girl said as she whizzed by on her scooter. A few seconds later there was the sound of a crash and the girl howling.

Cordelia turned and hurried to her. The girl was sitting on the pavement clutching her bleeding knee and trying to suppress her sobs. Her scooter, unharmed, lay on its side next to her. She wore a flowery cotton dress that was a tad too small and shoes that were a tad too big. Quite a few children in Silvertown didn't have shoes, or shared them with a sibling, so she was doing well.

'Oh dear,' Cordelia said. 'You have been in the wars.' She bent down to the girl's level. 'I recognise you. You come to the storytelling sessions at the library, don't you?'

The little girl nodded. 'Yes,' she said, her voice wavering. 'I liked that story about the girl what flied to the moon.'

It wasn't one Cordelia knew, because Jane ran most of the children's sessions, sometimes helped by Tom, a part-time member of staff. 'Shall I have a look at your knee?' Cordelia asked. 'I think it's bleeding a little bit. What's your name, by the way?'

'It's Lily, like the flower, my mum always says. My sisters are Rose and Daisy.' Her sobs had already subsided.

Cordelia gently prised the girl's fingers from her knee. It was just a graze and there was only the smallest amount of blood. 'You need to go home and give your knee a good wash,' she said. 'You don't want any nasty germs getting in there, do you?'

'Germs make you ill, don't they?' Lily said, the injury all but forgotten.

'They certainly can.' Cordelia reached for a hankie in her handbag. 'Tell you what, I'll tie this round your knee to keep it safe until you get home. How about that?'

Lily nodded again. 'Will the next story be about brave girls?'

Cordelia was busy trying to tie her hankie round the knee, sure it would fall off quickly. 'I don't know, sweetheart. You'll have to come next time to see. You all right to get back on your scooter now?'

Lily was up in a trice. 'Thanks, missus,' she said and was immediately on her way.

Cordelia smiled as she walked on, hoping that one day she would have children of her own. That they would be as lively and questioning as little Lily. She'd never discussed having children with her boyfriend Robert. Would he want them, she wondered. It would be terrible if they had different ideas about that. But then she remembered how often she'd seen him treating young patients, always kind and giving them plenty of time. Surely that was a sign he liked them.

She continued on her way. Despite it almost being time for church services, no bells rang. The government had forbidden them except for exceptional circumstances, and although Cordelia wasn't one to attend church, she missed the comforting sound of the bells. She passed a few families, dressed in their Sunday best, walking towards St Mark's. Many men would be in the pub soon while their wives struggled with rationing to find the necessary for what passed for a Sunday dinner.

The early-summer wind picked up, blowing her hair and bringing with it the smell of diesel from the docks and the mouth-watering smell from Mrs Donovan's bakery on the next corner. Many people in Silvertown had no oven so there was always a queue for bread. Some made their own dough but took it to the bakers' to be cooked. A flock of pigeons erupted from a rooftop opposite and swooped to pick up any dropped crumbs, making Cordelia jump and bringing her out of her thoughts from the wedding the day before.

Mavis had looked beautiful in Cordelia's dress, so different from her usual practical clothes. Cordelia recalled the day Mavis and Joe had met. It was when they found little Joyce as they were helping to clear a recently bombed house looking for survivors. Joyce had been one of them, but sadly both her parents were dead.

Yes, Joe had been kind and supportive towards Mavis all the time as far as Cordelia knew so she couldn't believe he'd done anything dreadful. What could have happened between them to make Mavis seem so edgy and jittery on what should have been her happiest day? Mavis could have been hiding something, but that would be unlikely. She was the most open person in Silvertown. It couldn't have been anything he'd done, could it? If not, what on earth could it be?

Deep in thought, she walked on towards her destination. Almost walked past it. All available women were expected to do some sort of war work on top of their regular jobs. Cordelia had chosen packing boxes for soldiers. It was easy work, requiring little concentration, which was a relief after a busy day at the library.

She went into the familiar building, a side room of a smaller Silvertown church. To her surprise, she didn't know either of the other two volunteers already there. Usually, she knew one or both of them.

'Hello,' she said with a smile as she took off her coat. 'I'm Cordelia, I'm sorry if I'm a bit late.'

'Don't worry your loaf,' the younger of the two women said. 'We've only bin 'ere five minutes. I'm Rita, and this 'ere...' she indicated the other volunteer, 'she's Elsie. I could do with a cuppa. Want to get the kettle on?'

Her middle-aged companion frowned. 'And I like to be called Mrs Lee, thank you very much.' She looked at Cordelia, who was busy filling the kettle. 'I'd appreciate it if you didn't call me by my first name. I may invite you to call me Elsie when I get to know you better.'

'Listen to 'er,' Rita said. 'You're a bit up yourself, ain't ya, Mrs Lee? But Cordelia 'ere sounds a lot posher to me.'

The fact that Cordelia was Lady Cordelia Carmichael was supposed to be secret. She never mentioned it except to influence officials occasionally. Better to keep it quiet.

''Ey,' Rita said a few minutes later when Cordelia passed her her tea. ''Aven't I seen you in the book van what comes to the factory?'

Cordelia smiled again. 'You have. I thought I recognised you.'

As she spoke, she began sorting out her table area, ready to fold
and pack boxes. 'Have you found books you like?'

Rita picked up a small piece of paper and gave it a lipstick
kiss before putting it into the box in front of her. 'To cheer up
the poor sod what gets it,' she said. Then she paused and looked
up. 'My boyfriend, Ben, 'is mum's about to peg it. Got any books
that might cheer 'er up?'

'Perhaps your boyfriend could come in one day, Rita, and
pick up a couple that might be right for her.'

Cordelia looked down at the unfolded box and the items to
load into them – tinned fruit, biscuits, sugar, boiled sweets, soap,
razor blades, toothbrushes and some warm items knitted by
other volunteers, hats, gloves and scarves. She began folding,
her mind still on the problem of what had upset Mavis.

They worked in silence for a few minutes with only the
ticking of the wall clock and the heating kettle to keep them
company, then Rita spoke again. 'Ay, you're the clever one,
Cordelia. My boyfriend Ben wants to do some... what do you call
it... family history. You got any books that might 'elp 'im?'

'Of course she has,' Mrs Lee said. 'It's a library.'

'You're right, Mrs Lee, but since we were bombed last year
we have fewer books in our temporary home. But I'm pretty sure
we do have some that would help. And the other librarians and I
would know other ways your boyfriend could do more research.'

They were interrupted by the door suddenly bursting open,
making them all jump. A gangly lad of about fourteen, wearing
a cap too small for his head, stumbled in, struggling to carry a
box almost as big as himself.

'Delivery for the soldier boxes!' he announced, proudly but
slightly out of breath. He took a step forward and his badly
fitting boot caught on an uneven floorboard. He fell forward,

dropping the box, arms windmilling. The contents spilled across the floor in a cascade of tins, packets and loose items.

'For goodness' sake!' Mrs Lee said, glaring at him. 'Be more careful, you clumsy idiot!'

Rita just laughed. 'Blimey, mate! You know 'ow to make an entrance, don't ya!'

Cordelia, practical as ever, worried about him, aware his cheeks were pink with embarrassment. 'Are you okay?' she asked.

'Yeah,' he said and hurried out without another word.

Mrs Lee sighed loudly. 'Young people these days,' she muttered. 'Hopeless!'

'Ay, mind your mouth,' Rita replied. 'I'm young and I fill just as many boxes as you.'

Silently Cordelia groaned. Was she going to be on duty with these two often? There was a war on and the last thing they needed was more stress.

They all continued sorting the fallen goods and finished their shift in silence. It was more peaceful that way.

Little could Cordelia know how the conversation with Rita would develop in the future.

4

Pale sunlight filtered through the small bedroom window, illuminating the faded handmade patchwork bedspread and sparse furniture. She'd died here, Ben's mother, only a few days earlier, and he had just returned from the funeral. His task now was to sort out her belongings. He couldn't bring himself to do it before. Couldn't even step into her room. This was the last action in closing the chapter of her life, and the weight of it was heavy on his mind.

Mrs Charles, the next-door neighbour, had lived alongside him and his mother since they'd moved there several years earlier.

'Take my advice, love,' she'd said as they shared fish paste sandwiches at the wake in a nearby pub. 'Horrible job sorting someone's stuff but get a system going. Things to be thrown away, things to go to the jumble, things to pass on and things to keep. I've 'ad to do it a few times so I know what I'm on about.'

Her advice made the task sound manageable, especially as his mother had very little. He'd seen Mrs Charles's living room, crammed with trinkets, photos and embroidered bits and pieces.

He'd always thought it looked homely, but now he was glad his mother had a simpler way of living.

His sister May had been too upset to offer much advice, sobbing into her hankie throughout the whole funeral and too overwrought to go to the wake. Ben had been disappointed, they'd always been so close, he was sure she would be the first to offer help and support. Instead, it was as if she needed help herself.

'I'm sorry, Ben, love,' she said, clinging to him after the ceremony. 'I know she was always proud of you, just like I am. You're my special boy.' She'd said that all his life and he'd been glad to have a big sister who took such an interest in him. A lot more than some of his mates did and several of them had a whole stack of aunts and uncles.

He hadn't been able to register his mum's death because the registrar's office had been bombed. One of his tasks was to find her birth and marriage certificates for when it reopened somewhere. She'd been a widow, she always said, and her husband had died when she was expecting Ben. So far, he'd only found her rent and ration books, always at the ready in the drawer in the old kitchen table. But his first task had to be to find her other paperwork. They rented the tiny house, and he didn't know if he could take over the tenancy. He didn't even know if there was a contract. Often there wasn't in these poor East End houses. Some landlords didn't give them, then they'd be able to throw out tenants at a moment's notice.

So he had to search her bedroom, although as a boy he'd never been allowed in. He stood in the doorway, his heart pounding, like a disobedient child. The room seemed to hold its breath waiting. Each step inside felt like a betrayal, an unwelcome acceptance that he would never see her again. He'd put off the moment too long.

Pulling open the worn dresser drawers, he sifted carefully through the contents. The top drawer held her underwear and nightclothes and a few accessories like scarves, gloves and knitted hats. He spread them out on the bed and sorted them into piles like Mrs Charles suggested. His mother wasn't one to spend money on herself and in any case never had much at all. So most of the contents of the drawers wouldn't be worth even passing on to a jumble sale.

The second drawer held three blouses, two hand-knitted jumpers and a cardigan. She'd worn all them so often it broke his heart to see them there, tidily folded but lifeless. He picked up a navy-blue jumper and pressed it to his face. Could he really smell the lavender soap she used or was it his imagination? Again, he put them on the bed. They could all go to the jumble, although he'd offer them to Mrs Charles first.

Sighing, Ben opened the bottom drawer. It was bedding and towels. Just enough of each to change his bed, his mother's and for them to have a towel each. He would keep them all, but first removed them to see if anything else was there. And there at the bottom was a big envelope with a single word on the front: 'Papers'.

Picking up the envelope, he went downstairs, put on the kettle and sat at the table while it boiled. The table's solid wooden surface held so many childhood memories. This was where they'd eaten their meals, where his mother had sorted out her weekly money and got ready for the knock of the rent man, where he'd done his childish drawings and later home-work from school. Now though, without the warmth of her pres-ence it felt alien, unwelcoming. As if he was seeing it for the first time.

The kettle began to whistle as he was laying the few docu-ments out on the table. He poured the boiling water into the pot, almost forgetting to only make half the amount he had been making ever since he was shown how. He'd let standards drop a little since his mother's death but made himself wash his cup and saucer and take it to the table.

A knock at the door brought him out of his sad reverie. It was Mrs Charles again. She was a stick-thin woman with a kind face, etched with the lines of a lifetime of hardship. Her eyes, though tired, sparkled with life.

'Here, I made these for you,' she said, holding out a plate. It held half a dozen biscuits. 'Sorry it's not much, love,' she went on, 'but tomorrow's payday and I'm running out of almost everything.' She looked over his shoulder. 'Sorting out her paperwork? Want a hand?'

He wanted to say no, but she'd been like another auntie for as long as he could remember. Until he went into the army. He couldn't leave her on the doorstep. 'Come on in,' he said instead. 'The kettle's just boiled. Share a biscuit and a cuppa with me.'

He pushed some of the papers aside, so she had a space for her cup and saucer.

'How're you getting on, love?' she asked.

He bit his lip. 'Well, it's been tough with Mum dying just when I... got discharged because of being partially blinded in one eye.' He couldn't go on, couldn't say how guilty he felt that he had been in hospital when his mother was going downhill. He'd written, of course, but she only wrote short letters back full of sympathy and saying all was well with her. It wasn't. 'I only wish I was here at the end. I hate to think of her dying alone.'

Mrs Charles reached over and put her hand over his. 'She died in her sleep, love. She wouldn't have known anything about it. It's the way we all want to go.'

He looked up suddenly. 'You saw her then?'

'You know what me and your mum was like, always popping

in and out. I knocked on the door to borrow some sugar and when she didn't answer I went round the back. It was a shock, I can tell you. I ran to get the doctor and that librarian lady what lays out folks around here.'

It was some consolation that his mother had died peacefully, but it still tore him apart. She could be strict with him, giving him a clout round the ear if he didn't behave, but he had lots of cuddles and love too.

'You make a good cup of tea,' Mrs Charles said, biscuit in one hand, cup in the other. 'You going to stay here now?'

He nodded. 'I suppose so. I've already got a job in one of the factories.'

But Mrs Charles wasn't listening. She was looking at one of the papers on the table and frowning. 'That's strange,' she said, pulling it towards her. 'This is your mum's birth certificate, isn't it?'

'It must be. I haven't looked through these papers yet. I only just brought them downstairs.'

Mrs Charles picked it up and peered at it, her brow furrowing. 'This is odd. It doesn't add up,' she muttered, more to herself than to him.

'What is it?' he asked, trying to hide the rising worry in his voice.

She didn't answer immediately but held the paper closer, squinting at the dates. 'I'm looking at her date of birth, that'd make her...' She began counting on her fingers. 'I must be getting it wrong. She'd have had to be fifty-five when she had you. That's... well, I've never heard of that.' He wasn't really listening and she spoke again. 'How old was your mum when she passed away, do you know?'

He shook his head. 'No idea. She always said you don't ask a lady her age. But she always seemed older than my mates' mums.'

'It'll be on her death certificate. Do you have that?'

He went to the drawer and took out the certificate the doctor had left. He'd been so upset he hadn't looked at it. 'It says... it says... she was seventy-nine.' His jaw dropped open. 'That's not possible.' His head filled with confusion and his stomach twisted with anxiety. 'This must be a mistake.'

Mrs Charles pushed the birth certificate towards him. 'That would tie up with this certificate. I'm sorry, love, but your mum wasn't your mum.'

5

'I'll be glad when we move out of this place,' Cordelia said, looking around their temporary library. 'I suppose we're lucky our old library will be repaired soon. This place is too small for the job.'

Jane looked at the clock on the wall of the school gym that was their current home. 'That's strange. Mavis is late. Not like her. I wonder if everything's okay after the wedding.' She grinned. 'Surely she'd never still have a headache.' She chuckled. 'Or still be in bed!'

They'd never got used to having the gym as their library. The emergency services had done a grand job of saving most of the book stacks and more than half the books after part of the library had been bombed. It wasn't the same though. The old library building had a long history, its weathered walls and creaking floors speaking of generations of Silvertown people using the knowledge and stories it contained. The musty scent of aged paper would have been eradicated when a portion of the building collapsed.

'I keep thinking of all the work we did to get the library

ready for the King and Queen's visit last year,' Jane said sadly. 'Fit for royalty it was.' She giggled at her silly pun, then looked at the clock again. 'Tell you what I don't miss, that's Bert knocking on the door dead on the dot of nine. Now he has to wait until all the schoolkids are in their classrooms.'

As if he'd heard his name, Bert strode in, squeezed past the crowded stacks and headed over to the newspaper table after a grunted greeting. As usual, he didn't look at the librarians but instead opened the papers at the sports section.

Two minutes later, Mavis burst in through the doors, her face flushed pink and hair escaping from its usual neat style. The soulless school gym echoed with the hollow thud of her footsteps as she crossed the polished hardwood floor. Devoid of the familiar scents of old books and tea at the old library, this cavernous room held only the scent of smelly children and cleaning products. Overhead lights glared down harshly, casting an unflattering light that accentuated the tension in her jaw as she negotiated her way towards her friends.

'Sorry, girls,' she said, avoiding their eyes. 'Couldn't be 'elped.'

Cordelia looked around. Bert was the only one in the library so far, so she called Mavis over to the makeshift 'office' she'd made by moving some furniture around to give herself a corner to work in. It wasn't completely private but needs must.

'Sit down, Mavis,' she said, indicating the chair opposite her desk that was really one of the school desks. 'What's up? You're never late and you never have a poker face. Something's wrong.'

Mavis sighed and put her handbag down beside her knee. The normally strong woman who never showed weakness sat shaking her head, a single tear rolling down her face. 'It's Joe. He's...'

Her voice, normally so confident, quivered. She stopped and

got her hankie out of her pocket. She fidgeted with the edges then wiped her face and blew her nose, still avoiding her boss's eyes.

Cordelia waited without speaking, sensing that, whatever it was, Mavis had to tell it in her own way and her own time. Her heart ached with worry for her friend. Only two days after their wedding, had Joe died? Had he left her? Had she found out something so unforgivable about him that led to this uncharacteristic emotional state?

Mavis took another deep sigh and gulped. "E's, well, 'e's been posted. Abroad. Don't know where. Went this morning. That's why I'm late.' Then her eyes opened wide, and her hands flew to her mouth. 'Oh, Cordelia, I'm so sorry. Your Robert's been gone ages and 'ere's me...'

Cordelia stood up. 'Let's go outside to talk. There's nobody in the playground and it'll be more private than here.'

She glanced over at Jane and indicated what they were going to do before opening the rear door of the gym and shepherding Mavis through it. They were lucky that it was a sunny day and there was a bench they could sit on nearby.

'Never mind me or Robert. This is about you and Joe. Did you know before the wedding? Jane and I thought you didn't seem quite yourself.' She paused. 'Even as beautiful as you were.'

Wiping away another tear, Mavis nodded. 'Yes, 'e told me the night before. We 'ardly got any sleep. Wonder I didn't have big bags under me eyes on me big day.'

Reaching out to hold Mavis's hand, Cordelia let her take her time. 'That is just awful for you both. And for little Joyce too.'

Mavis looked up. 'We didn't tell 'er 'til yesterday. No point in upsetting 'er and she'd be sure to say something at the do. Then people'd talk about nothing else, and I couldn't stand going over it again and again. Joyce doesn't really understand what it could mean. Just as well.'

Hearing Mavis's news, Cordelia's mind briefly drifted back to when she first heard that her boyfriend Robert was being posted abroad. A doctor in the local hospital, he had thought he was in a reserved occupation and wouldn't be sent away. But he was wrong. She remembered her heartache at the news, wondering how she'd manage without his love and affection, whether he would live or die. Mavis must be feeling all that now.

'I'm so sorry, Mavis,' she said. 'Going away before you've even had time to start your married life. It's so unfair. Mrs Taylor, the cook in our house, always said that the waiting for news was the hardest part of war. She wasn't wrong. It's the day-to-day not knowing that's the worst.'

'You know,' Mavis said, looking down at her hands, 'I've been on me own all these years. I brought up Ken on me own and I was only sixteen when I 'ad 'im. Then I adopted Joyce. Never 'ad two pennies to me name.' She paused and shook her head. 'Finally, I find a man I can trust, one who'll look after me, and that damn 'itler goes and takes 'im away. I hope that man rots in 'ell.'

They heard a bell ring inside the school, time for the children to change lessons. Cordelia stood up. 'One thing I found that has helped me is writing to Robert regularly. You'll have stories from the library and plenty of things about what Joyce is up to. It makes me feel closer somehow, as if it will keep him safe. Silly, I know.'

Mavis stood up. 'You know, when you first came to work at the library, I thought we'd never get on. Worlds apart in every way. But you're the best boss I ever 'ad.' Taking a deep breath, she put her shoulders back and braced herself. 'Now, enough of this self-pity, girl. Work is the best way to keep your mind off worries. Worrying never fixed anything. Let's go and 'elp our readers.'

They went back into the library and Jane immediately hurried up to them, concern on her face. 'Is everything okay?' she asked, looking from one to the other. The two friends looked at each other, Cordelia not wanting to say anything unless Mavis spoke first.

She did. 'Tell you about it later, you songbird,' she said, and then changed the subject, never the type to dwell on her problems. 'I reckon you could give the Andrews Sisters a run for their money. 'Ave you ever thought of making a bit of dosh from your singing?'

Jane laughed. 'Of course not. I just like singing a bit, that's all. I'm in the church choir and they get me to do solos now and then. Mind you, Mr Hubbard, the builder who does all the work for the library, he heard me. He was there in the evening. I told him not to, but he says he's going to ask the landlord of his local pub if I can sing there.'

'Well, blow me down with a feather,' Mavis said with a laugh. 'That's brilliant. Once upon a time I couldn't get you to even look our library customers in the eye. You'll be at the Palladium yet!'

6

Saturday mornings were always busy at the library. It was a day when schoolchildren could come to choose their books, listen to story time, and people working Monday to Friday could come in. The librarians were grateful to have been given a small side room in the gym for the children's section. Without that, the sound of children's voices would have echoed around, disturbing the readers.

Cordelia noticed Mrs Gregory, a regular patron, struggling to reach a book a little too high for her. 'Let me help you,' she said. The two knew each other well. Cordelia was aware that Mrs Gregory, a young mother of two with little formal education, was keen to educate herself. Her lifelong ambition was to be a teacher. 'Oh, I see you're looking for books on study skills. Good for you! Let me know how you get on. If you like, I'll see if Canning Town library has any others.'

Mrs Gregory's smile was all the reward she needed.

'Better get this stamped and get back before the little 'un wakes up,' she said. 'See you soon.'

Cordelia was walking along the stacks returning books to

their proper place when she saw a young man open the door. He hesitated before coming in and she wondered if he'd ever been to a library before. His clothes were clean and tidy but well worn. The elbows of his jumper were carefully patched and made her think of the 'Make Do and Mend' poster on one wall. As he looked around, he took off his hat and ran his fingers through his thick brown hair.

'Can I help you?' she asked, hoping to put him at ease. 'This is our temporary home so sometimes it's hard to find things.'

He gave her a strained smile. 'Yes, thank you. That would be... I'm trying to do a bit of research... into an old manor house. A hall type of thing.'

'Come on in then and I'll see what we've got.' She took him over to the right section and, taking several books from the shelves, laid them on a small table for him to look at. Then she paused and looked at him more closely, recognising his eyes – one brown and one hazel. 'Aren't you the kind man who got our library van started once, after it broke down?'

He grinned. 'Wasn't much, just the... spark plugs. Easy when you know what... you're doing.'

'Well, we were very grateful, and I'm delighted you've come to see us. Your name's Ben, if I remember correctly. Do you need any help explaining what each book is?'

He shook his head, thanked her and got out a notebook and pencil.

Many people in Silvertown had limited education so the librarians were used to giving support in a sensitive manner. The last thing she wanted was readers to feel patronised or embarrassed. So Cordelia moved a few feet away, pretending to tidy a shelf while keeping an eye on him. He opened the first book and, licking his thumb, began to turn the pages.

Seeing the gesture, she frowned. Most people licked a finger, not a thumb. But the action created a flicker of familiarity in her mind. Who else had she seen do that?

But before she could ponder on it more, he turned to her again. 'Excuse me, miss, I... do need a bit of help. I've got the name of the hall but I'm not sure it's right. Which book... would be best to look at first?'

She went over to his stack of books. 'What's the hall called?'

His cheeks coloured. 'I'd rather not say. It's... well, it's a private matter. I might have it... wrong anyway.' He looked around, probably aware that others could overhear their conversation.

'I understand,' she said, although she didn't. Picking up the biggest book, she suggested to him he start there. 'We do have a regular library user who might be able to help you. We call him the Prof. He's not here today but if you're interested I'll put you in touch with each other. He's involved with the history society and a kind man. He likes to be helpful.'

Ben nodded and went back to looking through the pages of the book. She couldn't help but notice that his hands trembled slightly. As she walked away, she wondered why she had a powerful urge to help him. Of course, she helped all library readers, but there was something about this young man, a vulnerability that made her want to do more. She shrugged and continued on her way.

But then a movement caught her eye. The young man gasped as something slipped out of one of the books and fell on the floor. She caught a glimpse of him hastily picking it up and tucking it away, his face flushed. It was a picture of two women in maids' uniforms. She couldn't see beyond that. She dithered. Should she say something? Tell him to put it back? But no one had ever looked at that book in all the time she'd been managing the library. Probably no one ever would again. She'd let him keep it.

The door opened again, and another man walked in. Without him saying a word, it was obvious to her that he was an American GI. After years of war and rationing, few British people looked as healthy and well fed as the Yanks, as they were called.

Like the other man, he was looking for some family research. Space was limited but she retrieved the relevant books and gave them to him, indicating a table he could use.

Hearing his accent and seeing his smooth brown skin made her heart jump. The previous year she had been very close to a black GI called Eugene whose gentle manner and quick wit made her heart beat faster. It was only her love for Robert that made her stop the relationship going further. But that didn't stop her thoughts returning to him regularly. She sometimes imagined what life would be like across the ocean. If she'd married Eugene, life would have been difficult – a white woman married to a black man in America. But there was no point in thinking about that so each time she did she shook the thoughts from her mind. Robert was her future and she loved him deeply.

Some local girls had already gone to the States and stories circulated about how they were getting on. Some sounded happy while others were desperately homesick. It was bound to happen when they were going to a new country and new relatives. One girl from Silvertown, Betty, had left only the previous month and her mother was waiting anxiously for news of her. The GI's presence caused a stir among the other patrons, with curious glances and hushed whispers following him. This was despite there being American working parties active in Silvertown. Cordelia noticed how some of the younger women subtly preened themselves when the GI was near, smoothing their hair or adjusting their clothes. She smiled. The GIs were often considered a much better bet than a local man. More money, more energy, better looks and great uniforms. No wonder people often said, 'Overpaid, oversexed and over here.'

It was time for her break, and she grabbed one of the newspapers and stepped outside. Finally, it seemed as if the tide was turning in the war. The best news was that the North African campaign had ended. That was where her beloved Robert was posted, working close to the front line in a makeshift hospital. Every night she prayed that the good news meant Robert would return home soon. It had been so long, she sometimes had to look at his photo to remind herself of his lovely face.

But she knew that soldiers could be moved from one theatre of war to another. There was no certainty he would return to England and letters frequently took ages to arrive. News was often out of date by the time they were read.

She flicked her way through the paper, conscious that she too used her thumb to turn the pages. She'd never been aware of that before. How strange.

She was putting the newspaper back on the desk when Ben approached her. 'Can I borrow... these books?' he asked.

'Only the biggest one, I'm afraid,' she said. 'The others are reference books so must stay in the library. Did you have any luck?' She pushed the library application form towards him.

He pulled a pencil out of his pocket. 'I'm not sure. I might have found the place.'

'What some people do is visit the area they're researching. But that depends on how far it is, of course. They go and ask locals what they know. Do you know where it is?'

'I'm not sure but I think... it's in East Anglia somewhere. I don't think I can go there. We work all the hours God sends at the factory. There's never enough sugar, is there?' He hesitated then spoke again. 'Do you have any records of... staff who worked in these big houses?'

Cordelia bit her thumbnail. 'That's a tricky one. I think you'd probably have to go to the area. Details of ordinary staff are unlikely to be printed in anything published. Why do you want to know?'

He shook his head. 'Just... wondered, that's all.'

The penny dropped. This was Rita's boyfriend. The one she'd talked about while they were packing boxes for the troops. Should she say anything? Sometimes having that personal connection helped people feel more comfortable in an unfamiliar place. Just as easily though this young man might feel as if Rita had been talking about him behind his back.

As Cordelia walked back to her desk, another penny dropped. East Anglia – that was where her family home was. Stonehaven Hall was in a beautiful part of Norfolk, with big open skies she never tired of.

It had to be a coincidence. After all, there must be many buildings like her parents' in East Anglia.

7

Mavis had left the library early that Saturday and the other librarians were tidying up at closing time, putting away books, newspapers and periodicals. Cordelia noticed Jane looking a little distracted.

'You okay, Jane?' she asked. 'You've been biting your nails. I've never seen you do that before.'

Jane put down the book she was checking. 'Tell you the truth, I'm so frightened I can hardly think. I've been asked to sing a solo at a wedding at St Mark's this afternoon.'

'Wow,' Cordelia said. 'That's so impressive. I know you told me you do solos in church sometimes. Surely that means you've had practice. People must really love your voice.'

Rubbing out some scribbles in the margin of the book she was holding, Jane shook her head. 'That's different. They all know me and I'm not the only one who does solos. They want me to sing "O Perfect Love". I've never sung that in church except when the choir is asked to sing at weddings, never as a soloist.'

Cordelia put her hand on Jane's arm. 'I'm guessing it's

someone you know who's getting married. They must know your voice. It's beautiful. I was green with envy when I heard you sing at Mavis's wedding.'

Gently closing the book and picking up another, Jane nodded. 'Yes, it's Jenny, one of the choir. She's lovely and I don't want to let her down.' She paused and looked up at Cordelia. 'I don't suppose you... you'd... come, would you? I'd feel so much better if I knew you were there. I'd ask Mavis but I know she's laying out a body for someone down her street.' She shivered. 'I don't know how she does it, but she says the dead can't do you any harm.'

Cordelia thought of all the things she'd hoped to do that afternoon – shopping, washing, writing to Robert and, if there was time, going for a walk. She certainly hadn't planned to put on a decent dress and attend a wedding. But Jane's need was greater than hers so of course she nodded. 'I'll just sit at the back though because they'll all wonder who on earth I am.'

Three hours later, Cordelia left her flat dressed in a pretty pale-blue dress and hat. The summer sun cast its bright glare over the remains of bombed buildings, making their jagged outlines seem more defined than ever, as if an artist had drawn them with a heavy hand and a thick black pencil. Each shattered wall and crumbling façade stood starkly in the sunlight, a haunting reminder of the days of the Blitz and the destruction and deaths they had all faced.

But nature never gave up. It was reclaiming its territory. Weeds and wildflowers, resilient and full of colour, sprouted proudly through the cracks on the pavement and over the debris. As Cordelia watched, they danced in the warm breeze, softening the harsh scene and bringing a smile to her face. They reminded her that even during dreadful times there was much to look forward to.

A little girl who couldn't have been more than five years old was carefully picking some of the wildflowers. 'I'm not stealing,' she said when she spotted Cordelia, as if waiting to be accused. 'They're for my mum. She's not well.'

'I'm sure they'll make her feel a lot better,' Cordelia said with a smile. 'You're a kind girl.' She picked half a dozen herself and gave them to the girl to add to her bunch before walking on.

The air was warm and plenty of people were out in the streets. She took a detour, and walked through Rathbone Market, enjoying the scents of fruit, vegetables and spices from foreign parts. She couldn't resist her favourite stall, one that sold second-hand books. The library had lost so much of its stock she was desperate to get more. New books were difficult to buy because of the fire in Paternoster Row where five million books had burned.

She remembered walking through the streets of the East End the morning after it happened. The air had been filled with a haunting sight – fragments of burnt paper fluttered around like blackened snowflakes. She could have cried seeing the remnants of never-to-be-read books as they floated on the breeze, their charred edges curling and slowly falling. Some pieces drifted aimlessly, like falling autumn leaves, others seemed to spiral upwards as if trying to escape their fate. She would never forget the sight or the smell of all those burning stories.

The stallholder knew her and greeted her warmly. 'When's the old library reopening?' he asked as he handed a customer her change. Even on a summer day he wore his usual outfit of thick trousers, a hand-knitted jumper and a tweed coat.

'At the end of next week, all being well,' Cordelia said, crossing her fingers. 'But we lost so many books in the bombings and it's hard to buy new ones. I don't suppose you have a secret stock of second-hand books we could buy off you, do you? We don't have much money though.'

He grinned and touched the side of his nose with his forefinger. 'You might be in luck there, dearie. I don't suppose I'll have anything like as many as you need but I've got a fair few in my shed.' He stopped and scribbled his address on a scrap of paper. 'If I'm not here you'll find me at home. Come and see what you want. I'll give you a good deal.'

Cordelia walked on; her heart lightened. Before the bombing they'd had a book drive and been given a reasonable number but most of them were gone now, destroyed by one of Hitler's bombs.

She walked on, past children playing hopscotch, past street vendors selling a variety of enticing-smelling foods, past shabby shops still open for business. And past the inevitable queues outside other shops. Everything was so scarce that if people saw a queue they joined it even if they didn't know what they were queueing for. Women spent so much time queueing as well as working and looking after their families, they got little time for anything else.

The grand stone façade of St Mark's came into view. The beautiful stained-glass windows had been covered up at the start of the war but the church was still an impressive sight, surrounded by trees and early summer blooms.

She joined the people walking in and several of them nodded to her even though she didn't know them.

Jane's friend looked stunning in her dress made from parachute fabric. Her headdress was a circlet of flowers. Her soon-to-be husband looked dashing if nervous in his army uniform.

Cordelia, who was never sure about her religious beliefs, found herself entranced by the beauty of the service, the obvious love between the happy couple.

Finally, the moment arrived for Jane's solo. Cordelia, who had been sitting on the end of a pew, leaned sideways so that Jane might be able to see her. She saw Jane take a deep breath as she stood in her place, the organist playing the opening bars. Jane's eyes darted anxiously around the congregation. Cordelia could see the fear on her face but also the determination. She couldn't help but feel anxious for her friend. Would she sing as beautifully as she knew she could or would nerves spoil her performance? As her friend began the song, Cordelia listened closely, her ears straining to catch every note.

But as Jane continued to sing, Cordelia felt herself becoming more and more impressed. Jane's voice was clear and strong, and she sang with such emotion it was difficult for Cordelia to hold back tears. She looked around and could see everyone was as entranced as she was.

She felt a powerful surge of pride and admiration for her friend who had had to be persuaded to sing at all. Nonetheless she had risen to the occasion and delivered a stunning performance. As the final notes of the beautiful song faded away, Cordelia knew this was a moment neither of them would ever forget.

When Jane stopped, there was a moment of silence, then slowly at first, a ripple of applause began, growing louder as more people joined in, moved by the emotional depth of her performance. It was an uncommon gesture, but one that felt like a collective appreciation of her skills. Jane didn't know where to look as her cheeks flushed, but the bride, her friend, went and gave her a quick hug before Jane rejoined the rest of the choir, relieved to be out of the limelight.

By the end of the service, Cordelia struggled to swallow tears. The beautiful words, the lovely church and the obvious love between the couple touched her heart. Would Robert arrive home safe and sound? Would they get married? So many things could go wrong before she got her happy ever after. If she ever did.

She had no plans to go to the reception at the Rose & Crown but walked with the congregation, going towards the shops before heading home. Jane caught up with her, breathless and excited.

'Was I all right?' she asked.

Cordelia smiled. 'You were better than all right. You were magnificent.'

8

GRAND REOPENING DAY!
Something for everyone!

In the heart of Silvertown, where poverty was a daily reality, the early summer morning saw many of its residents already hard at work or making their way to their various jobs. Their footsteps mixed with the clatter of cartwheels and distant factory noises. Labourers and port workers called to each other, laughing and insulting each other jokily.

In the distance, seagulls swooped around the boats on the Thames, hoping for a tasty snack. The deep rumble of machinery from the docks and factories punctuated the air. Another busy day was beginning.

Amid the rows of soot-stained buildings, chimneys puffed smoke into the crisp air, mingling with the faint aroma of baking bread from the nearby bakery. Despite the weariness of the people of Silvertown after years of war, they moved with determination, a sense of purpose.

None more so than the librarians on this special day.

It had seemed as if it would never come. They'd been beset by one problem after another, frustrating them in their efforts to serve the community as they had before. There was a shortage of materials and a shortage of workers as so many men had been called up. At least one of the librarians had visited their much-loved old building each day to check on progress, often leaving with a heavy heart.

Again and again, they had relived that dreadful day when part of the old library building was bombed and so many books destroyed. They'd been grateful to have the school gym as a temporary home, but it had none of the atmosphere of the old library.

'I thought we'd never live to see the day,' Mavis said, wiping a tear from her cheek.

'Remember how we all stood outside that night when it was bombed. We'd just got back from a night in the West End and couldn't believe what we were seeing.' Cordelia still remembered the night with a gut-wrenching emotional response. All around them ARP men and women had been at work putting out fires caused by incendiary bombs. It was such a contrast to the time they'd just spent in a glamorous restaurant, it was like walking into a nightmare film set.

Jane shook her head, remembering. 'I don't think it really sunk in 'til the next morning. We've been through the Blitz and loads of bombing, but it was still so hard to really believe what had happened. Didn't stop me going home and crying for hours though. My landlady thought someone must have died.'

'Not someone. But something very important,' Tom said. 'And not died, just injured. Yet here it is, risen from the ashes.'

They were standing outside the library, an hour before it was due to open, hoping that all their elaborate reopening plans for the day would pay off.

They'd had so much preparation to do. Everything had to be moved from one building to the other. Books had to be put on the stacks. By begging all and sundry they'd got more books to replace some of those destroyed. Not enough, but a useful number. Many people in the East End were not keen readers beyond newspapers so couldn't donate much. They'd had to reach out further afield, like the bookseller at Rathbone Market.

Each of them had taken on tasks in readiness for the big day. Jane had arranged a special story time in the morning, and a choir of children to sing after school in the afternoon. There would also be local musicians giving a performance in the early evening. Local newspapers had been invited.

Tom, who was very artistic, volunteered to take on the task of organising an art exhibition featuring local artists of all ages. He'd been surprised at how many people in the borough were unsung artists. Much of their artwork was pencil drawings on odd bits of paper, pages out of books, torn-off bits of wallpaper. With paper rationing they had to use anything they could get their hands on.

The drawings, and occasional paintings, reflected their lives and interests. As well as images of their favourite pigeons and pets, there were heartbreaking images from the trenches of the First World War or indeed the current war. Nightmare images of the Blitz, of destroyed buildings, of injured people being carried into ambulances. Drawings by women, less of them, tended to be of people, often children. Tom's favourite was of two women leaning over a garden fence chatting, washing blowing on the breeze behind them.

He'd spent much of his own time collating the works, going to markets and jumble sales to find frames. Often he repaired them himself too. Hesitantly, he'd approached Cordelia. 'Can I put one of my own paintings up? Would that be okay?' he'd asked. Of course she agreed. All paintings were for sale and a percentage of any takings would go to the library. That included his.

Mavis had organised information sheets about library services to be handed out and pinned on the walls. The following week the Missing Persons service, IIP, would move back into the library, continuing their essential and sometimes heartbreaking work. Then there were other activities – story time for children, quilting circle and book clubs.

'My favourite,' Mavis went on as the sun rose over the rooftops and cast a rosy glow over the library, 'my favourite was the time capsule we got the builders to bury under the building. I can't remember everything we put in it. What was it now? There was an out-of-date ration book, letters from all of us...'

'Articles from local newspapers showing the library before and after the bombing,' Jane added. 'Those sad drawings from children. So many showed bombings, grieving families and houses reduced to rubble.'

'But there were cheerful ones, too,' Tom said, smiling at the memory. 'Rainbows, kids playing on their old home-made carts, and of course children reading.'

The coalman rattled past on his horse and cart. 'Good luck today, you lot!' he shouted, giving them a wave. His horse shook his mane as if in acknowledgement.

'I wonder what the world will be like when that capsule is found, if it ever is,' Cordelia pondered. 'Perhaps men will go to the moon, doctors will cure horrible diseases...' Mentioning doctors brought Robert to Cordelia's mind yet again, not that he was ever far off. In North Africa he was treating diseases he'd never come across in England. She sighed. 'But enough of that. We need to get in there and get cracking.'

'I wish Joe was 'ere to see this,' Mavis said, biting her

bottom lip. She twisted her wedding ring round her finger. It still felt so new. Usually so steadfast, thinking of her new husband made her insides quiver and her heart skip a beat. She'd always prided herself on being strong, able to cope with anything life threw at her. Even cope with things thrown at people who came to her for help. Delivering babies, laying out the deceased, writing letters to official bodies or just listening to tales of hardship and sorrow. But it was like Joe's disappearance had stolen some of her strength, had undermined the person she had always been, the very foundation of her personality.

'Any news yet?' Jane asked, seeing the slight tremor Mavis was struggling to hide. She reached out for her friend's hand.

'None, but they say it takes a while.' Mavis looked at Cordelia and Jane. 'I wish your blokes were 'ere too. I'm not the only one, am I?'

Tom, who was a conscientious objector, shook his head sadly. 'War never does anyone any good, does it? Centuries of wars and it's as if we haven't learned anything.'

An hour later, local dignitaries had joined them, and they opened the door with a sense of history being made. A small crowd stood on the pavement ready to enter.

The librarians were delighted to see some of their favourite regulars, the Prof, Mrs Gregory and little Hetty, Bert, Floppy Flossie who pretended to collapse when she needed attention and Mr Booker who used Shakespearian language all the time. Seeing them brought wide smiles to the librarians' faces. They'd all visited the temporary library but seeing them here felt as if they'd come home at last.

Soon more people poured in. They looked around, exclaiming at the familiar and the new.

Cordelia clapped for quiet and explained the programme for

the day, although few of those present would be there all the time.

'You'll remember the services we have always provided. Books, of course, newspapers, periodicals. But also the children's sessions, the sewing circles, the IIP days where the volunteers can help you trace missing loved ones, and general advice.'

She paused as more people came in and nodded a greeting. 'In the future we hope to add workshops...'

'What're you going to teach?' Bert shouted. 'Bricklaying, welding? I'd like to see that.'

Cordelia managed to keep a straight face. 'I think that's outside our ability level, Bert. But if you'd like to volunteer your services...'

Growling, he looked away.

'The workshops will be on topics we've been asked for. Improving reading, maths, filling in forms, that type of thing.' She indicated forms on the desk. 'If you or anyone you know might be interested, just sign up over there and please spread the word.'

'Can you teach my old man to stay out of the boozer?' a woman shouted.

'We'd 'ave plenty of takers for that one,' Mavis responded with a laugh. They all knew that many Silvertown women struggled to feed themselves and their children because the men went straight to the pub on payday.

Cordelia laughed along with many others. 'One last thing before we have a special treat for you. And that is over there.' She pointed to a wall at the back. 'We've covered the wall with wallpaper we rescued from the basement. It's our memory wall. You can write any memories you like.' She paused. 'They can be anecdotes about Silvertown, about the library, anything others would be interested to see. Make it clean though, children will see it!'

'Pity! I know just the thing,' a voice from the back said, causing a laugh from most and tuts from others.

'Can I draw a pigeon wearing a gas mask?' Bert asked with a grin.

Cordelia smiled back. 'We'd all love to see that! But now, time for a very special treat.'

'Are we getting sweeties?' little Hetty called out.

'Let's see what happens later, shall we?' Cordelia said. They had done their best to provide refreshments but with rationing getting tighter every week it was a challenge. Luckily, a few library regulars had offered biscuits or other small treats.

She pushed that thought aside and turned to Jane. 'Ready?' Jane looked anything but ready to perform on this special day. Cordelia had been so impressed with her singing that she'd encouraged her almost every day to begin singing in public again. 'Who knows where it will lead?'

'Rotten tomatoes in the face, most likely,' Jane muttered.

One of her teachers at school had made her stand to one side when they had choir lessons. 'Your singing is enough to make the birds fall out of the trees!' she'd sniped. The others in the class giggled at Jane's discomfort and she wanted the floor to open and swallow her whole. No matter how many people told her her teacher was very wrong and her voice now was special, she still lacked confidence in it.

But Jane had finally given in and agreed to sing at the library reopening. Cordelia was delighted to notice she wasn't resisting the idea quite as much as she had in the past.

'So,' Cordelia continued. 'Because we are all meeting again in this grand old lady of a building, Jane is going to sing a favourite Vera Lynn song.'

People shuffled about, trying to see her as she stood by the circulation desk.

'Go on,' Tom said, giving her a nudge. 'Sit on the desk, you can show off your legs if you feel like it like a lot of singers do!'

To his surprise, she climbed onto the desk but kept her flowery dress firmly over her knees. Fear made her mouth go dry and she took a sip of water she had ready at hand. Mavis had told her to remember her success doing the solo at her friend's wedding if she felt nervous. It did help remembering the beauty of the day, the flowers decorating the pews and the affection evident between the newly-weds. What helped more was being back in the building she loved. Not only that but she recognised many of the people in front of her – regular library users and even some neighbours. They all looked encouraging.

'Right, everyone,' she said, struggling to speak loudly enough to be heard over the traffic noises from outside and the low-level hubbub of children in the room. 'I'll start this song, but I want us all to join in...'

She took a deep breath, and the room hushed...

'We'll meet again...'

Within a minute everyone was singing, joining in, celebrating the library reopening. The sound of happy voices reverberated around the old building, as if thanking the books for their knowledge and for their service. Several people walking outside were drawn in by the sound and came into the library to see what was going on. Some had never been inside before. Mavis was near the door and quietly welcomed them in. New readers were always welcome.

Jane became so engrossed she didn't notice the newspaper man making notes or his colleague taking photos.

Could this event be the beginning of a new life for her?

9

The reopening had been an unqualified success. The library hummed like a beehive all day, footsteps and voices echoing off the freshly painted walls as visitors discovered its treasures. Gone was the unpleasant tang of plaster and damp. The familiar smell of books with their old pages and leather bindings mingled with the warm breath of East Enders. The building had come alive once more.

'I love that everyone seemed so happy to see the place again.' Jane sank into the nearest chair, its wood sighing under her slight weight. The librarians had just closed the door, their feet ached and their throats were hoarse with speaking all day. 'I hope that reporter gives us a good write-up. That kind of publicity could really help us get more book donations and increase our readership.'

Mavis chuckled. 'It might not be book donations that the paper concentrates on. Did you see that reporter fella taking your photo, Jane? You'd just sat up on the desk and crossed your legs. You looked like a real diva.'

Jane's smile vanished. Her hand flew to her hair, checking

for stray strands. 'What? He took my photo? Whatever will George say?'

'He'll be the envy of all the blokes in his unit having a wife like you. I don't think you need to worry. You wasn't showing anything you shouldn't.' Mavis managed to sound cheerful despite the agony of still not knowing what had happened to her new husband.

Cordelia stood up and went behind the desk. 'Well, super librarians, before we tidy up, let's drink to our success. I have a well-hidden bottle of port and some nibbles here.' She carefully unwrapped the bottle, the label barely legible after years of careful storage. She wiped four dusty glasses she'd brought from home and poured generous amounts of port in each. 'Let's drink a toast to ourselves and our old library. Long may she live!'

They all had tears in their eyes as they sipped their drinks.

'That art display was popular, Tom. Some of the artists were excitedly showing their work to their friends and once or twice I saw people look at a drawing, then wipe a tear from their eyes.'

Tom flushed with pleasure at the praise. 'We don't get many art shows around here, do we?' he reflected. 'But today proves that people in Silvertown would be interested.'

Mavis laughed. 'I guess what's coming next, young man. You suggesting art classes in the library. Let's see if any other groups do them before we jump in. We've got more than enough to keep us busy.'

She'd been spot on, he had been about to suggest that. 'Did you see my painting sold?' he said, excitement in his voice. 'My first art sale! And it was so kind of the Prof to stand guard by the paintings and take orders.'

They paused again and took another sip of their drinks and more carrot and parsnip crisps. Cordelia reached behind her and picked up a pile of papers. She quickly glanced at them.

'Look at all these new subscribers. We actually ran out of forms. I never thought that would happen. My boss will be pleased. He's always on at me to get more readers.' She lifted her glass. 'Here's to you all, thank you for the amazing work you've all done.'

'Oh!' Tom said. 'I almost forgot. One of the men came up to me for a chat. He was one of the builders renovating the place. He said they'd found an old chest down in the basement. Thought we might be interested. He said it looked really old, and they didn't have time to open it.'

A silence descended on the group. The stress of the day, the joy of the reopening, forgotten for a minute, replaced by a prickling sense of anticipation.

A slow grin spread across Cordelia's face. 'Now that,' she said, her voice laced with intrigue, 'sounds like the beginning of a proper mystery story. Where is the chest hidden?'

'They tucked it under the circulation desk. You know that awkward space that just collects dust balls.'

The room seemed to grow colder. Cordelia's eyes flicked towards the desk, imagining the ancient chest lying there, hidden from view. 'What did it look like?' she asked, her voice barely above a whisper.

'Ancient,' Tom replied, his face lit with a mixture of excitement and dread. 'Really old, the man said. Heavy wood, metal fittings. Like it hadn't been touched in decades.'

10

'Excuse me, ladies.' The library had only been open half an hour the next day when the Prof approached the desk. 'I wondered if you'd seen page two of the newspaper?'

The four of them looked up. 'I never have time in the mornings,' Mavis said. 'Is it something about our open day?'

The Prof smiled his sweet smile. He turned the newspaper around so they could see the relevant page. Cordelia's eyes opened wide, and she took it from him and began reading out loud.

'"Silvertown Library reopens its doors." That's the heading,' she read to the others.

After months of struggle, the Silvertown branch library celebrated its grand reopening on Saturday, with an open day to welcome the community back into its newly repaired space. A steady stream of eager patrons, young and old, crossed the threshold to enjoy the special events put on by the librarians...

'Gosh,' Cordelia said. 'This is great. There are a couple of photos too. One of the outside and one of the art wall.' She turned to the page opposite and gasped. 'Look at this, Jane! It's you and you look absolutely amazing!' Sure enough, there on the opposite page was a stunning photograph of Jane sitting on the front desk, her face alight with joy as she serenaded the crowd. 'You look every inch the professional singer,' Cordelia continued.

Astonished, Jane snatched the paper from her and peered at it, unable to believe her eyes. 'Good grief,' she said, her mouth dry. 'I look... I look...' The other two peered over her shoulder to see the photo, and the Prof, who had already seen it, was smiling.

'You look enchanting, my dear,' he said. 'And your voice was enchanting also. I have been to concerts where the singers were nowhere near as good as you. I wonder if you have considered any professional engagements.'

Jane looked at him open-mouthed. 'Professional? Um, I'm not a professional. I just like to sing sometimes.'

Mavis nudged her. 'Yeah, but you sang at that wedding and at the pub. You're getting well known. Several people around town 'ave mentioned you.'

Jane's jaw dropped open. 'Me? They mentioned me?'

Mavis grinned. 'They did, cross my 'eart and 'ope to die.'

The Prof nodded, encouraging Jane to consider the possibility. 'You may not be professional, my dear, but you have natural talent. I am a firm believer in using and honing any talents we have.'

Jane was sitting still as a statue, as if she couldn't absorb what was being said. Cordelia, seeing her hesitation, put an arm around her shoulders. 'You are a wonderful librarian, Jane, with a special gift for helping children. We can each have more than one gift though. It looks as if this is a second one you have. I'm jealous.'

'Me too!' Mavis said.

Jane blushed, still too surprised to know what to say next. 'I don't know... I'm just an ordinary housewife and mother...'

'And librarian,' the Prof added. 'And singer.'

'And you ain't ordinary neither,' Mavis said, nudging her again. Mavis chuckled and, picking up a roll of newspaper, pretended it was a microphone. She sang the first few words to 'I'll Be Seeing You'. Then she laughed again. 'Come on, Jane. Before you know it we'll all be saying, "I used to work with 'er, right pain she was!"'

Jane play punched her arm. 'Stop it. You are all just being silly. It's just a stupid pipe dream and not even my pipe dream.'

The Prof leaned forward, his eyes twinkling. 'Jane, may I call you that? Sometimes the most extraordinary things happen to ordinary people. There are lots of quotes I like about this. "Jump and the net will appear..."'

'Jump where?' Mavis interrupted.

Cordelia interrupted her. 'He means take a risk and somehow it will turn out right.'

Mavis scoffed. 'Tell that to one of the blokes in our street. 'E's a gambler. Takes risks every day and loses a lot more dosh than 'e wins.'

The Prof laughed. 'Well, those are stupid risks. I believe in taking well-researched risks. In my life I've taken many and one thing I always ask myself is what can go wrong? Can I live with it if it does? I find it helps me to make a better judgement.'

Jane fiddled with the pencil she was holding, turning it over and over in her hands. What could go wrong, she wondered.

'I can see you're wondering,' Cordelia said.

Nodding, Jane bit her bottom lip. 'What if I try and it does go wrong? In any case, I wouldn't even know where to start.'

'Blimey O'Reilly,' Mavis said with a grin. 'No one's asking you to give up the day job, are they? You'd just continue being the world's best librarian.' She looked at Cordelia. 'No offence meant!'

'None taken.' She looked at Jane. 'Just think of the King. He's had a stutter all his life and rumour has it he's terrified of making speeches, but he does it. We're always glad to hear him too, even if he does have little hiccups.'

Jane had never been more pleased to see two elderly ladies approach the desk. She pushed the others aside to help them. The conversation was ended.

For now.

That night sleep was a long time coming for Jane, her head full of the conversation, but eventually she drifted off and the dreams came...

She was on stage, but not somewhere she'd ever been before. Somewhere beautiful, elegant, gracious. Crystal chandeliers floated overhead like some weird barrage balloon. The light from the chandeliers caught the jewels of the ladies sitting facing the stage.

As often happens in dreams, things changed, morphed. The room was at one time Victorian, then the library, then Victorian again.

Jane saw herself on stage singing. Her voice was as amazing as ever, but the song kept changing. There were snatches of old songs from the Great War, some Gracie Fields songs and some that sounded Indian.

From the stage, Jane saw a lady sitting perfectly upright, her dark hair swept up with an elaborate comb. It was unlike any she had ever seen, glittering, magical.

Jane was jolted awake by the sound of the milkman's horse and cart and the clatter of milk bottles being put on the doorstep.

Her heart thudding, she sat upright, unsure for a moment where she was. She remembered snatches of the dream. The comb. The chandeliers. The music. But none of it made sense.

Shaking her head, she looked at the clock. It was almost time to get up. Throwing the covers aside, she shivered. Somehow, she felt a connection with the woman in her dream, but how?

Then little Linda came into the room and the dream was forgotten. At least for now.

11

All thoughts of investigating the mysterious chest had been pushed aside because of the opening event, but now, although dog-tired at the end of the next day, they decided to open it. They dragged the chest out from under the circulation desk. Its once proud surface was now a tapestry of scratches and dents. The iron bands that reinforced it were pitted and corroded, proof of countless encounters with the elements.

'Cor, let's see what's inside,' Mavis said, excitement in her voice. But try as they might, they couldn't get the lock to budge however much they twisted and tugged at it.

Cordelia sat back and sighed. 'I don't know about all of you, but I'm too tired to fight with this now, much less inspect the contents.' She tapped the top of it. 'It's been down there waiting to be opened for goodness knows how many years. Another day won't do any harm. Why don't we just push it back and look tomorrow? We've still got tidying up to do.'

'I think it's a bit spooky,' Jane said, a frown on her forehead. 'If it was hidden away, whoever owned it didn't want it found. I feel a bit uneasy about it.'

Mavis laughed. 'Come on, girl. You just sang before a whole load of people and now you're scared of this. Where's your gumption?'

'Upped and gone, I think,' Jane replied. 'I'm too tired to think about it now. Cordelia's right, let's leave it until tomorrow.'

The other three groaned, got to their feet and began tidying. But even as they worked they were talking about the exciting find.

'I wonder why it was hidden?' Jane asked as she reorganised the children's area.

'It's like something from a children's book,' Tom replied with a laugh, remembering the sort of books he read as a lad.

'Perhaps it's full of secret codes to win the war,' Mavis said.

'It'll be the last war then,' Cordelia said, stacking books. 'It's been there too long for this one.'

As she continued on her way home the light was fading. Blackout curtains were already drawn tight in most of the buildings she passed, the last slivers of daylight surrendering to the indigo dust. Each step she took seemed to swallow a little more of the evening, the bomb sites around her dissolving into shadows deeper than the craters themselves.

Her feet ached but as her mind moved on from the events of the day, her thoughts returned to the chest they had found. Mavis insisted there had always been a rumour about hidden treasure in the building. Jane continued to feel uneasy about it as if the chest contained something evil, something best left alone. Only Tom and herself were open-minded as to what they might find. But his comments about books he'd read reminded her of games she used to play with her brother Jasper. If it wasn't cowboys and Indians, it was pirates. Of course, he was the pirate and she was his mate, or sometimes his captive. But a chest full of treasure was always part of the story he made up.

A smile touched her lips as she recalled how seriously Jasper had taken his role, determined to be the winner in whatever they were doing. He'd made eyepatches from old rags he'd begged from Mrs Taylor, the cook, and a wooden spoon as a cutlass. He'd bury his 'treasure' – usually some old buttons, or broken pieces of crockery – in the garden, drawing maps on scraps of paper which he soon lost.

Bored, wanting to read her book instead of play his games, Cordelia nonetheless went along with them. Could this chest, she wondered as she took her key out of her bag, hold a different kind of treasure? Not anything valuable like gold or silver, but something of a different kind of promise – part of the past, a story waiting to be told. The thought spurred her on as she walked up the stairs to her flat. Although she'd suggested waiting until morning to find a way to open the chest, explore the contents, she itched to try now. Perhaps Mavis's rumours held a nugget of truth, and tomorrow they would find themselves face to face with a different sort of treasure.

12

Morning light filtered through the blast paper on the windows, painting patterns across the dusty library floor. Cordelia, arriving earlier than usual, felt a prickle of anticipation run down her spine. It was probably her imagination, she thought, but the library seemed to hum with a different energy this morning, the silence thick with unspoken secrets.

She went through to her office. She'd seen a bunch of old keys somewhere ages ago. She put down her bag and took off her coat, trying to remember where. But everything had been moved after the bombing. It was possible the keys were buried deep in the ground, never to be found. She hunted through her desk, papers reminding her of the quarterly returns she had to submit. Then she hunted through the filing cabinets and her bookshelves. Nothing.

Chastising herself for spending her time this way, she nonetheless went to the circulation desk and started rummaging in the drawers there.

Then, when she was just about to admit defeat, she found them – the old keys. Half a dozen keys on a metal ring, the sort you'd expect a prison warden to carry. She remembered when she'd first started working at the library she'd tried them in every door, every cupboard, but they fitted nowhere. But still she couldn't bring herself to throw them away. If they hadn't been tucked away unnoticed, she would have given them up to the government for their Pots and Pans for Victory campaign.

She was so engrossed in what she was doing that a floor-board creaking behind her made her jump. Mavis's cheerful voice broke the silence. 'Couldn't wait for the rest of us to come in then?' she chuckled, her eyes twinkling with mischief as she saw what Cordelia was doing. 'I don't know what we'll find in that chest, but it'll give me something to write to Joe about.'

Cordelia looked at her properly. 'Have you heard from him?'

Mavis's grin faded. 'No, but I'm going to keep writing to him. I just know he's still alive. The letters will find their way to him sometime.' She paused and Cordelia saw her make an effort to put her fear aside. 'We'd better not open that chest before Jane and Tom get in or they'll murder us,' Mavis continued. 'Well, Jane might not. I'd never 'ad 'er down as superstitious but she seems to feel there's something odd about it.'

It was a busy day and none of them had time to look at the chest for several hours. The opening day had certainly had an effect. They had their busiest morning ever. New readers needed help finding books, others had decided overnight to come and join. The librarians worked flat out.

Finally, early afternoon, there was a lull. 'Shall we try to open it?' Cordelia asked the others as they sat drinking tea. 'I found a bunch of old keys...'

'The ones in the drawer in the circulation desk?' Jane asked. 'They've been there since before my day.'

Cordelia nodded. 'Shall we see if any of them work?'

Keeping an eye open for readers needing help, they began

moving the chest. It scraped across the floorboards, the groans of forgotten time bumping into the present. More dust motes rose into the beam of midday light, swirling like ghosts disturbed from their rest.

Despite their age, the brass fittings winked in the light coming through the window as Cordelia and Mavis hoisted the chest onto a chair. Ancient wood creaked under the weight of decades of secrets.

'Are you sure we should do this?' Jane's voice had a slight tremor. 'What if we don't like what we find?'

Mavis scoffed. 'Then we'll throw it away, won't we? This isn't Tutankhamun's tomb, is it? No terrible curses to worry about.'

Cordelia had the bunch of keys in her hand and picked the one that looked most likely. She hesitated a moment before pushing it in. The key resisted at first, but with a gentle wriggle and twist, it slowly sank into the weathered keyhole. The three women scarcely dared to breathe. She was about to turn it when Tom came back from his break.

'Hey, you didn't wait for me!' he said with a smile and stood next to them.

'Wiggle it about,' Mavis advised. 'I 'ave to do that with my front door key.'

'But what if it breaks?' Jane said.

Cordelia twisted it this way and that until it sank further into place. For a moment they all held their breath.

The chest hadn't been open for goodness knows how long, and each of them had been imagining what lay inside. Treasure, gold and diamond jewellery, maps, love letters, old photographs of seances, coins – all these ideas had floated through their minds. Now they would find out if their imaginings were anything like reality.

The lid resisted briefly then gave way with a groan that

seemed to echo through the library like the opening of a crypt. More dust motes danced in the shaft of sunlight that pierced the dark wood as the heavy lid creaked open.

For a moment, they all froze. The air that drifted up from the chest was stale and cold, smelling faintly of lavender and something else... something unfamiliar and unsettling. Was it metallic, sharp, almost like blood?

They all leaned forward to see the contents, heads close together. The inside of the chest was frustratingly dark, but their eyes soon adjusted.

'Shall I... do the honours?' Cordelia asked the others, who nodded silently.

One by one she removed the objects, handling them carefully to avoid damaging them. A leather-bound book with a tarnished clasp... a bundle of letters tied with red ribbon and, lastly, something wrapped in faded velvet. Each item was carefully placed on another chair, but when Cordelia picked up the velvet-wrapped item she paused and looked to the others for permission.

'Go on, then, you daft 'aporth,' Mavis said. 'Don't keep us in suspense.'

Carefully, as if the old velvet might disintegrate, Cordelia unwrapped the item. They all gasped when they saw the beautiful old comb, the sort that was used to hold up elaborate hairstyles. It was fashioned from intricate filigree of tarnished silver, the delicate metalwork winding and curling in an elaborate design.

Then Jane reached out for the comb and without hesitation lifted the top of it, which was hinged. What she uncovered made them all gasp.

Tiny stones glinted faintly in the dim light as Cordelia gently rubbed the comb with the velvet. 'How did you know what to do?' she asked Jane, who had once again stood back.

'I don't know,' she replied, her voice shaking. 'I just sort of knew.'

'Wow,' Tom said, turning the comb over in his hands. 'I wonder if those stones are real. It might be worth a bit. It's beautiful.'

The four of them looked at each other, then looked again at the items.

'Well, we have a mystery on our hands. We just have to find who this belonged to.'

13

At home that evening, Cordelia made herself a simple meal, then fetched the letters they had found in the chest.

'I think we should split up looking at this lot,' Mavis had said. 'We're all busy and, nosy as I am, I'm not sure I've got time to read everything.'

Tom nodded. 'I'd like to research the comb. I've no idea how, but I'm a librarian for heaven's sake, so I'll work it out.'

Cordelia smiled. They were all pretty good at finding things, but Tom was definitely the best. 'Well, I'll read the letters, if you look at the journal, Mavis, there's no hurry is there?' Then she looked at Jane. 'Do you want to be involved?'

Jane shook her head. 'No, it doesn't feel right somehow. I'll leave it to you. You can tell me what you find though.'

There were a dozen letters tied up with red ribbon. As Cordelia took them from her bag a faint, musty smell wafted up from the fragile parchment, a blend of aged paper and the subtle scent of wood from the ancient chest. She held them to her nose. Was it her imagination or could she smell a hint of vanilla or bergamot?

The fragrance briefly transported Cordelia back to the time when the letters were written. She had no idea when that was but allowed herself to imagine the hands that had carefully held the pen, writing each word with love. She immediately compared the paper these were written on with what she used to write to Robert. The 'blueys' were light blue, thin pre-gummed sheets that folded to form an envelope. Combining the letter and envelope saved weight. They cost 3d to send anywhere in the world. Squeezing all she wanted to say meant that her writing got smaller and smaller as the weeks went by. By comparison the paper these letters were written on was luxurious.

Feeling she must treat the mystery letters with respect, Cordelia gently untied the bow on the red ribbon and placed it on her table. There were no envelopes, only the letters written in a very old-fashioned handwriting, covered in a fine layer of dust.

She ran her fingers along the edges, feeling the texture of the paper – a tangible connection to the past and the history of the letter writer. She imagined she could hear the whispers of those long-ago voices, although she guessed the letters would only tell one side of the story. They must have been read over and over again. As she tried to open the top one it almost fell apart in her hands along the folds.

Even before she read the salutation, 'My dearest Evelyn', she guessed the letter was written by a man. The handwriting had a distinctive, formal style of years gone by. Each letter was crafted with deliberate, elegant precision – the strokes confident, yet flowing with an almost artistic quality. Perhaps the writer was an artist. Beside Evelyn's name was a tiny drawing of a bird. It was a style that spoke of an era defined by formality, and propriety.

Cordelia had seen photos of people of that era, and she imagined the writer. At home by a cosy fire, he might be wearing a velvet smoking jacket in a rich burgundy. Surely he would have a moustache that he fingered occasionally.

She had a notebook at the ready to record any important points so she could share them with the others. Finally, as if she had delayed tasting a fine wine, she began to read:

My dearest Evelyn,

How can I thank you enough for your wonderful gift? The leather-bound diary is something I will treasure for ever. I promise you I will use it to pour out my deepest thoughts and longings that I would share with no one but you.

They are calling this situation I find myself in the Indian Mutiny. I am horrified to report that it has erupted with a fury that none of us could have anticipated. I cannot tell you the detail, for I would never wish those images to be forged into your brain as they are in mine.

I think of you constantly, Evelyn. The memory of you, of your beauty, calms me in the most dreadful moments. I so long to be by your side, to feel your delicate hand in mine, to lose myself in your embrace. Alas, our secret love must remain in the shadows, lest it bring ruin down upon both of us. If only it were not so. Daily, I curse the circumstances that force me to keep our affections hidden, to steal so few precious moments together like thieves in the night. Yet, my darling, I would not trade those moments for all the treasures in the world.

I must bring this letter to a close, for the messenger awaits, and I must not miss him. But, dear heart, know that my heart beats for you and I long to be with you once more.

Your dearest

J x

Cordelia sat back when she finished reading the first letter, touched by the passion and longing it contained. She had read about the Indian Mutiny. The accounts of the British brutality and bloodshed horrified her. She couldn't help but wonder if the British response had been too harsh. It was no surprise that it bred resentment, tarnishing the empire's reputation and increasing a growing anti-colonial sentiment across the globe.

Yet J, whoever he was, was caught up in it. He must have had horrifying experiences. Reading his letter was like stepping back in time, listening to a voice from history. His letter provided a glimpse of human experience during the rebellion.

She was deeply moved by his love for Evelyn and wondered why the two had to keep their love hidden. There were so many possible reasons. Perhaps one of them was married or engaged to someone else, perhaps they were from different backgrounds, or their parents forbade their relationship. In that period attitudes would have been different from the 1940s when such restraints could still sometimes apply.

Cordelia gently put the letter aside and stood up. Turning off the light, she opened the curtains and looked outside. She peered out into the hushed, moonlit evening. As always, the blackout had covered the street in a blanket of darkness, save for the gentle glow of the crescent moon above. Her mind on the letter, she made out the shadowy silhouettes of nearby houses, their details obscured by the darkness. A couple walked by, using their shielded torches that wove a pattern on the pavement as they progressed. She opened her window and caught their laughter as they passed by.

What had happened to Evelyn, she wondered as she gazed at the night. Would the remainder of the letters reveal all? Why had they been in a chest in the library? And what was the significance of the beautiful comb?

Closing the curtains, she turned on the light and made herself a cup of tea, needing the strength to read more. The next letter read:

My dearest Evelyn,

I pray this finds you well, my love. Letters my colleagues receive from home tell of your struggles to find certain goods that are normally imported from India.

But you will be aware of things there. Here, the mutiny has spread at a terrible speed, engulfing more of the countryside each day. I will not tell you the details for fear of upsetting you. However, I find myself increasingly confined to the garrison, unable to venture out yet determined to help my compatriots whenever possible.

I console myself with memories of our time together. That time we had tea in that little tea shop with the pretty embroidered tablecloths you so admired. We had chosen it because it was far from either of our homes. You looked so beautiful, your skin pretty as a peach, your lips inviting. As much as we could, allowing for people around us, we talked about our feelings for each other and what we would do if we were free. Do you remember that day as I do?

Time grows short and I must go on duty. But know that I will return to you, the moment this madness has run its course. Meanwhile, you are forever in my thoughts.

Yours as always,

J x

As she worked her way slowly through the letters, Cordelia sensed the unwritten fear and desperation J felt about the situation he found himself in. It had been a bloody period, yet he had protected Evelyn from the detail.

With a shock, she realised this was exactly what Robert was doing in his letters to her. While he wrote about sandstorms and shortages of supplies, his letters must be as carefully worded as those from J.

How brave these men were. Yes, women at home suffered enormously during war. Deaths, shortages, rationing, bombings. But nothing compared to the men overseas. Another realisation forced its way into her head. She'd hidden the worst from Robert when she wrote to him. She didn't tell him about the dead and mutilated bodies she had seen, the burning buildings, the frantic race to air-raid shelters. No, she was protecting him just as he was protecting her.

14

It was Mavis's Saturday off and she decided to take Joyce to the church fete. Like most children in Silvertown, Joyce loved the variety of activities on offer. Her favourite was Pin the Tail on the Donkey, a close runner with Knock the Coconut Down and Hoopla.

'Will I win this time, Mummy?' Joyce asked as they walked towards the church.

'We'll have to wait and see,' Mavis said, squeezing Joyce's small hand as they approached the church gate. The sound of a brass band floated across the green, now mostly given over to growing vegetables. It felt as if there was an empty space between them that pulsed with Joe's absence, as it did so often. Mavis imagined she could hear his laughter, see him pushing Joyce on the swings and lifting her up for a better view. Would it ever happen again?

They were lucky, it was a lovely summer day with just an occasional cloud in the sky. The sun glinted off the barrage balloons as they drifted in the breeze, making them seem almost jolly. The old yew trees provided perfect dappled shade. As they walked closer, several people stopped to chat to Mavis and pat Joyce on the head. She scowled and pushed their hands away. Already, the area was crowded with local people, all wanting to forget about the war for an hour or two.

The church grounds looked jolly, with bunting, borrowed from the library, fluttering in the breeze. There were the usual stalls. Women selling second-hand books and repaired toys, tombola, guess the weight of the cake, a white elephant selection, handicrafts, a raffle and of course a refreshment stall.

The theme was 'Dig for Victory' and they even had a couple of Land Army girls selling vegetables. There were Make Do and Mend demonstrations along with a well-known chef demonstrating some new ideas for using rationed food.

'You'd never know you two worked on the land,' Mavis said to the Land Army girls. 'You look like film stars with your victory-rolls hair and scarlet lipstick.'

The taller girl giggled. 'You should see us the rest of the time, especially after mucking out the pigs. Yuck!'

The other one play punched her. 'She does more than that, I can tell you. She spends half her time reading those romances.'

'Well, you spend your time flirting with the village lads!'

The first girl raised an eyebrow. 'It's better than dodging the damn farmer. He's far too handy for my liking!'

Their youthfulness took Mavis back to the time before a brute had violated her. At sixteen she was left broken and pregnant. Ken had often asked who his father was, and had been angry with her for her silence. She couldn't tell him, could she? His father was that rapist. She couldn't bear to think what that knowledge might do to him.

She sighed and shook away the memory, giving her attention to the Land Army girls again. 'That's not good, 'e should keep 'is 'ands to 'imself!'

The girls grinned. 'Don't worry, we're more than a match for him. We can run faster! Now, can we sell you some lovely carrots? Picked them ourselves this morning. Or this bread made by Belle, the farmer's wife?'

The smell of the home-made bread took Mavis back to happier times. To Sunday mornings with Joe when he teased her about burning the toast. 'I'd love some of that. Me and Joyce'll 'ave it with jam for our tea.'

Joyce was jumping up and down with excitement, looking at the games for children. There was a Hoopla, a treasure hunt, Sink the U-Boat, and arts and crafts.

'What do you want to go on first?' Mavis asked, keeping in mind how much money she had set aside for the event.

'Sink the U-Boat!' Joyce said. 'Is Daddy Joe a sailor sinking the nasty submarines?'

'No, sweetheart, he's not a sailor, he's a soldier.' She didn't add that as far as she was aware he was in Europe somewhere so would have had to cross the English Channel. A dangerous crossing because of those very U-boats.

The familiar figure running the stall was Mrs Gregory, a library regular. 'Hello, Mavis and Joyce,' she said with her usual smile. 'You going to try to Sink the U-Boat, Joyce?'

Joyce nodded. 'What do I have to do?'

'It's easy-peasy.' She gave the girl four small balls. 'You throw the balls at the boat and every time it goes down you get a point. If you get three points you get a raffle ticket, then you might win a good prize!'

The tiny boat never actually sank, but if it went under the water, it counted, making it easy for children. Joyce threw the balls. The boat dipped. A point! She squealed with delight. Soon she was proudly clutching her raffle ticket. As she played, Mavis's gaze went to the street edging the churchyard. A telegram boy cycled past, his knees scabbed and his hair flying. A chill went through her. They rarely brought good news.

'Any news of your old man?' Mavis asked Mrs Gregory.

'I'm a lucky one. He hasn't gone abroad yet. Somewhere in Scotland from what I can make out. Isn't your son there?'

'Do you mean Ken?' Joyce asked. 'He's my brother!'

Mrs Gregory ruffled her hair. 'And I bet he's pleased to have a sister like you. Are you going in for the fancy dress competition? Hetty is.' She looked around. 'I don't know where she's got to, but you'll be sure to bump into her.'

As they walked away, Mavis's thoughts went to Joe again. They hadn't asked Joyce to call him Daddy after the wedding, but she had found her own compromise with Daddy Joe. Perhaps one day she would shorten that, but there was no hurry.

They went around all the stalls which took ages because Mavis knew just about everyone and had to catch up with news. Mavis bought a hand-knitted dishcloth from the handicrafts stall and Joyce won a bar of soap on the raffle. Now soap was rationed that was a valuable prize.

But Joyce's bottom lip stuck out. 'I wanted the sweeties!' she whined.

'We'll get you something on the way home,' Mavis replied. She was so proud of her daughter. There were times when she was difficult. But Mavis kept in mind the girl's problem background. The head of the children's home had warned her to expect much worse.

If only Mrs Anderson could see Joyce in her fancy dress outfit. Patched together with fabric from a jumble sale, it wouldn't win any prizes for sewing but looked enough like a nurse's uniform to come third. Joyce wore her Third Prize badge with pride, touching it frequently.

The fete was winding down when, worn out, they walked

home, pulling their cardigans around them as the sun hid behind a bank of clouds.

They were grateful to flop into a chair when they got inside. 'Want to sit on my knee and I'll read you a book?' Mavis asked. But it wasn't to be. A tapping on the door made her groan and pull herself up again.

When she saw who was there, her heart sank and her mouth went dry. A telegram boy. He looked no more than twelve and the corners of his mouth turned down.

'News for you, Mrs Smith,' he almost whispered.

Mavis was on the verge of telling him he'd got the wrong house, then she remembered it was her name now. She was Mavis Smith.

Frozen to the spot, she couldn't move. 'I don't want it!' she screamed inside her head. They only brought bad news.

'Got a neighbour you can be with?' It was something the delivery boys had all been instructed to ask.

Mavis nodded. Mrs O'Reilly would probably be in, not that that was important.

Her hand shaking, she reached out for the telegram and took it from the lad. She'd always felt sorry for them, having to give bad news every day, and most of them were under fifteen. No one wanted to see them. She searched in her pocket and found a thruppenny bit, which she held out. 'Thank you, missus,' he said, and jumped back on his bike.

Slowly she closed the door behind him and leaned against it, all strength drained from her legs.

Joyce looked up from her book. 'Who was it, Mummy?'

Forcing herself, Mavis headed towards their tiny kitchen. 'Nothing important, love, look at your book for a minute while I make a cuppa.'

She made her legs move towards the little kitchen and put

the kettle on, delaying the moment when she would have to open the telegram. Leaning against the cooker, she gripped the telegram so tightly it crinkled in her hands as her knuckles turned white. Her heart beat fast as she imaged the worst – news of Joe or Ken. It could be either.

Swallowing hard, she made herself open the envelope...

URGENT TELEGRAM
FROM: WAR OFFICE
TO: MRS MAVIS SMITH
DATE: 14 JULY 1943

IT IS WITH DEEPEST REGRET WE INFORM YOU THAT YOUR HUSBAND PRIVATE JOSEPH SMITH, SERVICE NUMBER 67587, HAS BEEN REPORTED MISSING IN ACTION IN ITALY. EFFORTS TO LOCATE AND IDENTIFY YOUR HUSBAND ARE ONGOING BUT INFORMATION REMAINS LIMITED AT THIS TIME.

YOU WILL BE NOTIFIED PROMPTLY IF ANY FURTHER DETAILS BECOME AVAILABLE.

WE EXTEND OUR SINCERE CONDOLENCES DURING THIS DIFFICULT TIME. SHOULD YOU REQURE ANY ASSISTANCE OR SUPPORT CONTACT THE WAR OFFICE.

SIGNED
COLONEL JAMES WARRINGTON
COMMANDING OFFICER.

Mavis read the telegram three times, willing the words to change. Missing. Not dead. Missing could mean anything – he could have got separated from his battalion, been injured and taken in by some locals, there were many tales of missing soldiers being found alive later.

The kettle's whistle pierced her thoughts, making her jump. She turned off the gas without being aware of what she was doing. Her hands shook so violently she had to grip the sink to keep her knees from giving way.

'Mummy,' Joyce asked, her hand slipping into Mavis's. 'Are you crying?'

Mavis touched her cheek, surprised to find it wet. She hadn't realised she was weeping. 'Just something in my eye, love.' She'd taught Joyce that lying was wrong but this time it was needed. There was no advantage to upsetting her unnecessarily.

'Can I have my tea now?' Joyce had moved to Mavis and wrapped her arms round her legs.

'Bread and jam today, love,' Mavis said, bending to kiss the top of her head. 'We'll get some more cheese tomorrow.'

She slipped the telegram in her pocket. Normality was what Joyce needed. She'd have time to break down later when Joyce was in bed.

As she spread the jam on the bread, Mavis's mind whirled. She tried to remember where Italy was. She knew it had been in the newspapers, but it was one of many so she couldn't really place it exactly.

Unaware of her mother's turmoil, Joyce chattered away about the fete, the friends she'd played with, what she'd enjoyed most. Her mind many miles away, Mavis managed to respond in the right places, to smile when a smile was expected. Yet the telegram seemed to burn a hole in her pocket.

'Can we go to another fete soon?' Joyce asked, licking jam from her fingers.

'I don't know when there'll be another one. If I find out about one we can go though.' Mavis began clearing up the things on the table. 'But now, let's turn the wireless on. It's *Children's Hour*.'

Joyce clapped her hands. 'Goody, goody. That's my favourite.'

Not five minutes after Joyce was in bed there was a knock at the door. It was her neighbour, Mrs O'Connor. 'Mavis, love,' she said, her forehead creased with worry. 'I've been out visiting my sister, but someone told me the telegram boy stopped here. Are you okay? Shall I come in to keep you company for a while?'

Mavis stood aside to let her friend in, then passed the telegram to her without a word.

Mrs O'Connor read it and reached out for Mavis's hand. 'It's not the worst news. He might be somewhere safe and sound. It happens sometimes, so it does.'

'He promised he'd come home to me,' Mavis whispered. 'He promised to come back.'

Her friend squeezed her hand. 'And he might well come back, sweetheart. No good assuming the worst. I expect you'll be going to the War Office tomorrow to find out more.'

But would the War Office have any news?

15

It was Cordelia's turn to collect the newspapers for the library. She had turned on the wireless while getting ready for work, hoping there would be some good news about the war. Over the previous few days, it finally seemed as if the tide was turning. Could it be that this was the beginning of the end?

She pulled her navy-blue and white dress over her head, the lace trim of the fabric soft and familiar against her skin. As she fastened the buttons, she breathed in the fresh morning air from her open bedroom window. Standing at the mirror, she fixed a row of white beads around her neck then ran a brush through her hair. Shoes were last. A quick check of her watch and she was ready for the day.

Just time to listen to the news headlines before she had to leave. She turned the wireless up as she finished getting ready for the day.

The voice of the newsreader was familiar, but his message was anything but.

'This is the BBC Home Service news. The Ministry of Defence has just issued a statement announcing that a limited number of troops fighting in the North Africa theatre of war will be returning to Britain.

'While some troops will be moved to other theatres of war, we can now confirm that the first wave of soldiers who have been fighting so bravely against Rommel's forces in North Africa will be arriving at Victoria Station in London in the coming days. Crowds are expected to gather to welcome these heroic men who have endured years of gruelling combat in the desert.'

Cordelia's breath caught in her throat as she listened, a spark of hope igniting in her chest as she absorbed the news. She had picked up her bag in readiness to leave but instead stood by the wireless, listening anxiously to the rest of the broadcast.

'The BBC will provide updates on arrival times and parade schedules as more information becomes available from the Ministry of Defence. It is anticipated that more contingents from the campaign will arrive over the next few weeks. Families across our brave nation are no doubt anxiously waiting for the safe homecoming of their loved ones.

'For now, we encourage all citizens to stand prepared to provide a warm reception to our courageous troops. Their dedication and sacrifice have brought us one step closer to victory.'

Excitement flooded through Cordelia's entire body, her heart swelling with a profound sense of relief and elation at the welcome news. But then she told herself to calm down. There was no guarantee that Robert would be one of the lucky ones. After years of agonising uncertainty, the possibility of his return seemed too good to be true. But excited as she was, she told herself to be realistic. The army would need doctors in other theatres of war, so he might be one of the unlucky ones. Her throat constricted with a mixture of hope and worry.

Stepping outside, the muted rumble of trams and the chatter of passers-by reached her ears. In the distance she could hear the rhythmic clanging of the factory hooters, a familiar sound-track to Silvertown's waking hours. The sun belied a chill from a brisk breeze that made her shiver.

Was the dream she had had that night been some sort of prediction? In the dream, the railway platform reached endlessly in either direction and she was the only person waiting for the train. There was complete silence apart from a strange whistling sound. She stood watching the train come in, then the doors being flung open. Soldier after soldier stepped down, their faces etched with exhaustion. But none were him, her love. She looked at the station clock. An hour had gone by since soldiers began alighting but still they came, an endless stream of identical uniforms. She saw herself, in her dream, feeling the weight of desperation as she realised he might never arrive.

Cordelia shook herself. This wasn't just a dream. If they were lucky, the reality would be his arrival in a few days.

Would he soon be walking these streets with her? Would their love return to how it was? Would he still be the same man or would he be changed by his experiences as so many were? Despite her worries, her footsteps seemed lighter as she walked along the familiar route to the library. Her mind on the BBC announcement, she hardly noticed where she was going.

She stepped into the road without looking and almost got run over by a lad on a bike. 'Watch out, lady!' he shouted after her. She hardly heard him. In her mind she was imagining going to the station to meet her love, their joyous reunion, hugs and kisses. Would he look the same? He would certainly be tanned, and she guessed he would have the lines of his dangerous work etched on his face.

She went into the newsagents and greeted Mrs Patel with a cheery, 'Good morning!'

Mrs Patel had her newspapers ready and she handed them over. 'Goodness, you are absolutely glowing this morning, Miss Carmichael. Has something wonderful happened?'

Cordelia nodded towards the newspapers. 'What might be good news. There's a chance my boyfriend might be coming back from North Africa.'

Mrs Patel almost jumped up and down with happiness for her. She reached to one of her jars of sweets. 'Here,' she said. 'Have a sweet on me! I'm so glad for you.'

But the happiness was soon to be squashed.

She went into the library bursting with the news, longing to tell her friends. As usual she was first to arrive and put the newspapers out on their special table, knowing Bert would be hammering on the door on the dot of nine to read them. But before she had time to check everything was ready for the day, Mavis and Jane came in. It was obvious before they even spoke that something was wrong. Their sombre faces immediately halted any thoughts of sharing her news.

'What is it?' she asked, going over to them.

Jane spoke for Mavis, who was struggling to hold back tears. 'It's Joe. He's missing in action.'

'But I'm going to damn well find out where he is!' Mavis said, steel in her voice, chin jutting forward. 'I've waited all my life to find the right man and as soon as I find him 'e's whisked away and damn well missing in action.'

Cordelia could have wept for her. Mavis's modest wedding had been so happy, so full of hope for their future together. Now that future might have been snatched away. 'Oh, Mavis, I am so sorry to hear that. The Missing Persons staff will tell you what to do. They're the experts.' She looked up at the clock. 'They'll be here in half an hour. I know it's their job to find people in this country after bombings, but I'd be surprised if they didn't have ideas for how you could find out more.' She put her hand on Mavis's and gave it a squeeze. 'Take as long as you need. We'll cover for you.'

Mavis couldn't concentrate on her library duties while she waited for the Civil Defence people, so she tidied the desk, made tea and fidgeted, turning a pencil over time and time again, going to the door and back again. A regular library user popped a book in the 'Books for the Forces' collection box. She was keen to chat to Mavis, which took her mind away from her worries for a few minutes.

Jane approached her and linked her arm in Mavis's. 'This is an awful time for you, love. Come and drink that tea you just made. Have a biscuit. You'll soon know what to do. Taking action will stop you feeling so helpless.'

As Mavis sipped her tea, memories of her time with Joe made her sob again. Walking through the Royal Victorian Gardens, admiring the vegetables growing there. Going to the flicks to see *Mrs Miniver*. Sitting side by side in her little living room listening to the wireless. Nervously introducing him to Joyce. Taking her to the park for picnics. And cuddling up in bed.

She was so deep in her memories that Jane had to nudge her. 'They're here, Mavis. The Missing Persons Bureau people.'

Mavis's heart leapt and she jumped up so quickly she almost dropped her cup and saucer on the floor.

'Good luck!' Jane said, squeezing her friend's arm.

Ten minutes later, Mavis was back with her. 'They're good, that lot,' she said. 'They've given me a list of places to contact to try to find out more.'

Cordelia had joined them, and the three friends made a list of steps Mavis should take, but readers coming up to the desk kept interrupting them. Nonetheless, by closing time, Mavis had a plan and her friends wished her good luck as they locked up for the night and went their individual ways.

When Cordelia returned home, she was thrilled to find a letter from Robert waiting for her. She turned it over in her hands. Would it tell her the good news she was hoping for? Impatiently, she took off her coat, poured herself a drink and sat by the window. The day was fading, golden light finding its way through the blast tape, casting patterned shadows across the room. Outside the sky was changing – a canvas of soft pinks and purples, its last rays painting the clouds as it sank below the East End buildings.

Sighing with pleasure, she picked up her letter opener and slit the top of the flimsy envelope.

My darling Cordelia,

Thank you so much for your last letter. As always reading about your life and events in the library made my heart warm.

But there may be some good news soon. The army might send me home. They need doctors who are experienced working in a variety of fields of war to train newly qualified doctors. Life in the desert has taught us so much about battlefield treatment that they can't teach in medical school. The heat plays havoc with everything – from keeping medicines stable to preventing wound infections. I wish I had had proper training before I arrived! I would love an opportunity to share my knowledge.

I miss our walks in Victoria Park and along the Thames dreadfully. Sometimes when I find time for a brief walk, I think of you while of course dodging scorpions... I try to imagine I'm walking with you instead of looking at the endless sight of sand and tents.

*If I learn more before I leave I will of course write to let you
know. But it is possible I'll be given very short notice.*
All my love
Robert. Xxx

Her hands trembling, Cordelia put the letter down on her
little table and sat back in her chair. Her heart raced, a mixture
of relief and anxiety coursing through her mind. She knew that
it would be impossible to put the hope of him coming home out
of her mind even for a minute.

But then she thought of Mavis, whose news had been the
opposite. This damn war. It had been going on so long, she
could hardly remember life before it. Before the sandbags and
shelters, before the drone of planes overhead, before the air-raid
siren making their hearts jump, before rationing, before they
could never assume they and their loved ones would be alive the
next day.

16

'So tell me about this mystery chest,' the reporter, James Cope, said. 'Readers of *East End News* love a mystery, especially one involving romance.'

It was early Saturday afternoon, and the library had just closed. Cordelia, Mavis, Jane, Tom and the reporter had gathered in one of the rooms at the back of the library. There was enough space there for all of them, plus a table where they could put everything they had found.

Mavis, Jane and Tom looked to Cordelia to speak on their behalf. 'It all started when the library was bombed,' she began. 'The builders found this small chest...'

As she began telling the tale, she thought back to all they had done to try to find out who the woman was whose letters they had found.

She had read the letters to the unknown woman called Evelyn from the equally mysterious J. The facts she had worked out were few – the couple were in a forbidden love relationship, the soldier involved in the Indian Mutiny, and both were literate. The latter point, and the fact that the chest was hidden in the library, suggested that Evelyn might have been a librarian years before.

The reporter scribbled frantically in shorthand as he listened to the story, then he looked up. 'This is fascinating, Shakespeare couldn't have done better. A forbidden love affair, a precious gift, a soldier fighting for king and country.' He looked around at them. 'Have any of you thought about writing a novel based on this?'

'I've thought about it,' Cordelia said. Ever since her time at Girton College, Cambridge, she had longed to become an author, to see her name on the front of a book. She had been secretly writing while Robert was away in what little time she had. The results weren't anything she would be willing to share, but she was happy the plot line was working well.

'That sounds like a story for another day,' the reporter said. He pushed his hair away from his forehead and flipped back several pages in his notebook. 'Let's see if I've got this right – between you you've studied the letters and the diary but not come up with anything you're confident about. Tom is still planning to research the comb further. Tell me, what are you hoping to achieve by an article in the newspaper?'

Cordelia shuffled the papers in front of her into a neat pile while she worked out how to answer. 'Two things. We obviously want to know more about the people involved and what happened to them...'

'And secondly,' Mavis said, interrupting, 'there might be some local people who are related to Evelyn and J. If so, they might want to keep these things.' She gestured to everything on the table. 'Just imagine – Evelyn might be the grandmother or great-grandmother of someone who lives in Silvertown now. They might even be people who come into the library.'

Tom grinned. 'I never knew you were so romantic, Mavis,' he said. She nudged him hard in the ribs.

'Did you notice any recurring themes or symbols in the letters? Sometimes small details can reveal a lot of the person's circumstances.'

Cordelia struggled to remember the fine detail of the letters despite having read them several times. Then she remembered something she had assumed wasn't significant. 'They did mention a garden a few times. It was obviously somewhere they met regularly, but they didn't name it.'

James Cope scribbled on his notepad again. 'Can you let me know tomorrow the name of the garden if you discover it? And do your best to try to find out where it was. It could be in another borough or even a private garden.'

Cordelia looked around the table, frustrated that with all their efforts they had come to no firm conclusions. 'I wish we'd managed to find out more.' She looked over at Mavis. 'There wasn't anything in the diary, was there? I'm sure you'd have said.'

Mavis picked it up and flicked through the pages. 'Just ordinary appointments and occasional initials, but none of them matched up. But there was something. One of my neighbours, who's as old as the hills, used to use this library. She's still got all her marbles and rattled off the names of people she'd heard of in the library. Mind, she wasn't sure if they were librarians or just volunteers. She said the names could even have been people who'd worked there before her time.'

Hope sprang in Cordelia's mind. 'That sounds promising. Did any name stick out as a possibility?'

Mavis nodded. 'Now, what did she say? Black something. I think it was Blackwood. Worth looking into.'

'I'm worried that we might be stirring a hornet's nest here,' Jane said with a sigh. 'What if we give away a long-hidden family secret?' She'd been going over this again and again in her mind. Suppose the secret was an illegitimate child or someone who went to prison, or some sort of violence or abuse. The descendants, even after all these years, might not want the old secret made public. She looked at the reporter. 'I wonder if we should be doing this at all?'

The room went still, and they all looked at each other. Then the reporter spoke. 'As a newsman I'd say you should go ahead. It's such a long time ago now. You've all tried your very best to identify the people.' He looked around at each of them. 'If nothing else comes of it, you will at least have raised public awareness of the library. You'll almost certainly get more readers.

'Scandals sell newspapers, you must know that. But... we are a local paper, and I think this story could run and run as we find out more. The boss always wants more column inches filled with something other than bombing details.'

'So we're agreed?' Cordelia asked and was relieved when he nodded. 'Jane, I know you were worried about this, concerned that family members might not want old secrets unearthed.'

Jane nodded. 'That's right. I'd be much happier if any article is written in a sensitive way. The East End is close-knit, it's quite possible that someone alive today will be a relative of Evelyn.'

They were about to get up when Tom spoke. 'Actually, there is one more piece of news. I've been in touch with the Victoria and Albert Museum. I'm going to see an expert there to find out if she can tell me more about the comb. I definitely think we shouldn't in any way suggest it's valuable or we'll be inundated with people trying it on.'

Cordelia looked over at the reporter. 'I know I can't dictate how you write the article, but after listening to all this, I hope you'll agree to write it as a "can you help solve this mystery" and in a way that won't embarrass any living relatives who may be found.'

He snapped his notebook shut. 'That's what I plan. Then we can keep in touch and hopefully I'll be able to write some follow-up articles. Local people will love it.'

Cordelia felt a wave of relief. They had a plan, and perhaps now the pieces of the past would finally fit together.

17

After Jane had left the library for the day, Mavis sidled up to Cordelia. 'I've got a wicked idea, boss.'

Cordelia was used to Mavis being bold and taking no nonsense from anyone, but wicked? That was new. She smiled, a glint in her eyes, life around Mavis was never boring.

'There's a talent competition at Tate & Lyle in three weeks' time. Why don't we put Jane's name down for it? She'll never do it herself.'

'Without her knowing?' Cordelia tried to imagine how Jane would feel. Outraged, probably. But then... experience told her that Jane needed encouragement now and then to try new things. Her confidence grew day by day, but this was something very different. 'She might be furious with us.' She tried to think through all the implications.

The truth was Cordelia would love to see Jane move on and perhaps make singing a new career. But then, she realised, she would lose an excellent librarian. Added to this, if she was honest with herself, she was a little jealous of Jane's talent. She thought back to one of her governesses, Miss Edwards, who tried to teach her to sing. They were always hymns; the governess was very religious.

Cordelia found the music dull and predictable. She'd rather have sung some of the songs she heard on the wireless in the kitchen when she spent time with the family cook, Mrs Taylor. But when she suggested them, the governess seemed baffled. It was obvious she never listened to anything but religious music. Worse, after a few lessons she told Cordelia she was hopeless, that she'd never have a halfway decent singing voice. 'Your voice is thin and reedy,' she said, as if it was all Cordelia's fault.

Even after all these years and her successes in other areas, the mere mention of singing caused a visceral reaction within Cordelia. Her throat constricted, palms growing clammy as vivid memories of those lessons forced their way into her mind. She could still feel the weight of Miss Edwards's stern gaze as she stood at the front of the room, voice shaking with nerves.

She remembered the way her heart raced, the thump-thump-thump drowning out the sound of her own voice. When she finally finished, Miss Edwards always reacted in the same way. A sad shake of her head, mouth turned down. Her expression crueller than any words.

During her time at university, Cordelia had sometimes had to give presentations. She had no more than normal nerves. She was talking about other things, not singing. It was a world of difference.

Since then, on the occasions she went to church, Cordelia just mimed the words of the hymns. She sometimes wondered if anyone noticed.

Shaking the memory away, she brought her attention back to Mavis's idea. 'Do we have to pay for her entry?'

Mavis smiled. 'Yes, but it's not much and...' Her grin turned cunning. 'I thought you could pay because you're loaded, and you can say it's a bonus.'

'Cheeky! And if she refuses to go for it, I'll have wasted my money, I suppose.'

Mavis merely smiled again and raised an eyebrow.

As Cordelia walked home later, she tried to imagine the scene – telling Jane she had a place in a talent competition. She was tempted to ask Jane's landlady, who everyone called Mrs S, to soften her up. But she pushed the idea aside. They'd only met once so it would be too much to expect of her.

Cordelia's gaze drifted to some wildflowers growing on a bomb site she was walking past, proof that life went on despite the war. Her thoughts were consumed by the hope of Robert's return. She longed to hear his voice, to feel the reassuring warmth of his hand in hers. Their conversations had always been a sanctuary for her, a space where they could talk freely with no fear of judgement.

His unwavering support had been a lifeline to Jane when he had explained the reason for the symptoms Jane's husband George showed when he returned from war broken in mind and body. Jane had dedicated herself to his recovery, juggling the demands of their young daughter and the family's finances. Remembering their ordeal heightened Cordelia's worry for Robert's well-being. Would he be the same man when he returned? Would all the dreadful experiences, the atrocities of war he had suffered, have changed him?

How long would she have to wait to see him again?

She shook her head. What was that quote about worry? 'Worry is like sitting on a rocking chair. It gives you something to do but gets you nowhere.'

So, her steps lighter, she forced her thoughts to the exciting possibility of Jane doing well at the singing competition.

18

Apart from the soft rustle of pages and the occasional creak of the old wooden chairs, the library was unusually quiet for a Tuesday afternoon, as if the building itself was holding its breath. Outside a bus rattled past, the conductor shouting the name of the stop.

Jane was restocking returned books in the far corner, quietly humming a cheerful tune under her breath.

Mrs Wheel, a sprightly older lady with a sharp eye for a good book and an even sharper ear for a good tune, sat at a nearby table, looking through a pile of books she'd taken from the shelves, trying to decide which two to take home. She always managed to sit where the light through the window illuminated the books. Her silver-grey hair struggled to escape her cloche hat. It should have looked old-fashioned but somehow looked elegant on her.

Mrs Wheel sat back in her chair and sighed. Having retired from her career as a music teacher, she was bored. Several schools had closed when so many children were evacuated but not all of them had reopened when many returned. She'd asked in every local school for work, but so far had only found enough for one and a half days a week. Much as she loved the library, she needed to be with people.

The first notes of 'You Are My Sunshine' drifted over the shelves, soft as a feather falling on your skin.

Her ears pricked up when she heard Jane's humming. Forgetting her books, she paused and listened intently, her glasses still perched on the end of her nose.

Jane was the other side of a stack from her, but Mrs Wheel, never one to delay pleasure, stood and walked round to her. 'Excuse me, my dear,' she said, going close enough to speak without disturbing other readers.

'Oh, Mrs Wheel.' Jane fumbled with the book she was holding and almost dropped it. 'You made me jump. I hope I wasn't disturbing you. Can I help you?'

Mrs Wheel was a petite woman with a youthful energy that belied her age. She had a warm smile and kind eyes that twinkled when she spoke – always with enthusiasm when it was about music or teaching.

Mrs Wheel took off her glasses, wiped them with her hankie, then put them back on. 'My dear, anything but. In fact, quite the opposite. I was enjoying your tuneful rendition of "You Are My Sunshine".' She paused. 'You sang at the reopening ceremony, didn't you? I was very impressed. You have great natural talent.'

Blushing, Jane tried to push aside the compliment. 'We've always sung in my family, even in hard times it cheers me up.'

'Oh dear.' Mrs Wheel looked concerned. 'Are you having a hard time at the moment?'

Jane picked up the dropped book and put it on the shelf. 'I'm sorry, I didn't mean that. I meant in general, with the war and so on.'

'Is there somewhere we can speak privately?' Mrs Wheel asked.

Surprised, Jane looked around and, spotting Mavis, indicated she was going to the back room. It was rarely used and felt cold and neglected.

The room was unchanged since before the bombing and was badly in need of some redecoration. A bare light bulb hung from the mottled ceiling and a Make Do and Mend poster adorned one wall, curling at the edges.

The room was empty, and Mrs Wheel, taking control, said, 'Come and sit down, Mrs Wilkins. I won't keep you long.'

Feeling a little unnerved, Jane did as she was asked. 'Is something wrong, Mrs Wheel? Anything I can help with?'

Mrs Wheel pushed her glasses further up her nose. 'You won't know but for many years I was a music and singing teacher. Since I retired I have too much time on my hands.' For the first time she looked uncertain of herself. 'You might think I'm a silly interfering old woman approaching you like this but...'

Jane sat silent, wondering where this conversation was going. Outside, they could hear children running along and shouting to each other.

'What I'm trying to say is, have you ever considered singing lessons?'

'Singing lessons? No, that's not something I've ever thought about.'

Mrs Wheel leaned forward and touched her arm. 'Well, my dear, you should. You have great talent. It should be nurtured.'

Outside a wind had got up and they heard a loud metallic banging. 'That'll be next door's dustbin,' Jane said. 'It often flies off when it gets windy.' She turned back to Mrs Wheel and waited.

'What I'm trying to say in my clumsy way, Mrs Wilkins, is would you like me to give you singing lessons to develop your talent further?'

Jane's jaw dropped open. 'Me? Lessons? But I haven't...'

Mrs Wheel touched her arm again. 'If you're going to say you don't have enough money, I wouldn't need paying. In fact, I should pay you. You'd be doing me a favour. Retirement is so much harder than I expected. I do voluntary work, of course, but I still have too much time on my hands.' She tucked some stray hair under her hat. 'You know, I always loved to sing and often sung around the house but my mother always shouted at me to stop. "You sound like a cat what's been run over," she'd say. Then when I trained to be a teacher it never occurred to me to teach music, but a friend heard me singing and urged me to give it a try. The rest, as they say, is history.'

She could see Jane was still uncertain.

'I once had a student who was very much like you,' she said. 'Uncertain of her abilities, uncertain whether it was even worth trying to improve them. She absolutely blossomed within a few lessons. The last I heard of her she sang at the Royal Albert Hall.'

Jane sat back in the chair, trying to identify her feelings. The Royal Albert Hall! Mrs Wheel was offering her a wonderful opportunity, not the Albert Hall but using her natural skill to progress her life. Was that something she wanted to do? What would George say? But then she remembered that quote someone – Mavis? – had said. 'Jump and the net will appear.' It wasn't much of a jump if she accepted this kind offer. If the worst came to the worst, she could just stop.

'I've got a daughter...' she began.

'Wonderful!' Mrs Wheel interrupted her. 'Bring her along. I've worked with children all my life and miss them so much.

She can join in or sit and read a book. I'm guessing she's prob-ably a keen reader if she's your daughter.'

Five minutes later, the deal was done. Jane would have a one-hour lesson every week and be expected to practise every day between lessons.

Mrs Wheel leaned forward and shook Jane's hand. 'It's a deal, dear girl. I'll scribble my address for you.'

Jane thanked her profusely and they went back into the main library, Jane's mind in turmoil.

Almost shaking with uncertainty, she went to the staff toilet. She stood looking in the mirror. Initially she saw doubt, then slowly a grin spread across her face, widening until her cheeks ached. She got her comb out of her bag and spent a few minutes trying different hairstyles in a way she hadn't done for many years. Looking in the mirror again, she saw a stranger staring back, someone shining with possibilities. Singing lessons! The very thought sent a thrill through her.

'Life is just a bowl of cherries,' she sang softly to her reflec-tion. Then she stopped, surprised that even though she had sung quietly, there was real strength in her voice. She could hear a group of girls walking outside, their chatter and laughter carrying on the breeze. Their energy and enjoyment of life somehow connected with her heart and mind. Perhaps it wasn't too late to find a new purpose in life.

Feeling excited and energised, she went to tell Mavis, but she was in the middle of signing up some new readers who weren't very literate and needed a lot of help. Impatience made Jane bounce off her feet and play with her hair, twisting it round and round her finger.

Eventually Mavis was free. 'What is it? I don't know what's 'appened to you but you're like a dog with two tails! Come on, spill the beans.'

Jane was so excited she stumbled over her words. 'It's Mrs Wheel, you know the lady who likes classical novels. She's a singing teacher and she's offered me free lessons. She said I've got natural talent.'

Mavis's eyes opened wide and her smile matched Jane's. 'Wow. You're on your way, girl, I said you 'ad talent. You'll 'ave to believe me now.'

19

'Not exactly a luxury dressing room, is it?' Mavis said, helping Jane into her elegant silver dress, another loan from Cordelia. It was the evening of the talent competition at Tate & Lyle Community Hall and they were in the ladies' toilet where female contestants were getting ready. Alongside them two other hopefuls were also putting finishing touches to their outfits. Mavis opened a window. 'Bit niffy in 'ere, isn't it!' she exclaimed, tugging the blackout curtain in place. The room reeked of perfume and make-up.

One of the other contestants, a young woman with jet-black hair and scarlet lipstick, turned to Jane. 'You as nervous as me, love? I'm shaking like a leaf inside.'

Jane hardly heard her. She was too busy putting on make-up, also borrowed from Cordelia. She rarely wore any and wiped it all off twice, convinced she looked like a clown.

'Come 'ere,' the girl said, snatching her make-up bag. 'I'll do it for ya. You'll never get on stage at the rate you're going.'

Five minutes later, Jane didn't recognise herself. Slim and

elegant in the borrowed dress, her hair up, she looked like someone from a magazine.

'There,' said the kind contestant. 'You look like the bee's knees. Just don't do better than me!'

'What are you doing?' Jane asked.

'Me and my friend are doing a comedy song and dance routine. It goes down well in the pubs and clubs.'

Jane nervously wondered how on earth the judges could decide between such different acts. As well as the song and dance routine, there was a talking dog, a ventriloquist, another singer, a juggler and a magician.

'If I mess up, I'll never forgive you for entering me into this competition,' she said to Mavis. 'I'd never have done it.'

Mavis just laughed. 'That's why I did it for you. Time you got braver about letting people know what a great voice you 'ave. Anyway, it wasn't just me. Cordelia was in on it too.'

'At least she had the good grace to lend me this dress.' Jane smoothed her nervous fingers over her slim hips and looked down at her silver shoes. She'd bought them in a jumble sales years before, knowing they would pinch but unable to resist them. They'd been in the back of her wardrobe all this time.

There was a sharp knock on the door. 'Five minutes, five minutes!' someone shouted.

Jane and the kind helper looked at each other and whispered, 'Good luck.'

All performers had to stand in the tiny backstage area until it was their turn. Jane was third and she waited nervously for the talent show to begin, listening to the buzz of the audience, footsteps as people arrived and other performers nervously cleared their throats.

'I can't believe I'm doing this,' a young man with a juggling kit said, his voice shaky. 'Someone bet me I wouldn't do it. I wish

I hadn't taken the bet. I've been practising for weeks but I'm sure I'll drop everything.'

Jane offered him a sympathetic smile. 'I know how you feel. I wouldn't be here if my friend hadn't entered me. We'll just have to do our best.'

The master of ceremonies called for silence and gave a brief introduction to the evening, then the faded burgundy curtains were pulled aside. The MC made a great play of announcing the first performer. 'I just know you're going to love him: he, or should I say they, had us all in stitches earlier.'

As he left the stage, there was a piano roll and a tall pencil-thin man with ears big enough to catch the wind strode on stage. It was the ventriloquist holding his dummy. It was dressed like a toff in a top hat and a monocle on its left eye. Soon he had the audience laughing at his corny jokes. 'Lord Snarkington here,' the ventriloquist said. 'He's convinced he's a much better ventriloquist than I am. He keeps saying, "If you let me do all the talking, this act would be a lot funnier!" And I say to him, "But then everyone would realise I'm not really the one talking, and the whole joke would be ruined!"'

Listening to the audience laughing, Jane was so sure he would win, she wanted to run away home. She would never get the level of applause he had as he took his bow. The next act, the talking dog, got belly laughs too and with each passing moment Jane got more nervous. Had she chosen the best song? The three librarians had spent ages discussing her options – 'We'll Meet Again', 'Jealousy', 'The Lambeth Walk', 'There'll Always Be An England'. After the library closed one day, they forced her to sing part of all of them and finally decided on another, 'The White Cliffs of Dover'. Mrs Wheel had said it was sentimental and showcased Jane's vocal range. She'd sung it so much since they'd made the decision that her landlady, Mrs S, told her she'd strain her voice. She wished she'd started her singing lessons earlier, but it was too late now.

Her thoughts were dragged back to the present when she saw the previous act leaving the stage. Her turn! Her heart beat so strongly she could hardly breathe. But Mavis came up to her with a glass of water. 'Sip this!' she ordered.

When the applause for the talking dog had died down, the MC began speaking again. 'Our next act is someone the book-minded amongst you might recognise. She is our very own Silvertown librarian Mrs Jane Wilkins, who will be singing a song well known to you all!'

20

Jane was frozen to the spot as the audience began clapping, expecting her to appear, but Mavis gave her a shove and the movement got her mind and legs working again. Cordelia had coached her on how to make an entrance: back upright, tummy in, breathing evenly, smile at the MC and the audience.

Then it was her moment. The stage lights seemed to blaze even brighter as she stepped up to the microphone. She took a deep breath, shifting her gaze to a point just above the audience to steady herself. The pianist played the opening notes, the melody immediately familiar to the audience.

As the last note of the introduction resounded, Jane began to sing.

'There'll be bluebirds over...'

Without being aware, Jane lost herself in the music. Her voice, pure and clear, soared, each note tugging on the heart-strings of the audience who had suffered so much. Initially silent, listening to her wonderful voice, they gradually began to join in. Soon the hall was full of the voices of the East Enders, their words filled with a palpable sense of longing and hope as the song's familiar and poignant lyrics echoed the emotions of the people who had lived through so much horror and loss.

Becoming aware of the sound of the audience, Jane let her voice soar higher, captivating everyone until the very last note. The echo of her final lyric hung in the air for a moment before the applause began, thunderous and overwhelming.

Coming back to the moment, it took Jane a few seconds to fully absorb the magnitude of the response.

Shouts of 'More! More!' echoed off the walls and several people stood up as they applauded.

Blinking in the lights, Jane looked around, amazed. Then she smiled – as if she would never stop – and bowed before the MC led her off the stage.

'That was a cracker. Marvellous, simply marvellous!' he whispered to her.

And suddenly she was back in the ladies' toilet with Mavis hugging her so tight she could hardly breathe.

'That was bloomin' top-notch!' Mavis said, her voice full of admiration. 'There'll be a riot if you don't win! Did you see the judges? They couldn't take their eyes off of you and they started singing too.'

Jane felt elated. Even if she didn't win, she knew she hadn't put a note wrong and felt proud of herself. She wished her mother had been there to see her, but then realised her mother would still have found something to criticise. She remembered all the negative things her mother had said to her – 'You're useless, you are!' 'I wish you'd been a boy.' 'Get out of my sight, you stupid brat.' The voices played in her head frequently, telling her she'd never amount to anything, making her scared to try. But with the help of her two friends, she had done it.

'Do you want to watch the other competitors?' Mavis asked, still holding her hand.

Jane shook her head. 'I'm just relieved it's all over. And I'm hot. I'd rather go outside for a few minutes to cool down and get my breath.'

They were joined by Cordelia, who had been in the audience and had come looking for them. 'You were fantastic, Jane,' she said, hugging her tight. 'You could give Vera Lynn a run for her money.' She checked her watch. 'Another forty-five minutes, then it's up to the judges to make a decision. If you don't win, it's a fix-up.'

They were in a narrow alley at the back of the community hall, not the best place with the smell of bins and litter.

'Do you want to go back in, Jane,' Mavis asked after they'd been out there a few minutes, 'or shall we walk round the block?'

'Let's walk.' Jane hadn't considered her very glamorous outfit and within three minutes she had wolf whistles from several men and admiring looks from several women. 'We'd better go back in,' she said before long. 'These shoes are too tight and I daren't take them off. This is my only decent pair of stockings.'

The three linked arms and made their way back, past the bins, past the litter, oblivious to it all of it. Jane's hurried breathing showed her nerves.

'I keep telling myself it doesn't matter if I lose. I'll still be me, George's wife, Linda's mum and a librarian.'

'A librarian with a wonderful voice,' Cordelia said, squeezing her arm.

The MC had called a half-hour break while the judges made their decision and many people had filed outside to smoke or get away from the smoky room, others hurried to the toilets or to get a drink or buy raffle tickets. Yet more stayed in their seats.

The three friends went back inside and joined the other performers in the wings. The judges had seats immediately in front of the stage, so they managed to catch a few words as they squashed together, trying to hear what the judges were saying – 'The ventriloquist was very funny.' 'The singer was magnificent.' 'Those dancers had legs to die for.' 'The talking dog needs elocution lessons!' Each time one of the performers heard themselves mentioned they tensed and either smiled or looked downhearted.

But they all knew that the judges voted by writing the names of their favourite performers on paper. It was impossible to see what they were writing, or to work out what their final verdict was. Jane, along with several others, was fidgety, too nervous to stand still.

After what seemed a lifetime, the judges handed the MC a piece of paper and the piano started again, bringing the audience back into the room.

'Welcome back, everyone. I'm sure you'll all agree with me,' the MC said, his voice booming, 'that we have had a wonderful show tonight. We've seen some terrific performers, let's give them all a big round of applause before I announce the winners.'

More agony, waiting until the applause stopped, then the MC held up his hand for the audience to settle down. He began to speak again.

'I am delighted to announce the top three our judges have chosen, in reverse order just to keep you all on the edge of your seats...' He paused and made a big play of opening the sheet of paper. 'Third place goes to... Rosie and Jean, the singing and dancing pair!'

Judging by the whoops and clapping, they had a lot of friends in the hall. They pushed the other performers aside and went on stage, smiling widely, to receive their prize, a small hamper of food.

'Please go and stand at the edge of the stage, girls,' the MC said. 'And second place,' the MC continued, 'is our wonderful ventriloquist Felix Hawthorn and Lord Snarkington. They both had us in stitches.'

Jane's shoulders dropped; it looked as if she wouldn't even be in the top three.

The ventriloquist pushed his way onto the stage, his dummy thanking everyone. 'Thank you very much,' it said. 'What do I get? I hope it's a big prize.' Another well-earned laugh.

The MC picked up another box. 'Your prize is four cinema tickets and a hamper of food.'

More applause. More agony of waiting.

Jane had given up hope and only Mavis and Cordelia behind her stopped her leaving in tears and going back to change into her normal clothes. 'I'm wasting our time,' she whispered.

The MC was speaking again. 'And now, I am delighted to announce our winner tonight. I'm sure you'll all agree with the judges' decision. The winner is... Mrs Jane Wilkins, our wonderful songstress.'

Jane's jaw dropped open, and her knees almost gave way. She had to be pushed onto the stage by her friends, almost stumbling her first few steps.

The MC laughed. 'Our wonderful prize-winner looks as if she doesn't believe it, but my dear, you had us all entranced.' He reached out his hand for Jane and she took it before she really believed her ears. 'I think I won't be speaking out of turn if I suggest you sing for us all again...'

The applause at this suggestion showed his idea was well received.

The pianist caught Jane's eye and gave her a thumbs-up sign and a big smile.

'If only my mother could see me now,' Jane thought,

standing as Cordelia had taught her again. 'I'd be delighted,' she finally said to the MC.

The audience hushed and the piano began the lead-in. That was all Jane could remember until she heard the tumultuous applause when she had finished. Could this evening prove some sort of turning point for her?

21

Ben hesitated at the door of St Mark's. It was his family's church, and he had been attending services there for as long as he could remember. He'd been a chorister, carried the donation plate around and, as his mother grew less mobile, helped her to her seat and to find the right pages in her hymn book.

Somehow today the church felt different, unknown, a mystery. The gaslights were insufficient for the lofty space, throwing unsettling shadows here and there. How had he never noticed them before? But it smelled the same as ever, of furniture polish, candles and old hymn books used by generations of Silvertown worshippers. The sign on the church noticeboard still held information about Sunday services, Sunday school and the women's Knit for the Troops sessions.

'Can I help you?'

The verger's words made Ben jump as they echoed through the space. He turned at the sound. 'Oh, Mr Gibson, you made me jump. I didn't realise anyone was here.'

The elderly verger smiled, showing many gaps where he had

missing teeth. 'We don't often see you here midweek. Can I help you with something?'

'I'd like to look at some old baptism records if that's okay.' Ben's mouth was dry, and he licked his lips.

'Doing some family research, are you?'

Ben nodded. 'Yes, I was reading about family history at the library and thought I'd like to give it a try. Can you show me where to look?'

He followed the verger to the vestry. They stopped at the door while Mr Gibson found the right key. 'Ah, here it is,' he muttered, turning it and pushing the ancient door open. The vestry smelled of beeswax and damp hassocks. 'Right, young Ben. What year are you looking for?'

Ben hesitated. He didn't want to give away too much. It was difficult enough accepting that the woman he always thought was his mother couldn't be. Now he wondered if his older sister, May, was in fact his mother. She was seventeen years older than him and he'd heard of cases like that before. But asking to see his baptism record should be safe. 'My own record. June 1923. No one seems to know where my birth certificate is.'

Mr Gibson nodded and went to an old cupboard in the corner. He bent down slowly to open the door, his knees creaking as he did so.

Sighing, Ben stepped forward to help carry the heavy ledger over to the reading stand.

Mr Gibson nodded. 'I'll leave you to it, let me know if you need any help. Have you got something to write on?'

Ben smiled his thanks and began to open the book. 'I think I'll be okay. I'll let you know if I get stuck.'

Two minutes later he began turning the pages, his stomach tied in knots. The register showed beautiful copperplate handwriting of a vicar whose name Ben couldn't make out. Each entry was precisely made in registrar's ink which had faded to sepia. Ben scanned the entries. Each one told a story:

May 7th: James Gordon, son of John James (Private, Essex Regiment, absent) and Amy Smithers (née Thomas) of North Woolwich Road, Silvertown. Previously Docker. (Now serving with H.M. Forces)

May 14th. Twins Mable and Margaret, daughters of William and Ruby Butcher (née Unwin) of Constance Road, Silvertown. Occupation Grocer.

With a start, Ben realised he knew Mable and Margaret. They had gone to the same school as him but a year or two ahead and always had an apple each day. Both were married with children of their own now. He still saw them occasionally around the town.

He turned the pages, forcing himself to concentrate, although he recognised so many names. His finger traced down each column methodically.

June 13th should be close to his date. The entries began normally:

Albert John, son of Albert and Helen (née Matthews), of Mill Road, Silvertown.

But something was wrong on the next page. Ben bent forward, squinting in the dim vestry light. He got goosebumps on his arms as he tried to make sense of the dates over and over again. Finally, he ran his fingers along the middle of the pages, between two. Yes, there was a ragged strip of paper.

A page had been removed. Neatly, so it was hard to see. Someone had used scissors or a knife.

Unable to believe his eyes, he turned the pages either side backward and forward, but he knew the page was gone.

'Everything all right there, young Ben?' Mr Gibson had come into the vestry unnoticed. 'You look a bit worried.'

Ben swallowed hard. Should he say? If his mother, or his sister, had removed the page, he didn't want to get them into trouble. On the other hand, someone else might notice. But he quickly reasoned, these records couldn't be looked at often.

'No, everything's fine, thank you, Mr Gibson.' He looked at his watch. 'I'd better get going. I'll be late for my shift.'

Struggling to calm his agitation, he set off towards the factory where he worked. His mind was a whirl. Surely it could only be his mother or sister who had removed the page. Why? What were they covering up? How did this fit in with them having moved to Silvertown years ago? He realised he had never known exactly when that was.

Feeling defeated, he knew the only option was to speak to his sister again. It wasn't a conversation he looked forward to.

22

Cordelia paused in the doorway of the packing room, breathing in the familiar smell of cardboard and tobacco. She smiled when she saw Ivy and Flo's grey heads bent over the table folding boxes. Her favourite evening volunteers. She'd been packing boxes for the troops for so long she did the work without thought. But having colleagues like Ivy and Flo made the time fly past.

Cordelia often wondered how women with families managed. Like her, they had to queue for everything, trudging from queues in one shop to the next, all the time hoping there would be something left for them to buy. It must be a stress even for a pair of spinsters like these elderly sisters.

They were always full of stories about people they knew and managed to make everything funny.

"Ello, Delia, love,' Ivy said as Cordelia walked in. She never managed her full name. 'Ain't seen you for a while. Thought you'd jumped ship!'

Cordelia took off her coat and hat ready to begin packing.

'I've been here. We just haven't overlapped. It's good to see you too.'

They'd already started packing the boxes. The contents varied a little from session to session but there was usually a tin of corned beef or similar, tea, sugar, basic toiletries, cigarettes and sometimes even something like a pack of playing cards or a mouth organ.

Flo and Ivy must have started early. They received the boxes flat and the first thing they had to do was fold them ready to be filled. There were already a dozen sitting on the table, and half a dozen full ones under it.

The room was as bleak as ever. Walls painted cream, now faded, a picture of the King on one wall and a clock on another. The wireless played George Formby's 'When I'm Cleaning Windows'.

All three women knew their work so well, they filled the boxes automatically, leaving plenty of time to chat. The sisters seemed to read each other's minds. Flo would push an item towards Ivy just as Ivy reached out her arthritic fingers for it without even looking. They often finished each other's sentences.

'So, what have you two been up to since I last saw you?' Cordelia asked. The sisters came into the library occasionally but because Cordelia was often in the office, she could easily have missed them.

'Nothing new,' Ivy said, putting a packet of cigarettes in a box. 'Cooking, cleaning other people's 'ouses, queueing, rubbing me old knees, they're paining me something rotten. What about you, sweetheart? Any news from that bloke of yours?'

Cordelia smiled, her eyes sparkling. 'Yes, I've heard he might be coming home to train other doctors, but nothing's certain.'

Ivy grunted. 'Bet the buggers send him off somewhere else all too soon though.'

Even though Cordelia knew that was likely, hearing Ivy say it brought her spirits down. Then she told herself to get over it. At least she would see him for a while. Plenty of women would never be able to see their men again. They'd been killed in action.

'Ivy!' Flo chastised her sister. 'Don't depress the girl before he's even got home. Mind you...'

Cordelia looked up from putting a tin of corned beef in a box. Whenever Flo said, 'Mind you...' and stopped, some gossip about people in the East End followed. Often the stories were hilarious. The sisters both looked at her as she got out a notebook and pencil.

'You stealing our stories again?' Ivy said with a grin. "Ow's that book of yours getting along then? We going to be in it?'

Cordelia thought back to her days at Girton College, Cambridge. There wasn't a girl doing English who didn't dream of being a bestselling author. They'd sat in the common room or under the massive giant sequoia tree if the weather was good enough, discussing books they'd been told to study. Virginia Woolf, Dorothy L. Sayers. They all imagined their names on the spine of books proudly displayed in bookshop windows.

Miss Hobson, their much-loved tutor, warned them again and again that writing a whole novel took more than ambition – it took time, energy and the ability to create gripping stories and relatable characters. Cordelia finally understood what she meant.

'I'm still planning it really,' she said, running her fingers across the edge of the notebook. 'I've got tons of notes, but it needs to be sorted out. And if I put you two lovely ladies in it, you'll be so disguised no one will ever know they're really you.' She looked up at Flo. 'Now, what were you going to say?'

'You know Pete, the old bloke down Barking Road, the one what keeps pigeons?' Flo started. 'You'd never Adam and Eve it but 'e's only telling people 'e can tell their fortune by listening to his favourite pigeon's cooing and that.'

'What!' Ivy's eyes opened wide. 'That sounds a lot of old cobblers. Surely no one's stupid enough to fall for that!'

'They are. Ask 'im everything, they do. Numbers for the football pools, will they win the marrow competition, will the girl they've got their eye on go out with them. All sorts.'

Ivy stopped working and put her hands on her hips. She shook her head. 'It never fails to amaze me 'ow stupid people can be. I won't be giving 'im any of my dosh, that's for sure.'

Flo laughed. 'I saw Mrs Simpson going in there last weekend. Dressed up to the nines she was. But that didn't stop 'er looking around, hoping no one would see 'er.'

'Hard times make people do things they wouldn't usually do,' her sister said, moving to the wireless and fiddling with the knobs to try to stop the crackling that threatened to overwhelm the music.

They worked for a few minutes, listening to the wireless, then Flo started again. 'Did you 'ear about the Joneses down Albert Road?'

'No, I don't know them. What happened?'

'Well, 'er old man, Bob I think 'is name is, got 'ome leave. Been in Scotland for ages. She was looking forward to 'im coming 'ome, got the place spruced up and everything...'

'But?'

'You'd never believe it. 'E'd only gone and got a girl up there in the family way. Young enough to be 'is daughter she is. 'E only came 'ome to tell poor Mrs Jones 'e's leaving 'er. I've always said you can never trust a man when 'e's away from 'ome. Like my old gran used to say, a man's never too old for a bit of 'ow's your father 'til 'e's in 'is box!'

Ivy nudged her so hard she almost fell over.

'What?' She looked from Ivy to Cordelia. 'Oh. Me and my big mouth. Your bloke's away, ain't 'e, Delia? But 'e wouldn't do nothing with one of them foreign girls, would 'e?'

Cordelia had sometimes wondered if Robert would be attracted to any of the nurses in the field hospital. He wrote about some of them occasionally, but she'd never picked up any hints that seriously worried her. But that didn't stop her wondering sometimes.

Then she had chastised herself, remembering how she'd been attracted to Eugene, the year before.

Lost in thought, the three women started folding more boxes, the pile of filled ones stacked up in the corner.

'Then there's the Crosbys next door but one to me,' Flo went on. "E's 'ome from somewhere abroad, don't know where. She was telling me 'e's very restless, can't settle down back 'ome. She don't know what to do with 'im. She don't say so but I reckon she'll be glad when 'e's sent off again.'

That story really hit home for Cordelia. She'd heard similar stories from Mavis, who knew everyone in Silvertown.

'Oh, I've only gone and done it again. Me and my big mouth.' Flo shook her head. 'I don't suppose you'll 'ave no trouble with your bloke, Delia.'

Little did she know, Cordelia thought, picking up a tin of fruit and absently reading the label. Little did Flo know that her story was one that flew at Cordelia's heart, lodging there like shrapnel. While she was thrilled that Robert was returning home, she had a knot of worry tightening in her chest. It had been so long since they'd seen each other. And while her life was much the same as when he left – the library, shopping, queueing and air raids – his had been dramatically different. He must have had experiences she could hardly imagine.

What if they didn't fit together as a couple any more? What would happen?

As she watched the two other women chatting, she didn't want to voice her fears. They'd think her crazy and ungrateful. After all, they'd think, your man is coming back. Neither of them had been married. They'd been what were called 'surplus women'. Women whose chance of marriage was destroyed by the deaths of so many men during the Great War. So many had died in that war there simply weren't enough men to go around, and many, like Flo and Ivy, never had a chance of marriage and children.

But grateful though she was, Cordelia still felt the worry about Robert's homecoming gnawing at her, wondering – what if... what if...

Her mind was brought back to what she was doing when she heard Ivy say to Flo, 'I reckon you should see that Pigeon Pete. His bird might know if anything's going to come of you and that bloke what always wants to sit next to you at the pub!'

23

Cordelia couldn't believe she'd let herself be talked into going with Ivy and Flo to see Pigeon Pete. Ivy had nagged Flo into seeing him and persuaded Cordelia to go with them. 'It'll be worth your while, Delia. Gotta be something for your book.'

For the last few weeks, a man who worked on the railways had been making a beeline for Flo every time the sisters went to the Spade and Bucket. He never asked her out but wanted to spend time with her, even buying her a port and lemon. As a result, Flo had had her hair permed and taken to wearing her precious lipstick when she spotted him.

Initially, Cordelia was surprised at this possible romance. Flo and Ivy always seemed much too old, but then she realised they just looked old. Life had been hard for them. They had only been in their late teens when the Great War started, so they must only be in their early fifties. Doing the maths made her look at the sisters again. They had lovely eyes and still a lot of brown in their hair. The wrinkles, such as they had, were laughter lines that made them appear warm and friendly. If they had money and time to work on their looks and clothes, they could look much younger.

The three of them got off the bus at the market. It sold food, clothes and bric-a-brac. Pete's stall was down one end along with other similarly unlikely offerings – from Cordelia's point of view.

One bric-a-brac stall they passed had a record player. The owner wound it up and put a record on. Soon there was a scratchy rendition of 'I'm Forever Blowing Bubbles' competing with the hubbub of market sounds. There were people selling off old household items like crockery and cutlery, others selling vegetables and fruit. There was Mystic Marge offering palm reading. She was dressed as a gypsy with a bright purple scarf on her head with small fake coins around it.

'Want your fortune told, ladies?' she shouted as they went past.

Cordelia looked at Flo – surely this was a better bet than a fortune-telling pigeon. But no, Flo insisted they walked on past Ernie's Elixirs – a stall selling home-made remedies and beauty products. And then past Paul's Penny Portraits. He did quick sketches of his customers for a penny. Cordelia was surprised he hadn't been stopped by the police because paper was rationed. But she saw one drawing he did, and it was surprisingly good. He captured the sitter in just a few strokes.

Pigeon Pete was next. He had a makeshift tent not unlike Mystic Marge's. In front of it was a table covered with a royal-blue tablecloth and a pigeon in a cage so big it almost covered the whole top. The pigeon walked up and down the limited space, cooing and pecking at the bottom of its cage where there were a few seeds.

Pete was a true showman. His white hair stuck out at all angles under a maroon fez and his clothes were a mishmash of styles and colours as if he'd raided a theatrical costume shop. Pigeon feathers hung down the sleeves. A sign proclaiming 'Feather Fortunes told!' was propped up in front of the birdcage.

'Come on. Come on, ladies,' Pete shouted, seeing their possible interest. 'Step this way! Let Feather prognosticate your future! Only fourpence a time!'

'What the heck does that mean?' Ivy asked Cordelia.

'It's just a fancy way of saying tell your fortune,' Cordelia replied. 'He must have swallowed a dictionary.'

'Fourpence is a lot for a load of old baloney,' Ivy said.

Flo nudged her. 'Ssshh, don't upset 'im or it might not work.' Then she turned to Cordelia and whispered, 'But if it stops 'er rabbiting on and on about Bertie it'll be worth every farthing.'

Flo had heard her. 'I do not go on and on. I just wonder—'

But Ivy was getting impatient. 'Never mind that. We've come all this way. You can't turn back now, Flo.' She nudged her towards the stand. 'Give it a go.'

Although fourpence wasn't a fortune, Cordelia had trouble letting Flo spend her very hard-earned money this way. 'You could always just ask the man at the pub,' she whispered in her ear.

Flo looked shocked. 'I couldn't do that. What if I've got it all wrong! I'll be a laughing stock.'

By now Pigeon Pete could tell he'd got them interested. 'Tell you what, ladies, I'll give you one go each for just thruppence a time. I can't say fairer than that, can I?'

As Flo stepped up for her turn, a whistle blew nearby. Pete's eyes widened.

'Police alert!' he hissed. Quick as a flash, he flipped over his sign so it now read 'Feathered Friend Fanciers Club'. He began shouting to people to join his club – 'Come in, ladies and gentlemen, you'll soon fall in love with these little beauties!'

As the policeman walked by, he was innocently feeding the bird.

Cordelia couldn't help but admire his quick thinking, although she'd often seen black marketeers dodge police in markets one way or another. She got out her notebook and wrote: 'Black marketeers – fortune-telling pigeon'.

She knew she'd never have time to write her book until the war finished, if it ever did. But she still liked to scribble down her notes. 'Character idea,' she added, 'market mystic with a flair for deception.'

When the policeman had gone past, Pete turned his sign back again. 'Sorry about that, ladies. I should have asked Feather here when to expect the constable.' He looked from one to the other. 'Now, who's going to be first? Step inside my tent and my wonderful bird will tell your fortune.'

'She's got a question,' Ivy said, pushing Flo so hard she almost crashed into the cage.

'How does it work? How does the bird tell my fortune?' Flo asked in such a timid voice she was hard to hear over the market noise.

Pete took off his fez with a flourish. The action got the pigeon to go near to him, pecking on the side of the cage. Pete rewarded it with a few seeds. 'My extraordinary flying friend here will give you an answer to your fortune. Just ask it a question to which it can answer yes or no.' He saw Flo looking worried. 'Let me give you an example. If you want to know if the love of your life loves you, just ask it a straight question. "Does – whatever his name is – love me?" Feather here will answer yes or no.'

It was so much hogwash, Cordelia didn't know whether to laugh or be furious. 'How does it do that then?'

'Excellent question, my friend,' he replied, looking at her.

'Feather listens to your question, then he looks into the future. He turns one way for yes and the other way for no.'

Now it was difficult for Cordelia to keep a straight face. 'Which way is which then?'

Pete tapped the side of his nose. 'That's for me to know, me and Feather. It's a secret between us.'

How convenient, Cordelia thought. Were her new friends going to take this seriously? Should she try to stop them? Then again, she thought, it's just a bit of fun and she would pay for them all.

'Oh, go on then,' Flo said, looking from man to bird and back again, excitement in her eyes. 'Feather, does Bertie, the man I see at the Spade and Bucket, fancy me?'

'No, stop!' Ivy said, agitated. 'You can't ask it like that. Ask if he'll ask you out one day. He could fancy you but not do anything about it otherwise, you daft thing.'

Flo's shoulders sagged as she nodded. 'Okay, you're right as usual.' She peered into the cage so close Cordelia worried the bird would peck her nose.

'Will Bertie, the man I see at the Spade and Bucket, ask me out?'

Pete did some dramatic movements with his hands then spoke to Feather. 'Feather, will you answer this beautiful lady's question?'

Cordelia noticed his final twist of his hand was clockwise. The bird noticed it too and obligingly turned that way.

'There, lovely lady!' Pete said. 'Feather here says Bertie will ask you out. And he's never wrong. I'd ask you meself if I wasn't already spoken for!'

Cordelia had to turn away to stop herself laughing. Then she saw the answer had bucked up Flo tremendously. It would probably give her the confidence to speak differently to Bertie next time she saw him. Thruppence well spent.

'Right, next lady, please!' Pete said, looking at Ivy. 'How can Feather help you today, my friend?'

Ivy had her question ready. 'Will I ever win a fiver at housy-housy?'

Pete repeated the dramatic twirl and again the bird turned the right way. 'This is excellent news for you, my love. What did you say your name was?'

'It's Ivy.' She was suddenly rather shy.

'Well, Ivy, my love, when you win that fiver you can buy me a drink because Feather says you're definitely going to win it one day!'

Then it was Cordelia's turn. As she'd watched the other two, she'd been wondering what to ask. She didn't want anything too personal. She had a million questions about her future with Robert, but she wasn't about to ask any of those.

'What's your question, sweetheart?' Bert asked, taking her hand and kissing it.

She almost wiped it on her jacket. 'Should I give up trying to write a book? That's my question.'

The dramatic twirl again, this time ending the other way. The bird turned anticlockwise. 'It seems we have a budding author in our midst, ladies and gentlemen,' he called out. Then he took Cordelia's hand again. 'Feather here thinks you should definitely carry on with your book!'

If only she had time, she thought. With work and Robert coming home it was likely she'd have to delay writing for the foreseeable future.

The next time she was working with Ivy and Flo, she learned that Bertie had indeed asked Flo out.

'We went to the flicks to see *Casablanca*,' she told Cordelia with a grin. 'He held my hand all the way through. Looks like you're never too old for love!'

24

As Tom had agreed to find out more about the beautiful comb in the mystery chest, he headed to the Victoria and Albert Museum in South Kensington. He knew it was very different from its pre-war days. Many of the exhibits had been moved for safekeeping to Welsh slate mines and parts of the museum were used as an air-raid shelter. Luckily, many of the specialists were still based there and he had made an appointment to speak to one of them.

Inside, his footsteps echoed in the half-empty galleries. The staff had done their best to ensure the exhibits looked inviting, but he couldn't help but think they looked like a stage set half completed. The ornate plasterwork of the ceilings loomed above him, a reminder of the museum's grandeur, but the echoing halls sounded hollow, as if the heart of the building had been sent to the Welsh slate mines along with the exhibits.

As with all public buildings there were war signs here and there. A notice about the air-raid shelter, sandbags piled discreetly near the entrance, signs like 'Every time you lend a shilling you help the war effort' and 'Carry your gas mask'.

'Can I help you?' The voice belonged to a woman emerging from a door he had just passed. Despite her advanced age, she stood tall and impressive, her steel-grey hair pulled back in a severe bun. A card pinned to her sensible black jacket identified her as 'Dr Janet Hammond, Senior Curator'.

'Ah, you're just the person I was looking for. I'm Tom Jackson. I phoned and made an appointment with you.'

She nodded. 'Something about a comb, wasn't it? Follow me.'

As she led him down corridors never seen by the public, he worried he would never find his way out again. But before long she stopped at a door with her name on and opened it for him.

'Sit down and show me the comb. I don't have much time, I'm afraid. I have another meeting in half an hour.'

Dr Hammond's eyes lit up when she saw the beautiful object, turning it this way and that and studying it closely.

'Most of our Indian collection is in storage. War safety measures of course but...' She paused, considering. 'I remember similar pieces to this one. Let me check what references we still have here.' They left her office and walked through another maze of corridors, their footsteps echoing off the wooden floors as she continued to speak. 'I've been here thirty years, believe it or not. I started as a junior curator when females weren't at all welcome, I can tell you. But I had a particular interest in Indian decorative arts, having lived there as a child.'

They entered a small office crammed with books and papers. Without hesitation, she took down one of the books and opened it on the desk. She flicked through pages until she found a section showing several photographs of combs.

As Tom watched, Dr Hammond ran her fingers over the photos. 'There! This is very similar to your comb. As I thought, the style suggests the Gujarat region, the stone setting is very distinctive.'

'So that's where it comes from?' Tom was amazed at her knowledge and expertise.

'Originally it would have been, but of course it could have been bought anywhere. Objects travel, don't they? Gifts, travelling traders and so on.'

Tom hardly knew whether to feel this information was useful or not. 'Could it have been commissioned?'

'It could. That wouldn't have been unusual. They were often gifts, many commissioned by the East India Company as presents to people they wanted to curry favour with. But many could have been made for personal gifts.' She saw his face drop. 'The most interesting ones, like this one, were those commissioned by British officers for their loved ones. Sometimes they were for Indian women – a common if forbidden liaison. But of course, many would have been sent home. Is it likely to be a love token?'

He nodded. 'Yes, that's very likely.'

Thanking her for her time, he left, unable to know how to feel. There was no proof, but what Dr Hammond had told him did fit the facts. Perhaps he could report at least a partial success to the other librarians. Would they be able to find any descendants of the lovers involved in this mystery? Just thinking about the two lovers made him feel sad. How must they have felt? What happened to them?

As Tom walked back through the echoing galleries, he took the comb out of his pocket and turned it over in his hands. What if the real story wasn't about the comb itself? After all, it was about the lovers, the people who gave and received the gift. A love token, it seemed. That was what it was. It wasn't just a gift – it was a connection, a commitment for the future.

25

Cordelia hurried through London's bomb-scarred streets towards Paddington Station. Despite the Blitz being over, there was still enough bombing and buildings collapsing to make her journey different each time. Nonetheless, she hardly noticed on this special day, she was too excited – Robert was coming home. The station's enormous iron ceiling arched overhead as she sought the right platform to wait for him. Its glass windows were still criss-crossed with blast tape.

Dodging through countless other people, she checked her watch. Yes, she was in good time, although trains so rarely followed the schedule, she would probably have ages to wait. She found a spot among the waiting crowd – mothers, sweethearts, children, all anxiously hoping their loved one would be on the next train. A woman clutched a baby close to her chest and Cordelia guessed it had been born while her husband was abroad. Soon they and two women nearby were chatting as if they'd known each other for years.

Finally the train appeared, its brakes squealed as it ground to a halt, the metallic clanking of its wheels echoing through the station. The acrid smell and noise of escaping steam filled the air, along with the cacophony of voices.

Cordelia pressed her hankie to her mouth, tasting coal dust. Her heart pounded like a drum, a mixture of excitement and anxiety competing with each other. She had hardly slept all night, wondering what her boyfriend's homecoming would be like. Surely their love would have survived their long time apart?

Train doors were flung open like pages of a book, each one with a story to be written. Cordelia lifted herself onto her toes, searching each face to spot Robert as quickly as possible. The clatter of boots on the platform, the shouts of happy greetings surrounded her. It was as if the platform itself was alive with joy and happiness. And then, finally, she saw him – Robert, his tall frame unmistakable despite his weight loss and haunted eyes. He was leaning on a stick and his skin looked grey, his hair lifeless.

Time seemed to stand still as she gazed at him – the man she had loved for so long, the man she had feared she might lose to war. Memories flashed through her mind – tender embraces, lovemaking, shared hopes for their future. All came rushing back.

For a moment they looked at each other and stood still amidst the moving crowd, drinking in each other's faces, everyone around them seeming to disappear. Cordelia saw in Robert's eyes the mix of love, relief, and something else – a shadow of experiences perhaps that she couldn't begin to imagine. Then, as if a spell had been broken, she ran towards him, arms outstretched.

'Robert, you're home!' she said, hardly able to speak for the tears threatening to fall. Like so many around them, they stood there locked in an embrace as if they were the only ones there.

Cordelia felt the rough fabric of his uniform against her

cheek, the warmth of his body, and the steady beat of his heart. The familiar, yet different, smell of him filled her nostrils and she breathed him in deeply, as if to reassure herself he really was there.

Robert dropped his stick and wrapped his arms around her, holding her tightly. 'Cordelia,' he murmured, his voice rough with unshed tears. She could feel the tension in his muscles, the slight tremble in his arms, and the way his breath caught as he fought to keep control of his emotions.

They held each other close, making up for what seemed a lifetime apart, then he bent to pick up his kitbag, but she beat him to it. They walked slowly towards the station exit, Robert leaning against her as well as using his stick. 'Just a minor injury,' he said, seeing her look. 'It's healing well. Nothing to worry about.'

Cordelia led him through the crowd, her voice soft and reassuring. 'It's all right now, Robert. You're home. You're safe.'

The scents of the city – a mixture of exhaust fumes, factory smells and the musty sweetness from countless chimneys nearby – filled the air as they walked. Cordelia kept her steps in pace with his, slow and measured, her hand firmly in his as if her mere presence would calm and reassure him.

As they walked, Cordelia studied him from the corner of her eye, noticing changes. New lines around his mouth and on his forehead, and when there were loud noises, a slight hesitation. Even the way he walked seemed subtly different.

She'd imagined their reunion so many times during her lonely nights in her flat. His injury did indeed seem minor, but although he held her hand tight there were gaps when he didn't speak.

'I've seen pictures of the damage from the Blitz,' he said as they sat in a taxi on their way to her flat. 'But it's much worse than I expected. What a terrible time you've had.'

She realised that she had become accustomed to the sight of damaged buildings standing like ancient ruins. Their exposed rooms told the stories of loss and heartache but had become everyday.

'The repair teams have done a great job,' she said, indicating half a dozen men who were patching up the front of a house. 'Some of them are local, but others are prisoners of war, and some are GIs waiting to be sent to the front.'

Robert shook his head. 'So much damage, so many lives ruined and all because of the madness of that monster Hitler.' He paused and turned to her. 'I'm afraid I've got to report to the Royal Army Medical College next week.' He squeezed her arm against his side. 'I told you in my letter they want me to train others. It'll be hard work, but nothing compared to being where I've been.'

Cordelia kissed his cheek. 'How long will you be teaching?'

His eyes sparkled with enthusiasm. 'At least six months. But let's not talk about it now. Let's just enjoy our time together.' He smiled at her. 'No more sleeping in a sandy tent tonight. I'll be coming home with you!'

She smiled, a twinkle in her eyes. 'You have no idea how much I've been looking forward to that!'

They climbed the steps to her flat, Robert taking each one slowly with the support of his stick. 'I should warn you,' he said as she groped in her bag for her key. 'I don't sleep so well these days – too many bad dreams.'

She opened the door and stepped aside to let him in. He only took a couple of steps then stopped and looked around.

'It's perfect,' he said. 'A real home, so cosy.' Then, without waiting to close the door, he dropped his kitbag and encircled her with his arms. 'I've missed you so much. More than you'll ever know.'

Their kiss lasted so long that a neighbour walked past and wolf-whistled.

'I think we'd better go inside,' Robert said with a smile.

'Sit down, my love,' she said, taking his coat. 'Let me get a drink to celebrate. I've been saving something special for today.'

He sank into her old settee with a big sigh of relief. 'You're the special thing I want. But I won't say no to a drink either.'

She continued the conversation as she poured their drinks. 'There's something I haven't told you. It's a surprise and I hope one you'll like. I've got a few days off and have borrowed a cottage so we can have some time away from the city before you start your new job.'

His smile broadened. 'A few days in the country? I couldn't have asked for anything more perfect.'

She explained where it was and what she'd been told about it. 'They've promised there will be no sandstorms!'

She put the wireless on, letting it play softly, and closed the blackout blinds as the evening light faded. Then she carried the drinks to her little coffee table and snuggled up to him on the settee. He was home and despite his injury he was well. Unless something dreadful happened, they could look forward to the rest of their lives together.

26

They were lucky to get the cottage for a few days. Some friends of Cordelia's friend Rosalind owned it. It was just what they needed – especially just what Robert needed – peace and quiet to get over his experiences in Africa.

The taxi dropped them off at Primrose Cottage. They put down their bags and stood outside the old building. They were fortunate with the weather. The gentle sunlight played on the old casement windows. Many panes of glass had circular marks showing they had been made many years before modern glass techniques had been invented.

The cottage was tucked away at the end of a winding country lane in Essex, its stone walls and sloping roof on one side giving it a storybook look. The front door showed the wear and tear of many years.

As instructed by Rosalind's friend, Cordelia lifted the third flowerpot on the left of the door and retrieved the key waiting there. Initially the lock resisted and her movements had to be carefully choreographed – a turn here, a push and pull there, a wiggle just so.

'I wonder how many days it takes to get used to that,' Robert said, watching her efforts. He stepped forward and hugged her as the key finally turned with a grinding noise that made him jump.

'Oh, it's a stable door,' Cordelia said when only the top half opened. 'I've always wanted one of these.' She leaned forward and pulled back the bolt inside, releasing the lower half. 'There,' she said. 'We're in. I hope it's as comfortable as it sounded.'

They stepped into the small hallway. Facing them were the staircase and several doors. The kitchen one was open, and they went inside.

The room wore its age like a comfortable cardigan, from the worn flagstone floor to the blackened cooking range that dominated one wall. Gleaming copper pots hung from iron hooks, their surfaces mellowed by decades of scrubbing. A deep sink was scratched here and there, showing its many years of use. Along one wall was a dresser. The top half had four shelves, each sagging under the weight of mismatched but pretty crockery.

'Oh, good,' Cordelia said, putting down her case. 'They remembered to bring food.' On the table was a box full of enough for their three-day visit. 'But that doesn't mean we can't go to the pub for a meal if we want to.'

Robert sat in one of the old wooden chairs. 'At the moment, I'll probably never want to go further than the front gate, but let's wait and see. One thing I do know is that I never want to be away from you for a minute.' He leaned forward and looked in the box. 'There's a bottle of cider here. It looks home-made. Why don't we take a glass and sit in the garden? The unpacking can wait.'

The small front garden was half turned over to vegetables – 'Help yourself to any that are ready,' they'd been told – the other half was filled with typical country flowers – dahlias, black-eyed Susans, asters and Japanese anemones. A wonky bench stood under the right-hand window.

Birds sung in the trees – a blackbird and others Cordelia didn't recognise. Then a movement nearby caught her eye – a squirrel running up a tree, its fluffy tail giving it away. In the distance they could just make out the faint trace of smoke and the bonfire smell made their noses wrinkle.

'This is heaven after North Africa and the East End,' Robert said. 'It's been so long since I saw so much green. I'm going to enjoy every minute of it, especially every minute with you.' He ran his hand along a section of hedge, enjoying the feel of nature instead of the feel of destruction and horror.

He pulled her round and hugged her tight, both feeling a powerful urge to get closer. But not yet. Not yet.

She was imagining sitting outside on that little bench after a country walk. The evenings were getting cooler, but they could wrap up in a blanket and just enjoy the peace and solitude. Enjoy being with each other, getting to know each other all over again after so long apart.

When they'd finished their drinks and the temperature dropped, they went back inside. 'I'll unpack the food if you want to go and freshen up,' Cordelia said.

Robert didn't need persuading. He took both their bags and headed for the stairs. Cordelia spent a while putting the food away and finding her way round the kitchen. She was so busy it took a while for her to notice how long Robert had been gone.

Worried something had happened to him, she crept into the bedroom. He was fast asleep on the bed, fully dressed. She stood looking down at him. She'd noticed the physical changes already but now she had time to inspect them more closely.

His face was deeply tanned, accentuating the new lines

around his eyes. He had always been slim, but now his cheek-bones stood out sharply and his clothes hung loose. Even in sleep there was tension in his jaw, as if he were grinding his teeth.

As she watched, his left hand twitched slightly and she noticed scarring across the back of his hand. He'd never mentioned the injury in his letters, and she wondered what had happened. His feet hung over the edge of the bed and she gently eased off his shoes.

She debated whether to wake him. His occasional odd behaviour showed the effects of his life in Africa. Perhaps he would sleep until morning. In his letters he'd mentioned working through the night trying to save lives, being too exhausted to think straight.

There was a handmade quilted blanket hanging over the back of a chair in the room and she gently put it over his sleeping form, careful not to disturb him. He grunted gently and turned over but didn't wake. It felt strange, off-kilter somehow, to stand here watching him sleep. He was her boyfriend, yet they'd been apart so long in some ways he felt like a stranger. She stood looking at him, remembering the first time they had made love. It had been before he went to Africa. Their chemistry had burned and their embrace was passionate, yet their love-making was tender and unhurried, as though they had all the time in the world to explore each other's bodies, the depth of their feelings, unravelling layer upon layer of their closeness.

Cordelia was about to leave the room when she heard his voice. 'Stay,' he said, his voice still uneven with sleep.

'I'm sorry, I didn't mean to wake you.'

He pulled her towards him and held the quilt up for her to lie next to him. 'I was just dreaming about you,' he said, kissing her forehead. 'I dreamt you were a nurse in the field hospital, keeping everything in order as if every person was a book in your library.'

She snuggled next to him, breathing in his masculine smell. 'You must be hungry.'

'I'm not sure I could stay awake to eat a meal. Would you be upset if I got into bed now?' He yawned. 'Not how I expected our first night in the country together to be.'

'We have two and a half more days,' she said, feeling overcome with love and compassion for this man who had been through so much.

Within a few minutes, his breathing slowed, and he nodded off again. Time for him to get undressed later, she thought.

Moving as gently as possible, she slid out of bed. She would make a simple cold meal and if he slept on she would stay downstairs reading a book for a while.

She moved around the kitchen, aware it had begun to rain. Opening the dresser drawer released whiffs of dried lavender and rosemary from old home-made sachets. From somewhere, perhaps from the pantry, came the sweet-sour reminder of stored apples, and beneath the sink lurked the familiar carbolic scent of old-fashioned cleaning soap.

She hunted for kindling and lit the Aga, glad that she had often seen their family cook do the same when she was a child. She found matches in the drawer under the kitchen table. The first match she struck sent a sharp, sulphurous tang into the room. As the kindling caught, there was the distinctive scent of wood just beginning to burn – fresh, resinous, with just a hint of pine from the smaller sticks.

She put the kettle on and cut a slice of bread, spreading strawberry jam from edge to edge. There was no hurry to prepare a meal.

There would be time later for talking, for finding each other again, for facing whatever changes war had brought to each of them, to them as a couple. For now, these days were enough.

27

They spent three days in the cottage. Robert wasn't strong enough for long walks, but they took short ones twice a day. The nearby narrow lane wandered between hedgerows humming with life. Wild roses and honeysuckle wrapped around each other, their sweet scents reaching them on the breeze. Birds hopped from tree to tree, chirping as if happy to be alive. Overhead, they were sheltered from the sun by oak and ash trees forming a dappled canopy. In the distance they heard a plane and instinctively looked up. 'Too far away to worry about,' Cordelia said with relief.

Robert held her hand as they walked on the sun-baked path, past wildflowers and grasses. A rabbit running across the path made them jump, then smile.

'This is bliss,' Robert said. 'No industrial or hospital smells, no noise, no rushing about. Is it like your family home?'

Cordelia remembered her childhood, the massive house they lived in and the grounds manicured with precision by a gardener. 'Well, it was certainly in the country but nothing like this. Our grounds were so big, we could forget about the rest of the world. But if we went into the village that was another matter.'

'Did you go on your own?'

She shook her head. 'Occasionally I went with my mother, but more often than not it was me and Jasper sneaking in there. Not that there was much to see. A small village green with a war memorial, a few shops, a down-at-heel village hall and cottages that needed a lot of work on them. Many were owned by my father.'

Robert frowned, trying to imagine her and her brother walking around the village. 'What did the pair of you do there then? It sounds boring.'

Cordelia remembered the village shop, the one that sold everything from cheese to saucepans to shoelaces. 'My brother used some of his pocket money to buy cigarettes, then he'd try to force me to smoke with him in the churchyard. He wanted a partner in crime in case we got caught.'

'Let me guess, you were too much of a goody-goody!'

She play swiped him. 'You're wrong there. I just didn't want to stink. I'd always noticed people smelled after they smoked.' She laughed. 'I suppose I was too vain. Mind you, I was tempted. I'd see those actresses on films smoking, always looking so sophisticated with their long black cigarette holders. I wanted to be like them.' She laughed at herself. 'So how is it that my life is so different? Not that I'd want to be a film star. You see them in the movies looking glamorous, but then you know they can't always be happy. From what you read, some of them turn to drink or even take their own lives.' She paused. 'No, I wouldn't want that life.'

'Do you think you could ever see yourself living in the country?' Robert asked, changing the subject.

Cordelia caught something in his voice beyond an idle question. She pulled a long blade of grass and twisted it between her fingers. 'Interesting thought. Is it something you think about?'

His pace slowed. 'Although we were run off our feet all the time in the field hospital, I still found time to think...'

Cordelia found her stomach doing strange things as she listened to him. 'And you thought...'

'Well, you know I became a doctor because I wanted to help people. Then I saw the job in Silvertown and it seemed perfect. A deprived area where people needed an unbelievable amount of support. And that was before the bombing even started.'

She nodded, remembering back to the time when she was trying to decide where to work. 'That's why I chose the library there. My family and friends all thought I was mad. With my qualifications I could have got a job in a nice area – one they thought more in keeping with people like me, like my family. My father was absolutely furious – he said he would be too embarrassed to tell people where I worked.'

Robert gently squeezed her hand. 'From what you've told me I can imagine your father's reaction. Status is obviously very important to him. But you followed your heart. That's one of the things I admire about you.' They stopped and turned to each other, kissing lightly before continuing with their walk.

At a wooden stile, Robert helped Cordelia so she didn't catch her dress. They emerged the other side into a sunny meadow dotted with wildflowers. It was a million miles away from the East End.

'What about you?' Cordelia asked, taking his hand again. 'Have you ever thought about being a doctor somewhere like this? It's not just people in the East End who are too poor to afford proper medical care.'

They sat down on a fallen tree, shaded by the branches of another. For a while they simply stayed side by side, their arms touching, looking around at the meadow, hearing the sound of cows somewhere nearby and a tractor in a field out of sight.

'You asked me if I'd like to practise somewhere like this,' Robert said eventually. 'The truth is I'm not sure. After working in the East End, then in the desert, then coming back to Silver-town, the idea of somewhere like this appeals. Not having the constant adrenaline from never having a moment to myself. But I don't know if I feel like that just because I'm worn out, through and through.'

She leaned towards him and rested her head on his shoulder, breathing in his familiar manly smell. 'Well, you can delay that decision until you leave the forces.'

He sighed. 'When the war is over, you mean.'

It was her turn to sigh. 'I wonder when that'll be. If ever. But surely it can't go on forever and Hitler seems to have given up on the idea of invading us, thank goodness.'

He kissed her forehead, breathing in the clean and elegant smell of her Je Reviens perfume. The floral notes, with hints of jasmine and something he couldn't identify, reminded him of the promise of its name which she'd once told him was 'I will return'.

'I think the tide may be turning,' he said softly, his voice displaying cautious optimism. 'It's too early to say really but it seems there is some reason to be hopeful.'

To her surprise, he stood up and she made to stand too. 'No,' he said with a smile, placing a hand on her shoulder. 'Stay just where you are. You look so beautiful, the woman I've dreamed of every night while I was away, the memory that kept me going even when I was feeling at my lowest.'

Then he dropped to one knee. For a dreadful moment, Cordelia thought he'd collapsed. But instead, he took one of her hands in his, his movement slow and deliberate, his gaze holding hers as if he would never let her go.

'Cordelia,' he began, his voice full of emotion. 'Since I met you, I realise what truly matters in life. Being with the one you love, the one you want to spend the rest of your days with, the one you could grow old with. We can't know what the future holds. With this war, we don't even know what the next week holds, but do you think... is it possible... that wherever we end up, you would do me the honour of being my wife?'

The words hung in the air between them, full of promise for the future. He looked at her, anxiety in his eyes, waiting for her answer.

28

Ben went over and over all he'd discovered in his mind. The more he thought about it, the more convinced he was that his sister May was covering something up.

He managed to get off work early one day and met her as she was leaving her work in the factory.

She smiled with delight when she saw him. 'Ben! What a lovely surprise. What are you doing here?'

He put her arm through his. 'I've come to take my lovely sister for tea and cakes at George's café.'

The walk to the café felt awkward, both stealing glances at the other, unsure what to say. Their steps were uncertain, as if they were walking on eggshells, each trying to judge the other's thoughts and feelings. The late-summer air did little to ease their discomfort, despite its warmth and the gentle rustling of the few trees that had survived all the bombings.

Ben shuffled his feet like a schoolboy, kicking a small pebble along the pavement, hands shoved in his pockets. He was tense, wanting to break the silence, to ask all his questions again, but he suspected that May would be evasive once more and the words stuck in his throat. They began to talk about insignificant things, the weather, the latest rationing restrictions, autumn on the way, but their words felt forced, unnatural.

May looked tired after her day at work, her usually neat hair escaping from her red and blue scarf. He hated the idea of adding to her burdens, but he was entitled to know the truth, wasn't he?

Her gazed fixed on the ground, May walked steadily, her steps more careful and measured than his. She clutched her handbag, as if someone might snatch it at any moment. She could feel Ben's eyes on her but was unwilling to talk about anything but trivial matters.

They navigated the crowded streets with forced smiles, nodding to passers-by and saying hello to anyone they knew. The sounds of Silvertown – the honking of cars, the distant clanging of the docks – filled the air but neither paid much attention.

As they neared the café, Ben paused briefly. 'May, I...' he began, but she quickly stopped him.

'Let's just have a nice cuppa, shall we? I wonder what cakes they have today.'

They gave their orders, tea and iced buns, then settled back, each reluctant to start. But May took the initiative.

'I think you've come to meet me to ask about Mum again, haven't you?'

He went pink to his ears. 'I must be transparent.'

She chuckled. 'I've known you since you were born. It's not surprising I can read you like a book.'

'I can't say the same for you,' he replied.

The waitress appeared at their table with their tea and buns on a tray. They thanked her and returned to their conversation.

May took the lid off the teapot and stirred the leaves with

her spoon. 'Well, I'll save you asking again,' she said, not looking at him. 'I still don't know any more. I remember you being born, of course, but I don't know anything else.'

'But surely...'

She poured the tea and passed him his cup. 'Surely nothing. Mum never talked about her childhood much, but I got the impression it was a tough one. Like me, she preferred to stick to the present and plans for the future. I never knew how old she was. She always said no one should ask a lady her age. Did you find anything interesting amongst her stuff? A crock of gold? Hidden treasure? You never said.' She grinned as she said this; their family had never had two halfpennies to rub together.

'There was something interesting.' Ben reached into his pocket and produced a much-handled postcard. It showed scenes from a Norfolk village – the war memorial, the post office, the pub and in the distance a grand manor house. 'This came from you,' he said, looking at it again. '"Got here safely," it says. "Very big house, I'm sure to get lost in it."'

Face suddenly rigid, May snatched it off him. 'Give me that!' Her face initially showed alarm then quiet reflection, and she sighed. As she touched the postcard, Ben realised it held a special meaning for her. 'I was a maid there,' she finally said, her voice little more than a whisper. 'Mum had no money so sending me away to be a maid solved two problems. I'd get fed and be able to send back a bit of money.'

Two people at the next table got up, their chairs scraping on the wooden floor.

'I didn't know you were a maid,' he said. 'You've never told me.'

She shook her head. 'It was before you were born and I wasn't there very long. When she was expecting you, Mum asked me to come back 'cos she'd need help.'

As she spoke, she fidgeted with her spoon, avoiding eye contact, her body language screaming that she wasn't being entirely truthful.

'But enough of that,' she said, her voice firmer. 'You got a girlfriend yet?'

29

Cordelia looked down at Robert, thrilled yet taken aback by his proposal. He hadn't been back from Africa long. Had they had time to truly get to know each other again, she wondered. As well as the separation, his experiences meant that he wasn't his usual self all the time. Sometimes he was quiet, as if the energy had been drained from him.

All this went through her mind in a flash as she looked into his loving eyes, saw the hope and longing there. Then she realised that she had always felt the same about him. He had always been the same. His letters from the front line, his personality in health and in sickness was always exactly what she'd hoped she would find in someone she wanted to spend the rest of her life with.

'Of course I'll marry you,' she said, her eyes sparkling, a tear running down her cheek. She leaned forward and kissed him tenderly.

When she released him, his face broke into a radiant smile. 'I'm afraid I haven't got a proper ring for you yet. Perhaps we could go and buy one together.' He pulled her up and they hugged each other, lost in the moment as they stood there in the lovely meadow.

'Have you been planning this?' she asked when they let each other go and slowly walked back to the lane. To their surprise, an army Land Rover drove along it, the driver giving them a cheery salute. It was a reminder, as if they needed it, that the war was still very much with them.

'I've wanted to ask you for longer than you can imagine,' Robert said, still holding her hand, 'but didn't dare until I was sure we still felt the same about each other – after my time abroad. Then, well, I was hoping to find somewhere romantic. This here today seemed perfect.' He looked around at the beautiful countryside, the flowers swaying gently in the breeze, the birds chirping, the smell of hay. 'I couldn't think of anywhere better than this.'

They climbed back across the stile and began walking towards the cottage. A farmer driving a horse and cart passed them. 'Morning, folks!' he said, and tipped his hat in greeting. In his cart was a dog who seemed quite at ease, his tail wagging as he saw them.

'I know there can't be any guarantees,' Robert went on. 'We both know the army is unpredictable. But I wonder, and I'm springing this on you, I know. Shall we get married soon, just in case the army change their minds and send me abroad again?'

Cordelia's breath caught. Feeling like a startled colt, she looked at him. 'That soon?' She laughed. 'You know everyone will think I'm in the family way!'

'Let them!' He grinned. 'None of their business. But what do you think of the idea?'

'I think it's wonderful, but I'm going to keep it a secret just for a little while. Hug it to myself until we've made some decisions about when and where.'

Mavis was third in the queue at the SSAFA office in Barking, the nearest to Silvertown. The WVS volunteers who came to the library and helped people find their loved ones only had information about local people, not servicemen abroad, but they'd told her to go to the SSAFA office.

On the first floor above a greengrocer's shop, and on a busy road, the office wasn't a quiet place to have a difficult conversation. The rumble of traffic and the sound of the rag-and-bone man shouting his wares drifted through the open window.

As she sat waiting, Mavis chatted to two other women who looked as anxious as she did.

'Why're you here?' one of them asked. A young mum, she was cradling a sleeping baby in her arms. 'I need some money. Can't manage now with this one.' She looked down at the baby and gently stroked his fair hair. 'Me mum's got me the essentials, all second-hand but good enough, but it's everything else. And I'm gonna have to find me own place. The people we share with are complaining about the baby crying.' She shook her head. 'I ask you! Babies cry, don't they? What do they expect? I'm Peggy, by the way.'

Mavis was glad to have someone to take her mind off her worries. She might not be rich but at least she could pay her bills. 'I'm Mavis. It's Joe, my husband. He's missing in action...'

Before she could finish her sentence, the other woman, older and exhausted-looking, spoke up. 'Oh, my dear, what a worry for you. Missing in action. Doesn't that mean they're dead but their body hasn't been found?'

This was exactly Mavis's fear, even though she knew it wasn't always true. The IIP helper had explained that to her. That didn't stop her mouth drying up and her stomach turning over. She could have killed the tactless woman.

Fortunately, Peggy nudged the older woman so hard she almost fell off her chair. 'You silly bint!' she said. 'That ain't true. And anyway, think this is what this lady wants to hear? I can't believe you said that!'

The older woman just grunted and turned her back on them.

'Silly sod!' Peggy adjusted the baby in her arms. 'I saw on the noticeboard that they help find missing soldiers. I hope you're lucky.'

Before they could talk more, Peggy was called over by one of the advisers. 'Good luck,' she whispered as she stood, struggling with the baby and her shopping bag.

Mavis read the notices on the walls while she waited to be seen. They were dog-eared, and she supposed they'd been there since the war started.

SSAFA, Soldiers, Sailors, Airmen & Families Association, helps people with finances, welfare support, housing, and locating missing soldiers.

The woman next to her still had her back turned so Mavis didn't try to have a conversation with her. Some people, she thought, had been left out when God was handing out tact.

As she waited, she looked at Peggy and two other women who were sitting being helped. She caught snatches of their conversations. 'That's all we can do, I'm afraid.' 'Go to this address, they'll help you.' 'You are in a spot, aren't you?' But listening didn't distract her from her own worry. It had been hard to concentrate on anything since she'd had the news. She'd been thrilled for Cordelia that Robert was home but couldn't help being jealous too. She hoped it didn't show.

Mavis wiped her brow with her hankie, worry making her unusually subdued as she watched Peggy explaining her situation to the adviser. A wave of longing washed over her. If only this hadn't happened – if only she could feel Joe's strong, comforting arms around her, hear his throaty laugh.

As each woman ahead of her left, her anxiety heightened. It would be her turn soon. She'd have to voice her worries.

Then a chair scraped as a tired-looking woman left one of the advisers, who promptly stood and waved Mavis over. As she walked towards her it seemed she could feel the tension of all those needing help, like a taut wire stretched to breaking point.

'Do sit down.' The kindly-looking woman smiled a greeting. 'I'm Mrs Erwin. How can I help you?'

Struggling to keep back tears, Mavis explained that her brand-new husband was listed as missing in action. 'I need to find out what's 'appened to 'im,' she said, her chin quivering. 'Can you 'elp? I need to know 'e's safe.'

Mrs Erwin began explaining the process they used to locate missing soldiers. Mavis leaned forward, her eyes watching the adviser's lips, anxious not to miss a word. But as the adviser continued, worry made her mind drift and her eyes focus on the window behind the woman. She noticed without wanting to that they needed cleaning.

'Are you with me, Mrs Smith?' the adviser asked. 'It's a lot to take in.' She leaned forward to put her hand on Mavis's arm. 'We'll do everything we can to help you. You're not alone in this.'

Grateful though she was, Mavis couldn't overcome her anxiety. 'What if... what if... he's...?'

'Let's just take it one step at a time,' the adviser interrupted gently, pulling out a form from her drawer. 'Let's focus on what we can do right now. This form will help me with the search. I suggest you take it to the little table over by the front window and complete it. Then hand it to the receptionist. We'll take it from there.' She attached it to a clipboard and handed it to Mavis with a pencil. 'Oh, there's another thing. There are some groups for women in your position, all giving each other help and support.' She paused while she looked down a list. 'There's not one in Silvertown, but there is one in Canning Town, St Margaret's Church on Barking Road. The meetings are on Tuesday evenings at six thirty.'

'I just turn up, do I?'

'That's right. You can go as often or as little as you like. And remember, we are here for you. That's our job. It's a difficult time for you but you're not alone.'

31

Back from her brief holiday with Robert, Cordelia waited until they were tidying the library after closing time to update her colleagues on what she'd learned from the letters they'd found in the mystery chest. Ignoring the sounds of traffic outside, she instinctively dropped her voice as she spoke about them, as if the stories held in the fragile pages might scatter like dust if she spoke too loudly. She placed the fragile yellowed pages on the circulation desk. 'I've studied the letters now...' She looked up at the others with excitement in her eyes.

Tom's eyes lit up with boyish enthusiasm. 'Any clues leading to hidden treasure?'

Cordelia laughed. 'There's still a lot of little boy in you, isn't there? No, but from what the mysterious J says, he must have been involved in the Indian Mutiny. I looked it up – that was 1857–1858. Only a year but from what I read in one of the books, it was a bloody battle. The Indian population were understandably unhappy about British rule.'

She reached for a thick leather-bound book she had taken home to study. She and Robert had been fascinated by what they learned, and she was glad to find something to keep his interest now he was home.

'Look at this.' She pointed to pages filled with vivid illustrations and dense text. One drawing was of a terrible battle, the violence in the scene painful to look at. 'I read some officers were sympathetic to the Indian cause. Can you imagine being stuck between duty and your conscience and having to fight like that?'

The others gathered round, peering at the book. Mavis pursed her lips. 'I 'ope J was one of the sympathisers. 'E must 'ave been nice for Evelyn to love 'im so much. Any clues as to who 'e was?' She felt low, if she was honest with herself, but gritted her teeth, determined not to show it.

'No,' Cordelia went on, 'but I'd guess he was an officer because his writing is so literate. He writes that their relationship must be kept secret. I wonder why.'

Mavis tapped the papers she'd been sorting into a tidy pile and clipped them together. 'Bet your life one of them was married.'

Jane laughed. 'You always think the worst, Mavis. There could be all sorts of other reasons, different classes...'

'Yeah, 'e wouldn't want to be seen with a maid, would 'e!' Mavis shook her head as she spoke. Then she told herself off. She tried so hard not to let her anxiety about her lovely husband affect her, but sometimes it did. She wished she hadn't sounded so harsh.

'There could be other reasons,' Tom joined in. 'Family feuds, different colour skin, different religions. All sorts.'

'I'm still not sure we should be poking our noses into this.' Jane was looking subdued. 'It feels intrusive. And their ancestors might still be alive and living in the East End...'

Mavis nudged her. 'They're all long gone, Jane. They're not going to come back to haunt us.'

Tom began sorting books on the return trolley as they spoke, putting them into order by the Dewey Decimal System to make shelving them easier. 'What you've found out fits with what I learned about the history of the comb. It all fits together.'

The clock on the wall struck the hour and both Mavis and Jane looked up. 'Goodness,' Jane said. 'I'd better go or Linda will be fretting.'

'Me too.' Mavis picked up her handbag. 'Joyce will be fed up with me if I'm late collecting 'er. We'll have to carry on with this another day. Why don't we all put our thinking caps on and chat about it tomorrow?'

Anything to take her mind off worrying about Joe.

32

Cordelia sat on the night train, going over the telephone conversation with her mother.

'It's... it's... your father. He's in the hospital. They say it's his heart. He's very poorly. Can you come?' The fear in her mother's voice made Cordelia shake. Her mother was always in control, elegant. But not this time.

Cordelia had just finished a busy day at the library, then filled boxes for the troops, but tired though she was, she knew she had to go immediately to see her father. She threw a few clothes into a weekend bag, locked her door and hurried to the station. No point looking at timetables this late in the evening. A variety of causes meant trains were frequently delayed, sometimes for hours and, if a track was bombed, delays could last days.

Relieved, she only had to wait an hour for her train and managed to squeeze into a carriage mostly filled with troops. One soldier, who looked barely old enough to shave, put her bag up on the rack, blushing as he smiled at her. His obvious youth made Cordelia look at the others. Their unlined faces and immaculate uniforms were a dead giveaway. They were new recruits and distracted though she was she sent up a silent prayer for their safety.

Too worried to want any conversation, she closed her eyes and was soon in a fitful sleep troubled by terrible dreams of her father dying. The train jolting to a halt woke her and she looked around, not knowing for a moment where she was. Night had overtaken them, and the blackout blinds and curtains made the carriage claustrophobic and stuffy.

'What's happening?' she asked the young man who had helped her.

'Bombing raid. We're in a tunnel. Let's hope it's one of them hit-and-run raids.' He paused. 'And pray to the good Lord that our tracks are still in one piece.'

The journey took nearly three times longer than it should. The only advantage was that by the time they arrived, it was early enough next morning for her to go direct to the hospital. Cordelia phoned her mother from a call box at the station and arranged to meet her there.

They sat at her father's bedside. He had a private room in the hospital, but they could still hear people walking past, trolleys being trundled along, and the ward sister's rubber-soled shoes squeaking as she walked past their door, marking time like a metronome.

Outside, ambulances wailed their approach. Each new siren made her mother flinch, as if every new casualty would somehow make her husband's condition deteriorate.

'What happened, Mother?' Cordelia asked. She had come direct to the hospital from the train and only just arrived. Her father was hardly recognisable. He was lying amidst the pristine snowy bedding, unconscious, an oxygen mask concealing the mouth that normally spoke with complete authority. His face, usually firm and determined, was gaunt, with shadows under his sunken cheeks. They had pulled their chairs a little way from the bed so they wouldn't disturb him while they spoke. 'You didn't say much on the phone.'

Her mother looked like a shadow of her normal immaculate self. The woman who never even left her bedroom without her hair and lipstick perfect, she was bare-faced, wore no jewellery and her clothes were creased. Sighing, she looked over at her husband. 'He's been getting a bit breathless lately. He will smoke those damned cigars all the time. "If they're good enough for Winston, they're good enough for me!" he always says.' She shook her head. 'I kept telling him to see the doctor again, but he always knew best. Then this morning as he was getting dressed he just collapsed. I was in my room so I didn't see it happen. I heard him groaning though...'

'Oh, Mother,' Cordelia said, leaning over and putting her hand over her mother's, aware that her own was trembling slightly. 'How awful for you.'

Out in the corridor, someone dropped a metal tray, making them both jump.

Their hearts were still beating fast when they were interrupted by a nurse and a doctor entering the room. The doctor introduced himself. 'I'm Dr McGrath,' he said, looking at Lady Carmichael. 'Are you the patient's wife?'

Cordelia's mother nodded. 'I am and this is my daughter Cordelia.'

'I'm sorry I didn't see you yesterday,' he continued. 'But now I'd like to examine the patient. Would you mind waiting outside while I do so? I'll speak to you both as soon as I'm finished.'

Without another word, he took out his stethoscope and they reluctantly left the room.

The corridor was bleak, smelling of disinfectant. Instinctively they went to stand by the window in search of fresh air. A willow tree outside was blowing in the breeze and another ambulance was leaving, on its way to the nearby road. The willow swayed gently, its delicate branches bending yet not breaking, much like Cordelia's hopes for her father.

'His heart stopped in the ambulance,' her mother said, her voice shaking. 'They thumped his chest a lot and got it going, but I don't think the doctors are very hopeful.' She paused and looked towards her husband's room. 'I suppose we'll know more in a minute.'

Cordelia knew that her parents had grown apart in recent years. Her mother was unhappy with the way he treated his tenants and with his attitudes to the poor in general. In years gone by, she wouldn't have taken much notice, but since the soldiers had been convalescing in a large part of their house, her views had changed. Listening to Cordelia speaking about life in the East End had contributed to that also. She wanted to ask her mother how she would feel if he died, but dread of the thought held the words back.

Several minutes later, her father's door opened, and the doctor called them back in. Cordelia held her mother's hand and they walked in together.

'Do sit down,' Dr McGrath said. He took a chair and sat opposite them. 'As you know, Lord Carmichael has had a very severe heart attack.' Cordelia saw the nurse glare at him and he lowered his voice. 'At the moment he is resting, and we have given him an appropriate dose of morphine, so he is not in pain.'

'Can't you do anything else?' Cordelia's mother asked. 'Surely there's something...'

'I wish there was,' the doctor replied. 'We're doing everything we can and keeping him comfortable is very important.'

Her mouth dry, Cordelia struggled to form the question she wanted to ask. 'Is he going to live?'

The doctor looked down at his hands. 'I always like to be optimistic but I'm afraid I can't say one way or another at the moment.' He looked at Cordelia's mother. 'I understand he enjoyed smoking cigars.'

She nodded. 'I was always saying they were bad for him, but he enjoyed them too much to stop.'

'I'm afraid they seem to have damaged his lungs as well as his heart. We'll just have to see how he does. If he survives the next twenty-four hours we can be hopeful.'

'But... but... if he does, will he be his old self again?'

The doctor shook his head. 'After a heart attack of this severity, most people have less energy. They must take it easy for the rest of their lives.'

It was impossible to imagine that. Cordelia's father had always been busy with his office work and trips to London to meet his financial advisers and goodness knows who else.

Outside they heard a trolley stop. The door opened and an elderly woman wearing a wrap-around apron came in. 'Cup of tea, anyone?'

Cordelia expected the doctor to tell her off. Consultants had a reputation for being God-like and an impatient God at that. 'Not for me,' he said, indicating himself and the nurse, 'but I expect Lady Carmichael and her daughter would welcome one.'

Soon Cordelia and her mother sat sipping their tea, watching her father for signs of movement, but there were none.

'You know, I can't remember your father ever being ill before.' Cordelia's mother shook her head. 'He thinks illness is a sign of weakness.'

'What, even after seeing all the sick and injured men in the convalescent unit?' Cordelia couldn't help but think of the men recovering in a large part of their home. They were blind, crippled or otherwise so injured in some way that they weren't fit to be discharged. Some never would be.

A nurse came in an hour later and took his pulse, temperature and blood pressure again. 'His figures are looking a little better,' she said. 'If he keeps this up, we may be able to be hopeful. It's too soon to be sure though.'

Cordelia sat back, her body still weak with worry. It had been years since she and her father had enjoyed a good relationship. Their views on life were too different. But she prayed to a God she wasn't sure she believed in to save him. Despite his treatment of his tenants, he wasn't generally a bad man.

Her mother moved over to sit next to her father and placed her hand over his. She looked over at Cordelia. 'Will things be okay at the library?'

Cordelia nodded. 'They know what's happened and they're all very capable. I'll phone them tomorrow morning and update them.'

'Can't you phone them tonight?' her mother asked.

'None of them have a phone, Mother. Not many people in the East End do.'

Her mother frowned as if trying to understand. 'People don't have phones? They can't afford them? That is just unimaginable.'

As she finished speaking, her husband opened his eyes and looked at her.

'Charles!' Lady Carmichael exclaimed, her voice a mixture of relief and fear.

Cordelia jumped to her feet. 'I'll fetch a nurse.' She was already moving towards the door.

She returned moments later with a nurse, who smiled at Cordelia's father. 'Good to see you with us again, Lord

Carmichael,' she said as she took his pulse. Then she slipped a thermometer under his tongue. 'Don't speak for a minute, there's a good man.' She chuckled. 'Wouldn't want you to swallow mercury, would we!'

After removing the thermometer, she read it, shook it firmly and made a note on his chart at the bottom of the bed.

'All in order. I'll get the doctor.'

Lord Carmichael had been silent during all of this action, his eyes moving around the room, then they settled on his wife and daughter. When the nurse had gone, he spoke, his voice shaky. 'What happened?'

'The doctors think you've had a heart attack, darling,' Cordelia's mother said. 'You've been unconscious for a while so we're very glad to see you awake again. The doctor will explain more.'

Cordelia took a deep breath, knowing that what the doctor told them might change the way her parents lived forever.

33

It was late when Cordelia and her mother returned home. Her father had thankfully managed to speak to them both for a short time then drifted back to sleep. A normal sleep rather than unconsciousness. The two women had looked at each other, relief draining tension from their faces.

'Perhaps...' Lady Carmichael said.

She didn't need to finish the sentence. 'Yes, it's a good sign,' Cordelia replied. 'Let's pray he continues to improve.'

At eight o'clock the doctor had insisted they went home. 'We will telephone you if there is any change,' he reassured them. 'In this wing we don't enforce visiting times so come back any time you like in the morning.' He put his stethoscope back around his neck and shook their hands. 'I think we can begin to have hope, although of course we can't give any promises yet.'

Back at home, they settled at the dining table, the familiar scent of Mrs Taylor's chicken pie wafting from beneath the silver serving covers. Steam rose as the maid lifted the lids, uncovering a golden-crusted pie nestled among the roast vegetables. The aroma, which would usually make their mouths water, seemed to mock their poor appetite.

'I'm not sure I can eat anything,' Cordelia's mother said. 'I'm too upset.'

Feeling the same, Cordelia picked at her meal. 'Mrs Taylor will understand if we leave some. She must be worried too.'

Cutting a small piece of pie, her mother nodded. 'She's been with us forever. The days have gone by when staff stayed with you until they retired. That was the case in my parents' day.' She looked down at the table, her fingers running up and down the cutlery 'I know you've always got on well with Mrs Taylor and I had a similar relationship with the cook before her. Mrs Edwards. It was her fault I have a sweet tooth.' She took a tiny bite of the pie and chewed it without tasting it. 'Mrs Taylor was just Nellie then – a kitchen maid.' Even as a child, Cordelia had felt sorry for the 'lower orders' – staff who were rarely seen by the family: the chambermaids, the kitchen help, the scullery maids and gardeners. In her mind's eye, she saw ghostly figures of maids from her childhood. She struggled to remember their names – Mollie, Dot, Jilly? Had she remembered them correctly? She remembered their slight frames bowed under the weight of heavy water jugs and smelly chamber pots.

She also recalled their tired faces, hair limp and damp escaping from once neat caps, dark smudges beneath their eyes. The narrow, bare servants' staircase seemed to swallow them, their breathing laboured and the swish of their skirts against the steps the only evidence they had been there. It was whispered that in the days when maids wore long skirts, one had been carrying a load of soiled bedding down those stairs and fallen to her death, her neck broken in an instant.

Cordelia had since learned they worked much longer hours than they would in a factory and for less money or freedom.

Who could blame them for leaving? She had vague memories of one or two who didn't stay long.

'Why did some of the maids not last in the years before the war?' she asked.

Her mother shook her head as if trying to remember. 'Some weren't suited, of course, and the housekeeper who oversaw those staff would give them notice. One or two just seemed to vanish. I would overhear the staff talking when they thought I couldn't hear. They seemed to have a lot of ideas why they'd gone. Theft and getting in the family way seemed to be the most popular suggestions.'

She looked over at the photos on the sideboard. One was of her own wedding day.

'Girls in my class never did such things, of course...' She stopped, then shook her head again. 'Well, I always suspected one or two who suddenly vanished for a year to "travel abroad to widen their horizons".' She made a gesture to put those words in quotes. 'They always seemed sad when they came back and would never talk about Rome or Paris or Madrid or any of the other places they were supposed to have visited.'

Cordelia thought about the people who came into the library hoping to find out about their family history. Not many, and usually looking for people who had moved on from Silvertown and on to greater things. They would come into the library with all the information they had – certificates if they were lucky, old, faded photos, family stories that may or may not be true. Often the librarians couldn't help much but were able to suggest ways to continue their searches.

The two women went to bed early, exhausted by the emotional day. Cordelia thought she would never sleep, thoughts of her father forcing their way into her mind like a never-ending film.

Outside she heard occasional footsteps as staff or patients from the convalescent unit walked about. Once or twice, she heard someone cry out as if having a terrible nightmare. But she also heard an owl hooting, and the chur-chur-chur of a nightjar. Her curtain was half open and as she lay there she saw shadows as clouds crossed the moon and hoped there would be no bombing for the East End or anywhere else.

She was surprised at how terrified she was that she might lose her father. Lose the man she had struggled with for so many years. She realised it wasn't just the fear of his death that scared her, but the thought of losing the chance of having the father she'd always longed for. A father who was loving and attentive, interested in her and her life. But she remembered talking to Jane when Jane's mother died. Her mother had been a difficult, critical woman and Jane always hoped she would change. That she would become the type of mother Jane longed for. It wasn't to be.

Aware that she might be watching her own father's mortality unfold, Cordelia faced a new worry: Robert. He hadn't met her parents yet and she could already hear her father's dismissive tone. 'Not suitable,' he'd say. 'Not like us.' He clearly thought that was the only important criteria for a good husband. She had explained how Robert had studied for many long years at medical school – the endless long nights of study, the humble part-time jobs to keep his finances afloat. All would count for nothing with her father. She knew he didn't value such things as personal drive and motivation. To him, when he thought about suitable spouses for her and her brother, status, money and family background were foremost in his mind. Not what they themselves wanted, but what he thought was appropriate for people of their standing.

34

'Come in, Jane, lovely to see you.' Mrs Wheel's greeting was as warm as ever.

The house was one of the larger ones in Silvertown, on the edge of the borough. Mrs Wheel's late husband had been a factory owner, so they were better off than most.

The room smelled of lavender and furniture polish and the dark wooden piano glowed like a conker. Dappled sunlight came through the bay window, illuminating the highly polished surface. The room had a feel of faded gentility, from the antique furniture to the patterned velvet curtains. Larger than her living room at home, Jane loved the feeling of space, of being able to move around without worrying about crashing into something.

Jane ran her fingers over the upright piano, wishing that one day she could learn to play. A memory popped into her mind, something she hadn't thought about for years. Her grandmother had a battered old piano in her living room, not entirely in tune, but she could play anything entirely by ear. She loved nothing better than belting out a tune with the family at Christmas or at the local pub, encouraging everyone to have a good old sing-song. Jane must have been very young and didn't know all the words but enjoyed singing along with everyone else.

'Right,' Mrs Wheel said, bringing her back to the moment. 'Take your coat off and we'll get started on the scales.'

Jane put down her things and stood by the piano as she had been taught.

'Jane, don't slouch!' Mrs Wheel said sternly. As she spoke, some of her steel-grey hair slipped from its pins and she automatically tucked it back in. 'Always remember, stand upright, shoulders back, chin parallel to the floor! You won't be able to breathe properly if you're slouching.'

Embarrassed she'd forgotten, Jane did as she said, ready for what came next.

'Take a deep breath, Jane. Feel your diaphragm expand.' Mrs Wheel demonstrated by putting a hand on her own stomach. 'Now, exhale slowly, control the air flow. You are in charge.'

Next came the trills, where Jane had to vibrate her lips, producing a sound that always made her want to giggle. It certainly made Linda laugh when she practised at home.

'And now the scales.' Mrs Wheel struck a key on the piano. 'Now let's begin. Do-Re-Mi-So-Far-Mi-Re-Do,' she sang, her voice clear and strong despite her age. Jane copied her notes, tentative at first but with growing confidence. As she sang, she felt the vibrations in her chest, her throat opening to reach the higher notes. Even she, who could be critical of herself, could tell her voice had already begun to improve.

'Let's get you singing a song you haven't sung before.' Mrs Wheel sorted the music sheets and pulled one to the front. 'You'll know it. It's from the film *Casablanca*.' She looked over to Jane, who smiled. It was one of her favourite films.

'Is it "As Time Goes By"?' She'd often sung it around the

house and used to sing it to Linda to get her to sleep when she was a baby.

'It is,' Mrs Wheel said. 'I've chosen it because it's a lovely melody and perfect for developing your vocal control. And because the lyrics are emotional, you'll have to show you can express feelings through your voice.' She sat at her piano stool, smoothed her skirt and adjusted the sheet music before she began to play.

'You must remember this...' Jane began and continued with the beautiful song, making an effort to use every technique she had learned.

When she'd finished, Mrs Wheel turned round on her stool and clapped her hands. 'That was excellent, Jane. You have progressed so quickly. I assume you are practising between our sessions.'

Jane nodded. 'My landlady, Mrs S, says our house is always full of music. Luckily, she likes it.'

'Sit down a minute,' Mrs Wheel said, moving to an armchair. 'I want to talk to you.'

Jane immediately thought she'd done something wrong or that Mrs Wheel wasn't going to give her any more lessons. She'd refused payment so Jane would hardly blame her.

She sat on the edge of the padded armchair like a schoolgirl expecting to be told off.

'Relax, Jane,' Mrs Wheel said with a sparkle in her eyes. 'I have excellent news for you.'

Jane's eyes opened wider, and her heart raced. She couldn't imagine what that would be.

Mrs Wheel smiled again. 'Now, I think your first reaction to what I'm about to suggest will be to say no, so I want you to keep an open mind...' She paused and tucked her hair in again.

'There is an opportunity for you to sing to the troops at Woolwich Barracks.'

'The troops?' Jane echoed, her voice trembling. She stood up abruptly, and began pacing the small space between the piano and the armchair. 'But I'm not ready. I'm not good enough.' But even as she spoke, her heart pounded with a mixture of excitement and fear as she realised she loved the idea. Singing for the troops like her husband George. She knew how much it meant to them to have some entertainment.

'Nonsense!' Mrs Wheel's voice became stern. 'I will not listen to that. You won that talent competition fair and square and everyone loved you. This is an ENSA concert so there will be other acts and at least one other singer. You will certainly sing at least one song alone but perhaps sing one or two with others. Think of it as doing your bit for the war effort.'

Jane threw herself back in the armchair. Sing for the troops? Could she really do that? It would be completely different from singing in the church hall. 'I... I...' she began, but even as she hesitated, her mind raced ahead. She could borrow a glamorous dress from Cordelia, Mrs S would look after Linda and perhaps George would be lucky and get a weekend pass so he could see her.

'Well?' Mrs Wheel asked, watching her thoughts race across her face. 'Will you do it? We need to get practising some songs.' She stood up and moved to the piano without waiting for an answer. 'I thought "As Time Goes By". It would suit your vocal range perfectly.' She swivelled round on the piano stool. 'Come on then, girl. Stand up, let's get practising.'

35

It had been a month since Cordelia's father had had a heart attack, and he'd just been discharged from hospital.

'Normally they keep them in longer,' her mother said when they spoke on the phone, 'but because we can afford to have a nurse for him, they agreed to discharge him now. The doctor will come regularly.'

Despite their difficult relationship, Cordelia was delighted her father was recovering, albeit slowly. Now she was on the train on her way to visit him. She hadn't seen him for ten days and then he had seemed a shadow of his old self. Quieter, less aggressive. Her mother had told her he thanked all the hospital staff who had helped him when he left, even the porters. Had his brush with death changed him, she wondered.

The train was as crowded as ever, full of troops going on leave, loud and jolly, filling the air with cigarette smoke and laughter. She watched them with a mix of admiration and envy. Their camaraderie and resilience impressed her. She caught snippets of their conversation, their laughter interspersed with serious talk about where they would be sent next.

If the news was to be believed, they would soon be sent abroad to fight, and some would probably lose their lives. Thinking that brought her mind back to Robert. They had been together regularly since he returned from North Africa, and she had been delighted that his initial nervousness had almost disappeared. Soon she would bring him to meet her father.

The train slowed and she stood up and picked up her luggage, ready to open the door and step onto the platform. To her surprise, her mother had learned to drive, and she would be waiting for her.

'Thanks for coming, Mother,' she said as she stepped into the car. 'It's always a relief to get off those stuffy trains.'

Her mother patted her arm and then opened a window. 'I'm afraid you reek of cigarette smoke, but it'll soon go.'

As they drove to Stonehaven Hall, her mother gave Cordelia the latest news of her father's health.

'He's still frail, and must sit in a chair a lot, but I see an improvement every day. On good-weather days he sits in the garden. To my surprise his nurse, who seems very up to date on medical matters, makes him go for short, gentle walks. She even makes him exercise twice a day. She says he mustn't let his muscles wither. He grumbles a bit, especially as he has to lean on her arm for support, but he does it.'

Cordelia remembered how her father was always busy, spending hours at his desk or up in London doing whatever business he did. 'How has he been in himself? It must be very frustrating for him not being able to do everything he usually does.'

'I think you'll see a change in him, Cordelia,' her mother said as she drove up the drive to the hall, narrowly missing a rabbit that ran across the path. 'I don't know if it's because he hasn't recovered his strength, but he seems much calmer... much kinder, actually. I probably shouldn't say this, but I am enjoying the way he is at the moment.'

Cordelia could hardly believe her ears. That was the last thing she expected to hear.

On both sides of the drive at Stonehaven Hall convalescing soldiers were weeding or planting the vegetable patches, all part of the Dig for Victory campaign.

'I love seeing them out here,' her mother said. 'Their matron told me it's not only good for their physical health, but their mental health is improved because they feel they are achieving something. They certainly are, they provide most of the vegetables they need and occasionally bring a small box round for us too. Mrs Taylor is delighted.'

She pulled round the side of the hall, the entrance the family now used. Her father was there sitting in a wicker chair, a blanket over his knees and a book on his lap. He was near the remaining flower garden and although he was looking at it, his mind seemed miles away. Cordelia was relieved to see a little more colour in his cheeks and remembered how grey and withered he had been in his hospital bed.

She got out of the car, taking out her weekend bag, and went over to him. 'Hello, Father,' she said, kissing his cheek.

He turned and looked at her. At first it was as if he wasn't sure who she was but she could see recognition dawning and he smiled. She blinked fast. She couldn't remember the last time he'd smiled at her.

'How are you, Father? You look so much better than last time I saw you.'

'Cordelia,' he said, and his voice was much gentler than normal. 'It's good to see you. Is Jasper with you?'

She shook her head. 'It's an awkward time to leave the farm and Scotland is so far away. He wanted to leave as soon as he learned you were ill, but Mother decided to just keep him informed. But he sends you his love.'

'Ah, yes, I have received a couple of letters from him. He seems to have matured, finally.'

She sat down on a nearby bench, eyes scanning the garden where he'd been looking.

'You must be thirsty after your journey, Cordelia. I'll fetch us some tea,' her mother said, and disappeared inside.

'The flowers are looking lovely,' Cordelia said, thinking it best to keep the conversation light.

'Your mother has been helping the gardener every day, light stuff of course, pruning and the like. I enjoy watching her. It's important to grow the vegetables, but we must have some beauty too.' He looked around. 'It's only since I got home that I've noticed your mother makes sure there are one or two vases of flowers here and there in the house. They brighten the place up, don't they?'

Cordelia watched him carefully, noticing subtle changes in his demeanour. He seemed more willing to speak to her and her mother, interested in their lives and conversations.

'How are you feeling now?' she asked.

He sighed and closed the book on his lap. 'A little better. I suppose I must be if I'm back home, but I still feel weak, and they tell me I'll never get my full strength back.'

The pain in his eyes was dreadful to see and Cordelia longed to throw her arms around him, but guessed he wouldn't appreciate that even if he did feel more human.

'It was a wake-up call,' her father continued. 'The vicar came to see me several times and we had some long talks. It made me realise that... well... I hadn't always got my priorities right.' He twisted his blanket between his fingers. 'I was brought up being told that emotions were a sign of weakness and making money to keep the hall going was paramount. Now I... I... realise I need to value you and the rest of the family, not just material wealth.'

They were interrupted by a soldier wheeling himself round the corner of the house. As soon as he spotted them, he stopped. 'Oh, sorry, mate,' he said. 'I've come too far. Didn't mean to disturb you.' With a struggle, he turned the wheelchair round and headed back to the front of the house.

Once, her father would have been furious, outraged that someone should take liberties as he would have thought. Instead, he just continued talking as if nothing had happened. 'Now, where's that tea?' He looked around and caught sight of his wife and the maid approaching with a trolley laden with tea things. 'The doctor tells me I must lose some weight,' he mused. 'But one cake a day can't hurt, can it?'

Cordelia's breath caught in her throat. She'd never heard her father speak with such vulnerability. It was such a change from his usual impatient and self-important way of speaking. She longed to reach out, to offer comfort, but worried that would be a step too far for him.

'One cake a day sounds allowable,' she agreed. 'And don't worry about the past. We all have things we wish we'd done differently.'

He reached out and touched her arm with his shaky hand. It was the closest they'd come to an embrace since she was a child. She wasn't sure it had even happened then. For a moment, they sat silently until the sound of rattling cups and saucers got their attention.

'Excellent timing,' her father said as Cordelia's mother and the maid reached them. 'I can have one cake, dear, can't I?'

Dear? Cordelia was speechless. She couldn't remember her father ever using a term of endearment to his wife. Looking at her mother, she saw she was glowing, delighted at such a small change in his approach to her.

When the tea and cakes had been distributed, her father spoke again. 'How is Jasper? Is he still enjoying the farm? It sounds as if it'll be the making of him.' He sipped his tea. 'After his behaviour in London I thought I might have to cut him out of my will. He'll get my title when I pass on, of course, but I can decide if he gets the money.'

'You'd be very proud of your son,' Cordelia's mother said. 'I hear he's doing extraordinarily well. He's managing the farm, looking after the finances and even thinking of introducing sheep.' She took a tiny bite of a small cucumber sandwich. 'I believe he has a girlfriend too. A local girl, but he's not saying much yet. Her name is Fiona and she's a nurse.'

Her father swallowed his sandwich and nodded. 'A nurse? Well, I've met a lot of them recently and damn fine things they were too. The doctors wouldn't be able to manage without them.'

They talked about the hall, Jasper and the hospital until Lord Carmichael was tired and asked to go in. The nurse, who appeared as if by magic, helped him into a wheelchair and pushed him into the house.

Cordelia and her mother sat silently at first, drinking more tea and finishing the cucumber sandwiches. Then her mother spoke. 'He seems to be a changed man, Cordelia. So much more relaxed and able to enjoy the small things in life. I hope it lasts.'

36

'First time is it, love?' another performer asked Jane. She was dressed in a revealing sparkly dress with feathers in her hair. 'Here, have a sip of this, it's guaranteed to melt those nerves. I'm Maisie, by the way.'

She handed over a flask, but Jane hesitated. It would be sure to contain alcohol and what if she got tipsy and forgot her words? 'I'd better not, but thank you.'

'Okay, let me know if you change your mind. Nice dress, by the way.'

Jane looked down at herself and smiled. Cordelia had let her borrow a different dress this time, a silver slinky number with a split up to the knee and bare shoulders. She looked in the spotted mirror in the room the army had allocated to the ENSA group. She hardly recognised herself with her perfect hair and make-up. Hands shaking slightly, she adjusted a small brooch on her dress that Mrs S had given her for luck. 'I wore it to my wedding, ducks,' she'd said.

It was only two weeks since Mrs Wheel had persuaded her to sing for the troops. Someone had dropped out, another singer, and they were looking for a replacement at short notice.

'But won't they want a professional?' Jane had asked, her mouth dry.

Mrs Wheel shook her head. 'There are so many ENSA groups all over the place that they often struggle to put together enough talent. And it's not unusual to have amateurs. I'm afraid that means you won't get paid though, apart from expenses.'

Getting paid was the last thing Jane had thought of, but the first Mavis had asked about when she told her the news.

"Ow much will they pay you then?' she'd enquired in her usual blunt way.

Wondering if she was making a mistake, Jane bit her lip. 'Mrs Wheel, my teacher, says it's good practice and there might be someone in the audience who can help me get further with a singing career.'

Cordelia had joined them and caught the end of the conversation. 'A singing career,' she said, her voice warm and encouraging. 'Goodness, that's a wonderful thing to aim for and you certainly are good enough. That's fantastic, Jane.'

As she looked in the mirror again, Jane wished her friends were there to give her support. But she wasn't alone much longer. Three more girls came in, all dressed in mock army uniforms – khaki shorts and shirts with the sleeves rolled up. They all had army caps on the back of their heads. 'You the new singer?' the tallest of the three asked. 'I hope you're better than the last one. When she started singing all the dogs outside started to howl.'

Her friends nudged her so hard she almost fell over. 'Don't take any notice of her. The important thing is the troops are always happy to see us. And you, dressed like that, looking a million dollars, they won't want to let you off the stage.'

'Thanks.' Jane blinked in surprise at the compliment, her voice trembling as much as her knees. 'I've got to go to the WC.'

Once there she relieved herself, then went through her scales, hoping no one could hear her. Then, terrified, she suddenly realised she had no idea what she was going to sing. Her mind was completely blank. She lightly slapped herself on the cheeks. 'Of course you know it! It's... it's...' Then an image from the film *Casablanca* came into her mind and she relaxed. 'You must remember this...' The opening words came into her mind. She could almost hear Mavis telling her not to be so silly, or Cordelia encouraging her with praise.

'Five minutes! Five minutes!' someone called, and she came from the WC and joined other performers in the wings, relieved she wasn't on first. She peeked around the curtains and terror seized her when she saw that every seat was filled and there were men standing at the back too.

Jane could hardly remember anything until it was her turn to go on. Then, almost in a daze, she walked on stage and was immediately overwhelmed by cheers, wolf whistles and foot-stamping. She grinned and gestured for them to calm down, then surprised herself by saying, 'Down, boys!' That got a burst of laughter.

And as with the talent competition, once she started singing, she was lost in the music, lost in the emotions of the song and her love for George. He hadn't been able to get a pass to come to see her but had made her promise to sing the song for him when he got home.

I'm so proud of you. I've told all my mates my wife's a singer. They're all dead jealous. Make sure you get a photo taken this time!

And seemingly after no time at all, the song finished and there was a moment's silence. Eyes wide with fear, Jane wondered if the audience had hated it. Had she sung the words wrong somehow? Missed a note? Made the dogs howl?

Then she was taking her bow amidst wild applause, cheering, whistling and calls for more. She was so overwhelmed she could hardly breathe and just stood for a few seconds until the master of ceremonies came on and thanked her, calling for another round of applause.

Backstage there was a flurry of performers congratulating her, one giving her a hug, whispering, 'You were magnificent, darling!' in her ear.

The tension that had been there all the time gradually left her like a boa constrictor unwinding and releasing its grip. She leaned against the wall, taking one deep breath after another. Then she shook her head and moved so she could see the other acts. She wanted nothing more than to sit somewhere quiet but couldn't miss the other performers. Her first time in an ENSA show, and it might never happen again.

But before the show had finished, a man came backstage and approached her. 'Mrs Wilkins? Jane? Can I see you after the show?' he whispered. 'I'm from the BBC.'

37

The man from the BBC invited Jane to talk to him after the show finished, suggesting the barracks canteen, or the mess hall as it was called. Puzzled by his request, she followed him through several corridors, still wearing her glittery dress and uncomfortable shoes. It was the first time she'd been to a barracks and realised this sort of building must be familiar to George after all his time in the army. What a lot she would have to tell him when she wrote. And perhaps something else – something this man she was following was about to say.

The mess hall buzzed with men who had been at the show, and several congratulated her before she even sat down. Long wooden tables and benches filled the vast space, arranged in neat rows, all spotlessly clean. The walls were painted in military green and here and there were motivational posters saying things like 'Loose lips lose wars!'

Although Jane could see the serving area was empty, the smell of an earlier meal still drifted through the air. It must have been stew, she thought, smelling meat, potatoes and carrots. Her stomach rumbled; she'd been too nervous to eat before the show.

'Come and sit down, Mrs Wilkins,' the man said. 'May I call you Jane? My name is Roger Lister.' He pulled a bench aside so she could slide in without having to climb over in her tight dress. 'I expect you're curious as to why I've asked you to meet me.'

She looked at his face, wondering if this was some sort of elaborate ruse. But he had honest eyes, green and friendly with plenty of laughter lines. His fair hair was going thin, and he'd combed some of it over, trying unsuccessfully to cover the gaps.

'Well, yes.' She struggled to keep her voice strong. 'I can't imagine why you would want to speak to me, Mr Lister.'

He pulled out a notebook and pencil. 'Please, call me Roger. I hope what I'm about to say will please you just as you delighted your audience this evening.'

Jane shifted on the bench. The narrow skirt of the dress tugged at her, putting her at risk of showing this strange man her thighs. 'Um, I was glad they liked the song.'

'They loved it, and they loved the way you sang it, Jane. You have a very fine voice and bring real emotion to every word.'

She blushed at the unaccustomed compliment from a stranger. 'I don't mean to sound rude, but why have you asked to speak to me?'

He wrote her name on his notepad. 'I'm sorry, I should have explained sooner. At the BBC they have talent scouts looking for people who could perhaps be on their shows. In fact, I first heard you at that wedding reception in the Underground station, but didn't know then how to contact you.'

Jane heard the words but couldn't for the life of her make out their meaning. A talent scout? What could that have to do with her? 'I... I don't understand.'

'Jane, I am one of the scouts, and I go to shows like this one looking for people with exceptional skills who I believe the BBC would be interested in. You are so talented I would like to offer you an interview with the researcher at the BBC.'

They were interrupted by two soldiers leaning over their table. 'Lovely voice,' one said. 'Almost made me cry, that did.'

'You see, Jane,' Roger said as the man walked on. 'That man speaks for many. Your voice would sound wonderful on the wireless. We need good singers for several of our shows. I can't make any promises. That is not within my grasp, but I would like to put your name forward, as I said.'

'But... but...' Jane was struggling to absorb what this man was saying. The BBC might be interested in her to sing for them? Surely that couldn't be right. He must have made a mistake. 'Are you sure you mean me? I'm no one special.'

He smiled and nodded, his eyes twinkling. 'Yes, you, Mrs Jane Wilkins. You have real talent.' They spoke for a while longer as he described the BBC process. 'They don't move along very quickly,' he added. 'So don't be downhearted if you don't hear anything for a while.' He dug in his bag and produced a business card. 'Take my card. You can contact me if you have any questions.'

'Would I... I... be paid if they accept me?' She worried about sounding like a money-grabber.

He smiled as he began to get ready to leave. 'That's an excellent question. They would pay you but don't start planning an exciting new life. It won't be much and will depend on whether they invite you for a one-off show or a regular slot. I'm afraid I can't be more specific than that.'

After he'd left, Jane slowly walked back towards the dressing room, the man's business card clutched in her trembling hand. The possibility of singing for the BBC seemed both thrilling and terrifying. She knew that the war had changed the way the BBC produced its radio shows. There were more patriotic programmes, including live music. She remembered hearing ENSA programmes on the wireless. 'Stars in Battledress' was a famous ENSA unit. She'd heard comedians like Charlie Chester, Jimmy Edwards and Tony Hancock on comedy shows. Their silly jokes always brightened her day. Then there were some famous singers, both male and female, too. She wondered briefly if she might even meet one or two of these famous people in the future. It was an exciting thought.

She paused and leaned against a wall, trying to slow down her racing heart. She closed her eyes and imagined how proud George would be when she told him. Some husbands resented their wives being successful, but she knew she could count on George to give her all the support and encouragement she needed. But success, even modest success with the BBC, was sure to change them, change their relationship. Would it still be as strong, she wondered. But he and their daughter would always come first, she was sure of that.

Whatever came next, she knew her life had just taken an unexpected turn. Even if this came to nothing, it proved that her talent was special.

Taking a deep breath and straightening her back, Jane made her way towards the dressing room.

To her surprise, several of the performers were backstage, having an impromptu party. Drinks were flowing and a couple of people were already quite merry.

'Hey, here's our singing star!' a man who was a juggler said. He walked towards her with a glass of something alcoholic in his hand. 'We heard a rumour that the BBC scout dragged you away after the show.'

Immediately everyone stopped speaking and looked at her, waiting for her to answer.

Startled, she took a step back and stuttered, her face reddening.

'Is it true?' someone else asked. 'It's what we all dream of.'

Jane nodded, her heart pounding. The words tumbled out almost incoherently. 'Um. Yes, he was a scout, but it must be a mistake...' Even as she spoke, a tiny voice in the back of her mind whispered, 'What if it's true? What if this is real?'

'They don't make mistakes like that,' the juggler said. 'I hear they don't pay much but it could lead to all sorts of opportunities.'

'Don't underestimate yourself,' a dancer exclaimed. 'You have the voice of an angel. I could see it in the soldiers' faces – you moved them. It takes special talent to do that.'

A chorus of agreement followed, and Jane felt a warm glow of friendship for these people she'd never met before. She took another sip of her drink, feeling the tension beginning to seep away.

Embarrassed but happy, Jane smiled. 'Thank you, everyone. Hearing those words, it... it... means a lot to me.'

'Come on, everyone.' The juggler clapped her on the back so hard she spilled a few drops of her drink. 'Let's celebrate her success. To Jane, our rising star and all the opportunities in the future!'

Taking a big gulp of the drink she'd been given, Jane almost spluttered it over him. 'You said opportunities? What do you mean?'

She heard someone say, 'Lucky sod, wish that was me!'

But the juggler was speaking again. 'Your own show. A record deal, all sorts.'

Jane laughed. 'Don't be daft. This is just me.'

But a part of her wanted to believe it. Even being a minor part of a wireless show would be astounding.

38

'No, we don't know where Daddy Joe is at the moment, love,' Mavis said. She struggled to hold back tears as she finally told Joyce that her new daddy was missing in action. She'd delayed doing so, hoping to have news, but none had come so far, and Joyce had noticed they hadn't received any letters from him for a while. All Mavis had received was a letter from SSAFA confirming that they would search for him.

Joyce fiddled with the buttons on her blouse. 'Is Daddy Joe lost? Can't he find his way home?'

Mavis put her arms around the little girl, wishing she could protect her from bad news. Being an orphan, she'd had more than enough already in her life. 'We don't really know what's 'appened, sweetheart. When the brave men like Daddy Joe are fighting things get a bit muddled up and sometimes they can't tell where people are.'

'Like Tibby next door when he went missing for a whole week?' Tibby was the black and white cat she was fond of. 'He was lost, wasn't he?'

"E was,' Mavis agreed. 'But 'e found his way 'ome. We just 'ave to 'ope that Daddy Joe does too.' She hoped one day Joyce would simply call him 'Daddy' but didn't want her to forget that she had once had her birth father. Nosy Mrs O'Connor next door had several times told Mavis she was daft not to insist on it, but Mavis was adamant. 'She'll change in 'er own good time and if she doesn't... well, it's not that important. She'll know 'e loves 'er.'

'Can I go and play?' Joyce asked, bouncing back as they did at that age. 'Where's my skipping rope?'

'In the sideboard where it always is.' Mavis pointed and pretended to be impatient. 'Be near enough for me to find you when it's time to eat.'

When she'd gone, Mavis tidied up then sat to begin a letter to her new husband. New in the sense they'd hardly been married when he had to go to war. She'd got no further than 'Dear Joe' when there was a knock at the door.

Frowning, she looked at the clock. It was too early for the rent man. But her breath caught when she opened the door. There stood a soldier wearing the same uniform as Joe. For a crazy second she thought it was him. But of course, it wasn't. This man was shorter, his hair and eyes were darker, and he carried a bit more weight.

'Mrs Smith? Mavis?' The man took off his hat and tucked it under his arm. 'Are you Joe's missus?'

From hope a second before, Mavis now felt worry. Had this man come to tell her the worst?

'Yes, I'm Mrs Smith.' The new title still gave her a thrill, despite her fear. 'Do you want to come in?'

He nodded and stepped inside. 'I'm sorry to come without warning or anything, but I thought you'd like to know something I'd heard.'

'Sit down, sit down.' Mavis swallowed hard. Her nerves jangled. 'Do you want a cuppa?'

'I'd kill for a good cup of tea,' he said with a wan smile. 'But while you're making the tea, I'll get myself a fag.'

Mavis's knees went weak. 'Go ahead.' She opened the window. 'What's your name anyway?'

'It's Victor, Vic everyone calls me. You get that kettle on, and I'll tell you what I know, not that it's much.'

Hands trembling, she made the tea and put her last few biscuits on a plate. Joyce would grumble when she realised they'd all gone but needs must. Then, terrified about what she might hear, she sat opposite the man. Was Joe injured? Dead? She couldn't bear the thought of it, although she'd thought of little else since she found he was missing in action.

'What is it? 'E's not dead, is 'e?' Her voice was little more than a whisper.

She watched him impatiently as he bit into a biscuit before saying more. 'I don't know if you know he was in Italy...'

'The telegram I got said 'e was there. I couldn't take it in. 'E 'adn't been gone long.'

Vic put half a spoon of sugar in his tea and stirred it. 'He'd probably only just arrived. Anyway, what I heard was he'd been taken prisoner. I can't say for sure if that's true, but I spoke to some bloke who lives in Canning Town, and we got chatting. He knew your Joe and saw what happened.'

Swallowing so hard her mouth went dry, Mavis managed to speak. 'What did 'appen?'

'An ambush or something, he didn't really tell me the details. But the good news is that he didn't think Joe had been killed or anything.'

As always happened when she had a visitor there was a tap

on the front door. Mavis sighed. 'Give me a minute.' She went to the door.

Mrs O'Connor from next door again. Always had to know what was going on.

'Got a twist of tea, love?' she asked, trying to peer over Mavis's shoulder. Much as Mavis liked her, she wasn't going to fall for her excuses again.

'I'm busy just now. I'll drop some off later. Excuse me, gotta go now.' She almost slammed the door in the woman's face.

When she turned round, she saw Vic was lighting a Woodbine and hurriedly handed him an ashtray. Her mouth dry, she poured more tea before she spoke again.

'So 'e's alive. Thank goodness for that.'

'The thing is...' Vic took a deep drag of his cigarette. 'The thing is... there's a rumour that Italy is going to surrender.'

Her heart sang with hope. 'So 'e'll be 'ome then?'

Another long drag. 'I wish that was true. The thing is, he was in the north of Italy. If that's true it means his prisoner-of-war camp will be run by Germans now.'

Mavis blinked hard, trying to remember what she'd read about the war in that area. The trouble was the government hid a lot, so reports weren't always reliable.

'But I thought I'd read our army was winning there. Did I get that wrong?'

'It's hard to know because everything is so censored,' Vic replied, flicking ash into the ashtray. 'But from what I've heard that's happening in the south of the country. They'll have a lot to do to take the whole country. It'll take ages, I'm afraid.'

He had no more to tell her and when he'd finished his tea, said a sad farewell.

When he'd gone, Mavis threw herself on her old settee. Prisoner of war! He was a prisoner of war! People talked about it a lot. The government didn't let much information out, but people talked. They were allowed to get letters and, even though they were censored too, they'd learned enough to know life was horrible in the camps.

Normally tough as leather, Mavis could hold back the tears no longer and cried for ten minutes, sobbing like there was no tomorrow. Then she pulled herself upright, washed her face and gave herself a good talking to. If this Vic was right, at least her Joe was alive. The SSAFA people might know more. She had to think of the positives.

She sighed and stood up. She had one thing she did when she needed to work off some worry. Housework. She got out her cleaning cloths, mop and the Vim and scrubbed until her home was sparkling clean.

39

The shrill whistle of the factory horn echoed through the sprawling munitions plant. The end of another long shift. May wiped her brow with the back of her hand and smiled a relieved acknowledgement to the other girls nearby. They were a motley gang, mostly East Enders but some from as far away as Scotland. May often wondered why they'd come so far south.

'You got a date tonight?' one of her colleagues asked.

May shook her head and rubbed her aching back. 'I wish I had the energy. Or a man I wanted to go out with.'

The next shift came in and took their places. Some people said the war was winding down, but the government still demanded just as many shells.

Clocking off at the machine on the wall, May walked towards the door, doing up her worn navy coat. Outside she took a deep breath. No one ever said the air in Silvertown was fresh, but it was heaven after being stuck in the factory. The smells of gunpowder, grease, metal and chemicals never seemed to leave her though. They clung to her clothes like an unwelcome guest.

But a welcome surprise awaited her: her brother Ben,

looking as familiar and handsome as ever. He smiled as he saw her, yet instinctively she saw something was amiss. Something in his eyes gave it away.

'Is everything all right?' she asked when she'd given him her usual hug.

He squeezed her arm. 'Everything's fine. I just wanted to take you for a drink and a pie if you fancy it. Got some more questions too.'

'A pie and a drink sound great,' May said. 'I'd have had a jam sandwich at home. No energy to cook tonight.'

The wove their way towards the George and Dragon, passing crowds of factory workers bustling about their evening routines. They passed a woman selling hot chestnuts, who called out to them, 'Come on, you two, get your tasty treat 'ere!' Children darted here and there playing war games, girls skipping. There was an endless number of rhymes to skip to. This one was:

> Strawberry jam and chocolate cake,
> How many slices can Betty make?
> One, two, three...

Despite the lively atmosphere around them, there was a strained silence between Ben and his sister again. It saddened him and he hoped they would soon be back to their relaxed friendship.

The George and Dragon was as busy as ever. Inside there were few females although a group of three elderly women sat knitting and chatting in one corner. The bar was thick with working men who had just finished their shift, leaning against the wooden bar, weariness lining their faces. There was so much smoke in the room it was like looking through fog.

'Payday,' May said. 'I wonder how many of this lot will drink away the week's housekeeping before their families see a penny of it.'

Ben nodded. 'It makes my heart ache when I see so many children with rickets – their poor legs so bent they can't walk properly. And a lot of them don't even have shoes.' He indicated the men at the bar. 'More money spent on food for the family and less on beer would solve that problem.' He got out his old brown wallet. 'But enough of that. What would you like to drink?'

'Half of stout, please.' She was aware he didn't have much money and if she drank a pint she'd want to fall asleep.

Drinks collected, they found a tiny corner table. It was hardly private, but their conversation would probably not be overheard. There was chatting, the clink of glass on the bar, the thudding of darts in the crooked dartboard and the background hum from the factories.

Ben noticed how tired May looked. 'Are you okay? You look a bit down.'

'I'm fine.' She picked up her stout and took a sip. 'It's been a long week.'

'Ben!' the landlord shouted. 'Your pies are ready.'

As he went to fetch them, the pub door opened, causing a draught. He glanced round and saw a middle-aged woman entering. She looked as weary as most workers at the end of the day. Her hair was trying to escape from her knitted hat. Her hands were red and rough, a sure sign she was a laundry worker.

But he hardly noticed her as he turned to put the pies on the little table. What he saw there almost made him take a step backward. His sister was sitting with her head bent, face close to her drink. Her shoulders were hunched, and her hair fell over her face. It didn't take a detective to realise she was trying to avoid the woman who had just entered.

'What is it?' Ben said as he put down the steaming pies. 'You look like you've seen a ghost.'

May pulled the plate towards her without looking up. 'Something like that,' she muttered.

She'd only taken one bite of her pie when a shadow fell over the table. 'Well, I never. Blow me down. It is, isn't it? It's you. Mary... Maggie... no, May. Fancy seeing you after all these years. You haven't changed a bit.'

Without being invited, the woman dragged a chair towards their table and sat down. Her rough hands spread possessively on the tabletop.

'Fancy us meeting like this. How's life been treating you, sweetheart?'

'I'm fine,' May said, still not looking up. Her fingers held her knife and fork so tight they were going white.

'And who's this?' The woman's gaze fixed on Ben. 'Not your young man, surely?'

'My brother,' May said shortly. 'Ben, this is Mrs—'

'Jameson, love. Though you wouldn't know. I wasn't married in them days, was I? We had some good laughs, didn't we, up there in the big house.' Ben noticed how May seemed to shrink into herself with every word the woman said. There was no stopping her. 'I often wondered what happened to you after that business with...' She had dropped her voice as if trying to whisper.

May's chair crashed backwards as she stood. Her handbag caught her half-finished drink, sending the contents across the table like a dark stain.

'I need some fresh air,' she announced, and snatching her bag she darted for the door, leaving her barely touched pie behind.

'Did I speak out of turn?' Mrs Jameson asked. There was

something in the way she said it that made Ben uneasy. 'Funny how some people like to forget all about their past, ain't it?' She pulled May's pie towards her and cut off a chunk.

Ben stiffened. 'What do you mean by that?' His voice was harsher than he intended.

Mrs Jameson chuckled, the kind of smile that didn't reach her eyes. She took a slow, deliberate bite of the pie, her cruel eyes never leaving his. 'Oh, nothing, love. Just that some folks like to pretend they're something they're not. Can't blame 'em. Fresh start's often a good idea, I'm sure. But the past has a funny way of catching up with you, don't it? Especially when it's a past like hers.'

Ben's eyes hardened. 'I don't know what you're trying to say, and I don't want to know...' He made to stand up, but she hadn't finished yet.

'Oh, I'm not trying to say nothing. Just making conversation, that's all. Trying to help a nice lad like you out.'

He pushed his chair away and put on his coat. 'I understand enough to know when someone is a troublemaker. I'll thank you to keep your thoughts to yourself.' He didn't wait for a response. Without another word, he headed for the door, tight with anger.

Through a window he'd caught a glimpse of May hurrying down Metal Lane. The opposite way to her route home.

Outside she was nowhere to be seen. He looked up and down the street, struggling to see past people going about their business. A dog was picking through some rubbish. A couple were walking arm in arm.

What had made May so upset? What was it this Mrs Jameson with her smirking look was alluding to? Should he go to May's house to see if she was okay? But he had no way of knowing where she'd gone. Not home, apparently.

He realised he hadn't even had an opportunity to ask her the questions he'd been pondering on.

Reluctantly, he decided he would have to ask her the next time he saw her. He still worried though. She'd always been so good to him. He hated seeing her upset. She had always been there for him, a sister who had been a second mother more times than he could remember.

And was it really so important to find out who his father was? Did it matter? If he ever found out, would it change anything? He had no hopes of the man being someone rich or famous. Whoever he was, there was a good chance he wouldn't welcome finding out he had an illegitimate son.

As he walked past a shop, he caught sight of himself in the dusty window. He started at his own reflection as if it were unfamiliar to him – like a word that's been said so many times it loses its meaning. Everything he thought he knew now seemed uncertain. His mother might not have been his mother after all. If not, who was she? Who was he? He'd built his own life around being his mother's son, felt her love and support throughout his whole life.

Now those certainties seemed to be drifting away like shadows at dusk, growing longer and stranger until their familiar shapes became blurred. Each memory he retrieved seem to transform in his grasp – holding his mother's hand on the way back from school, telling her about his day, watching her prepare a meal for them both. If she wasn't his mother, were those memories real? Who was she?

40

Cordelia had been visiting her parents more often since her father's heart attack. Each time she'd been relieved to see him gradually improving, not just his health but his mind. When he first returned from hospital he tired easily and found doing the accounts and other work he always did too much of a strain.

This visit was special. Robert was coming the next day to meet Cordelia's parents for the first time.

'Are you sure they'll want to meet me when your father's not completely recovered?' Robert had asked when Cordelia suggested it. 'A lot of people – especially men, in my experience – hate others to see them when they're not at their best. It makes them feel vulnerable, less of a man.'

She'd previously talked it over with her mother on the telephone and been assured her father would be well enough for visitors.

Her father had gone to rest after luncheon, and they went to sit in her mother's study. The sun drifted through the windows and the scent of late-summer roses filled the room.

The maid had brought in a jug of Pimm's, with a sprig of mint floating on the top. 'This is a treat,' Cordelia said. 'I haven't had this since I left Girton College.'

They sat in companionable silence as they sipped, looking out over the windows at the flowers and the topiary bushes shaped like animals.

'It's so peaceful here compared to the East End,' Cordelia said. 'I love hearing the birds and seeing so much greenery.'

Her mother smiled. 'But I'm guessing you'd soon get bored here. You like more excitement in your life, don't you?' She sipped her drink again. 'Your father and I were thinking it was about time we met your young man. We're so glad he's coming.'

Cordelia smiled. 'He's hardly a young man. He's been a doctor for years, and served in North Africa. It's aged him, but he's recovering well.' She looked around. 'Being somewhere tranquil like this rather than in the East End with all its problems would probably do him the world of good. There was another bombing raid last night so he couldn't just leave them to it. Soon he'll be off to his new job training others in desert medicine.'

'I'm so glad he's well enough to work again,' Lady Carmichael said. 'Is he ever tempted to take a nice, easy rural GP practice?'

Cordelia tried to imagine it. A country practice with no bombing, less grinding poverty and a cottage hospital to refer patients to. Once upon a time she'd have laughed at the idea. Robert was so lively, so involved with the local community. But since he'd returned from active duty, she could sense that the constant struggle to treat so many poor and injured people was taking its toll. His skin, once so fresh and firm, was often grey and more lined than it had been before he went away.

What would she do if they lived somewhere like that? She'd

pondered on that question often and they'd discussed it briefly. Look for another library to manage? Take on some other work to benefit the local community? She shook her head at the idea of playing the doctor's wife, it was too much like her mother's role as lady of the manor.

Perhaps she could write that book that had been in her mind for longer than she liked to admit. It was often said that you should write about what you know. That would leave her some choice – daughter of the lord of the manor, Cambridge under-grad, and East End librarian where every day she heard stories that would make great reading. Some would make your hair curl.

While her mother poured more Pimm's, she let her mind flow, imagining herself at a book signing, holding her very own book in her hands. But then she shook her head. If that ever happened, it was a long way off.

'You look miles away, my dear,' her mother said, handing her a fresh glass.

Cordelia smiled. 'I was just thinking what a country home would be like.'

Her mother laughed. 'I often think about what a busy life like yours would be like. Sometimes I think I could have done more than just be Lady Carmichael.'

'It's not too late,' Cordelia said. 'You are already very involved with the convalescent unit and if you found any aspect of it really appealed you could follow it up.'

'Be a nurse?' her mother asked, grinning. 'I don't think that would be quite suitable. But you're right. Since the unit started and I've listened to what you're doing, I find myself wanting to help people more.' She took a sip of her drink. 'I'll give it some thought. There's life in the old girl yet.'

Robert arrived late the following afternoon. As soon as she

heard the taxi stop outside, Cordelia ran to the door and threw herself into his arms. He wrapped her in his loving embrace, whispering endearments she could hardly hear. Then he held her at arm's length. 'I know it's only been a few days, but I've missed you so much, my love. Would you—'

She didn't hear the rest of the question. Her mother appeared at the door.

'You must be Robert. We are so pleased to meet you. Come in, come in. You're just in time for a pre-dinner drink.'

Robert stepped into the entrance hall. Not the usual very grand one which was now part of the convalescent unit, but still impressive enough to make his eyes widen slightly. Cordelia watched him, a mixture of pride and nervousness making her mouth dry.

'Welcome to Stonehaven Hall,' came a deep voice from the drawing room doorway. Lord Carmichael stood there, still thinner than he had been but looking more like his old self.

'Thank you, Lord Carmichael.' Robert stepped forward to shake his hand. 'It's an honour to meet you, sir.'

As they moved into the drawing room for refreshments, Cordelia noticed Robert's eyes darting around him. She took her childhood home for granted but seeing it through his eyes made her notice the luxury around her. The expensive furniture, the rich tapestry curtains, the thick carpet.

They sat with their drinks beside them then Lord Carmichael spoke. 'Tell me, Robert, if I may call you that. Cordelia tells us you've been serving in North Africa.'

'Yes, sir. It was... quite an experience – very unlike being a doctor in this country. Cordelia may have told you my next posting will be in this country training other doctors on desert medicine.'

Lady Carmichael topped up their glasses. While she hadn't said much, Cordelia could see she was listening carefully.

Lord Carmichael took his glass from her. 'Tell me, doctor, what do you think of our chances out there?'

'Father,' Cordelia interrupted. 'Could we delay the war talk until after dinner? I'm sure Robert would love to hear about your work and the work Mother is doing with the soldiers in the convalescent unit.'

Her mother nodded agreement. 'When we've finished our drinks why don't I show you the rest of the house – or more accurately those parts we still have use of.'

On the whole, their stay went well, although occasionally a flash of Lord Carmichael's old impatient self appeared. Each time it happened, his wife gave him a look or touched his arm and usually it appeared to calm him down. He never went as far as apologising but would turn the subject around with a softer tone.

Those flashes worried Cordelia. Did they mean that when he recovered more strength he would go back to his old ways? His habits of largely ignoring his family and engrossing himself in his business? Only time would tell.

On the journey back, Cordelia and Robert discussed the visit. She squeezed his hand. 'What did you think of my parents?'

The corners of his mouth turned up. 'Your mother is wonderful. She has coped with so much, so many changes and now your father's illness. I admire her tremendously...'

She raised an eyebrow. 'And my father?'

'He took me aside at one point when you weren't in the room and quizzed me about how much I earned. He didn't look impressed. Wanted to know about my family too.'

'Oh dear, old habits die hard with people like him. Think

nothing of it. Overall, it seemed to go well, although I worry about those occasional outbursts and what they might mean for my mother.'

He kissed her cheek. 'My mother always used to say, "Worrying about tomorrow only steals the happiness of today." We'll just have to wait and see. The main thing is we have each other.'

41

The librarians were fascinated by the information Tom had discovered at the museum, but it got them no nearer to knowing who 'Evelyn' was. It had been a while since Tom's visit to the V&A but they were so busy that the mystery of the contents of the chest had been pushed aside.

'I'll go to the history society offices,' Cordelia volunteered. 'The Prof often mentions it – if I'm lucky he'll be there.'

She had a day off and looked forward to doing some research, although she wished Robert could have joined her. Their opposing schedules left little time to spend together. Pushing the thought aside, she stepped into the historical society building, a narrow structure wedged inconspicuously between a greengrocer's and a newsagent. She walked past it twice, its unassuming façade and faded notice easy to miss.

Inside, a steep staircase greeted her, its worn wooden steps creaking faintly underfoot. Each step felt like a journey back in time, as if the air itself got heavier with the weight of years gone by. At the top, Cordelia entered the first room and paused, taking in her surroundings. The musty scent hit her first – a blend of aged paper, dust and something faintly damp. It reminded her of the library in the depths of winter when the doors and windows stayed closed, and the smell seemed to settle like an old blanket.

'Can I help you?' an elderly man asked, looking up from his book. Then he registered who she was. 'Miss Carmichael! How nice to see you. What are you doing here?'

It was the Prof, the wonderful man who spent a lot of time in the library and was always willing to help anyone.

Cordelia smiled and shook his hand. 'I'm so glad to see you here. I thought you might be involved with the history society.'

'Bring that chair over here, Miss Carmichael, and we can talk. We don't get many visitors, so I doubt we'll be interrupted.'

She pulled up a chair so she could sit opposite him. 'I'm hoping you can help me – well, all of us at the library really. We found this old chest...'

His eyes sparkled. 'How exciting. It sounds like the beginning of a mystery story. But I interrupted you. Do go on.'

Cordelia explained about the contents of the chest and the steps they'd taken so far to find out more about the mysterious Evelyn.

'That is absolutely fascinating. I don't know how much time you have, my dear,' he replied. 'I have an idea where we can look in our archive if you come with me. We can look together.'

She followed him to a back room, where shelves were crammed with boxes of historical records. Her breath caught as she scanned the shelves, each box, each book, each folder promising secrets from the past. 'This is like a treasure trove,' she murmured, running her hand over the dust-covered spines of old records and folders. The sheer volume of material made her heart race. Somewhere in this room she would surely find the answers they had been looking for.

The Prof confidently went to one section of the room and began taking down files and folders, sending clouds of dust into the air. He moved quickly, flipping through newspaper clippings, birth, death and baptismal records, faded maps and old logbooks.

He pushed several folders towards her. 'Let's look together. I have a feeling we're going to be lucky. Blackwood is an unusual name for the East End. It was lucky she had written it in her journal, or we would have no way of knowing where to start looking. Nonetheless we have a lot of records for the relevant period.'

Finding so many interesting items, Cordelia had to keep reminding herself to keep focused or she'd be lost down the research rabbit hole. More than once she thought that being a librarian meant that she felt at ease in this room. Perhaps one day when she didn't have to do war work she would volunteer in a history society.

An hour later, the Prof gave a little cheer. 'I've found her, my dear. I thought it would take much longer. This is luck.' He held up two pieces of paper joined together with a paper clip.

Her heart racing, Cordelia took them from him. They were so old the writing was faint and difficult to read.

'Go over to the light,' the Prof said. 'It'll be easier there.'

What she read made Cordelia both delighted and sad. The first was a copy of a death certificate. The elaborate writing was hard to decipher. The second was a newspaper cutting, crumpled and faded with age.

'Oh, it's a death certificate.' Her heart sank as she read the contents. The dates matched, and the name was right. Evelyn. It was her. Cordelia's hands trembled as she tried to make out the cause of death. To come so close to the truth only to find it ended in tragedy, although Evelyn had lived to a good age. She squinted and tried to read the cause of death. 'I can't make this out. Can you see what she died of?'

The Prof took it from her. 'I think it says appendicitis. Treatment wouldn't have been so good in those days. Poor thing, it's a painful way to go.'

Outside, the greengrocer rang a bell and bellowed, 'Come on, ladies, fresh fruit and veg. Keep your old man 'appy! You won't get it cheaper nowhere else!'

Cordelia studied the certificate again. 'I've just realised when she died she was still single. She can't have married the soldier who was writing to her from India and who sent her the beautiful gift. How sad. I wonder what happened to her. Or him. Did he survive the Indian Mutiny? Did he end up marrying someone else? We'll probably never know.'

As they spoke, the Prof was putting the folders back in their place, keeping the two documents relating to Evelyn on one side. 'Be of good cheer. Military men are easier to trace, there are always good records. I'd be more than happy to research him for you. When it's my turn on the desk here I'm sometimes stuck for something to pass the time. A project like this would be just the ticket.'

Cordelia was distracted by looking at the obituary for Evelyn.

We are sorry to announce the death of Miss Evelyn Blackwood. A librarian, Evelyn was well known in Silvertown and beyond because of her charitable and voluntary work. She helped a wide range of local people from helping children learn to read to reading to elderly people. She had no family but will be much missed by everyone who knew her.

A librarian, like me, Cordelia thought. A life spent helping others, but haunted by what might have been. Never finding another love. She felt a deep pang of kinship with this woman she would never meet, as if across the decades they shared some unspoken understanding.

Deep in thought, she finally looked up. 'I'm sorry, I got distracted. This is what history is all about, connecting the past with the present. Now what were you saying?'

The Prof smiled. 'I easily get distracted when I look at old documents. It always leads me to wonder what happened to the people. I was saying I'd be very happy to continue the research. Would you like me to do that?'

She almost hugged him. He was always so kind, so gentlemanly. 'I'd be grateful if you'd do that. It looks as if Evelyn had no relatives for us to search for. Even if he had some, we wouldn't want to disclose what we know about their relationship. There is very little to go on though, just the initial J.'

'I can see your point of view. Who knows what upset that could cause even all this time later? But don't worry about finding him, there will be clues I can follow in army records. Could I perhaps have the letters? I'd give them back of course, but they may offer clues I can follow up.'

Cordelia kicked herself for not thinking of this. 'Of course, Prof. I'll drop them off tomorrow if that's okay.'

As Cordelia prepared to leave, she glanced back at the treasures crammed into the space. She felt a sense of gratitude towards all the people who had carefully kept the documents down the years.

A few days later she received a note from the Prof.

Dear Miss Carmichael,
    I have found several items relating to J. I believe his name

was John Findlay. He appears to have died during the Indian Mutiny and I cannot see any trace of descendants.

I have a suggestion. This story is so romantic. I wonder if you and your colleagues would agree to a display at the library showcasing the relevant items. I would be very happy to help you organise this.

Cordelia smiled as she finished reading the note. An exhibition in the library – it was perfect, and she was sure it would be of great interest to the community. Evelyn and the soldier's story deserved to be remembered, not just as a tale of loss but as a testament to enduring love. She couldn't wait to tell the others.

42

Having no luck talking to May, Ben decided to go back to the library as the friendly head librarian had offered to help him in his search.

Cordelia finished helping a reader then turned to him. 'Hello again. How can I help you?'

He smiled, thinking what a kind face the librarian had. 'You offered to help me when I came in last time, Miss Carmichael. Do you have a few minutes? I'd like to show you something.'

Nodding to Mavis to let her know to take over, Cordelia led Ben to the far quiet corner of the main reading room. 'How can I help? I remember you were trying to trace a country house. I can't remember if you told me why. But you don't have to, of course.'

They settled down at the old wooden table, hidden from much of the library by shelves full of books on world history. They were rarely borrowed.

Ben took a big envelope out of his bag. 'I've got a picture of somewhere my sister worked as a young woman. She was a maid. It may not have anything to do with my father... oh, I didn't mention but I'm trying to find out who he was. He might well still be alive. This is confidential but I think that my sister may actually be my mother.'

His look made her feel anxious for him. 'But you're suspicious of something that happened in the house. Is that correct?'

'It's not like May, that's my sister, to be secretive about things...' He began opening the envelope. 'I could be completely wrong. Perhaps she had a horrible time working as a maid. You hear stories of them being worked to the bone. It's probably nothing to do with whoever my father is.'

He handed the dog-eared postcard to Cordelia. At first, she saw the back with the brief message from May to their mother. There was no date on it and the post office frank was too smudged to read. It told her nothing.

But when she turned the card over her heart skipped a beat and she gasped.

'Are you okay, Miss Carmichael?' Ben asked, seeing her face go pale.

Shocked, she hesitated to answer. Questions ran through her mind like a loose thread in an old jumper, but she told herself not to be irrational. Just because Ben's sister once worked at Stonehaven Hall didn't mean anything. Over the years her parents and indeed grandparents must have employed dozens of staff. She knew that it was only since the war started that they had struggled to find people to work for them.

She turned the card over again, then studied the picture, faded and creased here and there. Finally, she looked at him. Should she tell him? No doubt there was nothing sinister about his enquiry, but something felt wrong.

'I'm... yes, I'm fine,' Cordelia whispered, her fingers tracing the outline of Stonehaven Hall. 'It's just... I know this place. Very well.'

Ben leaned forward. 'You do? Have you been there?'

Cordelia sighed and brushed her fingers through her hair. 'I grew up there. This is my family home.'

The silence that followed seemed endless. Ben's eyes moved from the postcard to Cordelia's face and back again. She could see he was struggling to process this information. He was frowning as he made connections that she hoped weren't there.

'Your home?' His voice shook. 'Really? So you would have been there when May worked there.'

Cordelia's mind raced backwards and forwards, trying to pinpoint dates.

Ben's eyes were full of hope. 'Do you remember May?'

Sitting back in her seat, Cordelia's mind raced back through the relevant years. Her parents had had so many maids. Their faces blended together, some friendly, some ignoring her as simply a child, doing only their essential work.

Then she remembered one. A maid with kind eyes who would often chat to young Cordelia as she went about her work, telling stories of life in the East End of London. It was a place that sounded exciting to the little girl. Tales of ships and markets and street vendors shouting out their wares. The maid would describe the smell of fresh bread from the baker's shop mixing with salty smells from the Thames. Tales of children playing in the streets, their mothers hanging out washing between the buildings. She taught Cordelia some rhyming slang which made them both giggle.

Those stories gave the girl who had limited exposure to the world a glimpse into somewhere quite different. The maid – it could have been May – it must have been, although sometimes people called her Mary – made it all sound exciting. These stories must have influenced Cordelia's decision to find employment in the East End. Now though, Cordelia realised May had carefully edited her stories, filling them full of magic, leaving out the hardship and hunger she must have experienced. For the first time she understood another way May was different. Most of the maids came from local towns and villages and spoke with a Norfolk accent. They often claimed they couldn't understand May's cockney sayings and speech.

Then, without warning, the stories stopped. May had disappeared and no one would tell Cordelia where she'd gone. The other maids quickly hushed her when she asked, shooting nervous looks at her father's study.

Now, looking at Ben sitting opposite her, she saw something in the shape of his eyes that reminded her of the kind maid. But it was so long ago she could be imagining it.

Ben repeating his question brought her back to the moment. 'Do you remember her, Miss Carmichael?'

'I think so...' Her fingers ran round the edges of the postcard. 'I was young, so it's possible I'm thinking of the wrong person. Was she sometimes called Mary?'

Ben nodded. 'Yes, she was by some people.' He opened his jacket pocket and took out a photo. 'Is this her?'

Her hands shaking, Cordelia studied the photo of a maid standing in Stonehaven's kitchen, wearing her black and white uniform with an expression that was hard to read. It was a long time ago so she could be wrong, but she didn't think she was.

'Yes, I think that's her, but I might be mistaken,' she finally said.

The tension seemed to drain from Ben's shoulders and his face lightened as if a ray of sunshine caught it. He reached for the photo, excitement shining in his eyes.

'I knew it,' he said, relief changing his voice. 'She denied it, but when I saw the way my sister behaved when she saw this postcard it was obvious something was up. What was she like then? Was she happy there?'

Cordelia didn't know how to answer that. She'd been a child, hardly old enough to see beyond what she was faced with. Not mature enough to read between the lines or understand body language or facial expressions.

'Happy? She was always cheerful when she was with me. Mind you, I know life below stairs could be tough. The hierarchy was strict, and anyone seen to miss the rigid standards was treated harshly.'

Ben sat back and looked at the postcard again. 'So, it's difficult to tell and she won't say a word. I don't know what to think.'

Cordelia's heart went out to him. To live his life never knowing who his father was and now facing a mystery about the woman who he'd always believed to be his sister. It must feel like some sort of torment.

She imagined his whole sense of who he was was in the balance. Every belief he'd grown up with was slipping away, leaving him adrift in a sea of confusion.

As they'd been speaking, other memories came to Cordelia's mind. She couldn't trust them – children see the world differently from adults. However, they might hold some truth. But she decided to say nothing at this stage. She could easily be mistaken.

'Ben, I'm not even sure I'm right and it's her. Next time I visit my parents I'll try looking through old records. If I find anything certain I'll share it with you.'

43

Cordelia spent several restless days after her conversation with Ben. Her mind was a whirl of concerns, possibilities about the meaning of what she had learned. Had May left Stonehaven Hall because she was in the family way? If so, who was the father?

Stories of maids being taken advantage of by 'upstairs' men were common. Could one of those be her father? His brother, who used to stay regularly over the years? Or even one of the guests who stayed from time to time? Or might it be one of the 'below stairs' men?

Finally, she decided to visit her family home on her next day off to see if her father would tell her anything. Knowing his personality, she wasn't hopeful. If he was the guilty man, he would be sure to deny it. Apart from that, how on earth would she approach such a sensitive subject? Was she mistaken to even consider it?

But she made a big mistake. She didn't check if her father was at home and, when she got there, she discovered he was in

London for a few days. Though disappointed, she was relieved that it was a sign of his continuing recovery.

Nonetheless, she was happy to be back in her old home. To see all the military men recovering from their injuries. As always, some were in the garden, often walking with a nurse. Others, she knew, would be inside, either bed-bound or undertaking some sort of recuperation exercise.

Even more, she was delighted to see her mother looking well and happy.

'Cordelia, darling,' her mother said. 'How lovely to see you. I had no idea you were coming.' She hesitated. 'I'm so sorry but I must go out for a couple of hours and your father is in London for three days. I hope you are staying tonight at least so we can catch up.'

As soon as she left, Cordelia went into her father's study. She always felt like an intruder there and she paused at the doorway, letting the uncomfortable feelings in her stomach settle before stepping in.

Her father had always made it clear that he never wanted to be disturbed when he was at his desk. She and Jasper knew they'd be in trouble if they tried to get his attention when he was working.

Even after all these years, it smelled the same – cigar smoke, furniture polish and his woody cologne. Taking tiny steps as if he could hear her all the way from London, she tiptoed over to his desk. The top drawer was locked, and she couldn't open it without doing damage. The middle drawer was full of correspondence and the third one held leather-bound ledgers arranged by year.

Cordelia realised she was holding her breath as her fingers ran along the spines of the ledgers until she found the one with the crucial years. She hesitated before pulling it out. She had no right to be poking through her father's papers. In any case the ledgers were probably full of boring lists of incomings and outgoings for the house and estate. But could she just walk away without at least having a quick look?

Then, as she was about to replace the ledger and shut the drawer, she remembered Ben's face, taut with concern. No, if she could help him in his quest, she would. Taking another deep breath, she placed the ledger on the desk. It fell open easily despite its age. Its pages were filled with her father's distinct handwriting. Expecting a boring list of incomings and outgoings, she read down the columns of names and dates. Purchases for Stonehaven Hall, staff wages, repairs, charitable donations, rents collected, investments, staff names and dates when they began or left. She found the list fascinating; each entry told a story. What were 'sundries'? Items that her father didn't want anyone to know about?

Then, when she'd all but given up hope, there it was – May Gardner – employed 25 February 1926. Dismissed August 1926. But what caught Cordelia's eye was the notation in red ink beside the entry. 'Refer to private papers.'

She'd seen nothing marked like that while searching through the desk, no papers marked 'Private'. Then she remembered her father had a safe behind a painting of a Suffolk landscape on the wall next to his desk. Knowing she was wasting her time, she swung the painting back. The safe was the type with a wheel to turn. She'd have to know the numbers and she had no idea. If she turned the dial and didn't leave it exactly as she'd found it, he would be sure to spot it.

Giving up the attempt, she was about to close the painting when a voice behind her made her jump.

'What are you doing here, Miss Cordelia?'

Cordelia spun round, her heart thumping. Then she realised

it was Mrs Taylor, the family cook who had been like a second mother to her.

'Oh, it's you!' she said, struggling to keep the tremor out of her voice. 'I'm so glad to see you.' She hesitated, wondering if she should own up to what she was doing. 'Can we go to the kitchen and have a cuppa? It's been so long since we had time together and Mother will be out for a while yet. I'll explain what I was doing then.'

Mrs Taylor smiled broadly. 'Of course we can, ducks. Your dad is away so your mum won't be wanting a big dinner this evening. Follow me. Like you don't know the way!'

The kitchen was warm and familiar, taking Cordelia back to the many times in her childhood she'd spent there. She and her brother were left to a nanny or tutor and only saw their mother and father for about an hour a day. They couldn't have been more different from this lovely lady with her flour-coated apron wrapped round her soft, cuddly body. The kettle was steaming gently on the Aga, and Mrs Taylor put some tea leaves in the old brown pot.

'How are you, Mrs Taylor?' Cordelia asked. It seemed as if the warm-hearted lady never aged, although her back was a little bent these days. Her fingers too.

Mrs Taylor poured boiling water into the pot. 'Can't complain. Arthritis is a bit worse, but I don't let it bother me too much.' She sat opposite Cordelia and pushed a plate of biscuits towards her. 'Here, girl, have one of these. I bet you don't have time to do any baking.'

Cordelia reached for one without hesitation. 'No time even if I had your skills.'

They talked about general issues then Mrs Taylor put down her cup and looked Cordelia in the eye. 'So come on now. What were you up to, poking around your father's study like a burglar? Out with it, young lady.'

Biting into another biscuit, Cordelia wondered how to approach the subject. She trusted Mrs Taylor not to tell her parents, so there was nothing to lose.

'A young man, Ben, has been coming into the library. It's a long story but he's trying to find out who his father is. Come to that, he's not even sure who his mother is.' She went on to explain what had happened so far. 'Then I realised you must have been working here at the same time as his mother. Or the woman who he was brought up to believe was his sister but he now thinks must be his mother. Her name was May, sometimes called Mary. Gardner. Do you remember her by any chance? She left in August 1926, quite suddenly I believe. She was a cockney, so the way she spoke would have made her quite memorable, I think.'

Pouring more tea, the cook bit her lip. 'That's a long time ago, love, and maids come and go.' Her shoulders sagged as if under a great weight. 'Some things are best left alone.'

Nodding, Cordelia suddenly wondered if she was doing the right thing in helping Ben. But then she recalled again his quiet look of determination again. She could hardly blame him for wanting to understand his parentage.

'It sounds as if you do remember her.' She spoke gently, not wanting to pressure this lifelong friend. 'Was she in trouble when she left?'

Mrs Taylor stood up and began putting flour and lard in a bowl to make pastry. Her fingers, nimble despite her arthritis, worked without her mind having to take notice. 'If she's who I think you're talking about, we never knew. But I'd bet a penny to a pound she was in the family way. You can often tell by a change in a girl's body, even in the early days.' Lifting the flour and lard which now resembled breadcrumbs, she added some water to the mix. 'Does your father know you're asking about this girl? Or that the lad, what did you say his name was – Ben – is asking around?'

Cordelia remembered the subtle features of Ben's face that reminded her of her father. She could easily be mistaken though. It proved nothing. 'Do you think my father might be responsible? Was he having a dalliance with the girl?'

Squeezing the pastry into a damp ball, Mrs Taylor avoided her eye. 'Your father would have already been married then. You know that. You were a child yourself. But... I sometimes heard rumours that he... well, he wasn't always the most... faithful of men. People talked about his regular overnight trips to London for a start.' She dusted a patch of table with flour and put the pastry on it with a thud. 'You know what staff are like – they miss nothing. There were whispers below stairs. I heard he particularly favoured May. Can't say I know it's true though.' She fetched her rolling pin out of the drawer. 'Mind you, in those days your parents had people to stay regularly. Your mother's mother, God rest her soul, your father's brother Edward and more friends than I can recall.'

'I vaguely remember that,' Cordelia said. She remembered the excitement on evenings when there was a party or a big dinner. Her mother, always well dressed, looked beautiful in her evening dresses and diamond jewellery. The staff were rushed off their feet getting everything ready. She was never invited, of course, but she would hide at the top of the stairs or behind the furniture and watch people coming and going. It was exciting but frightening at the same time in case she was spotted. 'May was always nice to me,' Cordelia said, remembering her bright eyes and warm smile. 'Quieter than the others. She didn't tittle-tattle but told me lots of stories of the East End.' She watched as

Mrs Taylor rolled out the pastry. 'If this is right, do you think my mother knew?'

Wiping the flour from her hands, the cook took a hankie from her pocket and dabbed her eyes. 'In my experience, women often have an idea what their husbands are up to. But life is difficult for them if they try to do anything about it. Better to not know. Your mother's always been considerate towards staff but probably wouldn't know anything about their private lives.'

Cordelia thought about Ben, searching for answers. His sister's stubborn silence on the subject. She thought about her mother, who always treated her father with respect. How she had maintained her dignity even if she had suspicions.

'What on earth shall I do with this information?' she asked to herself more than to Mrs Taylor.

'That's not for me to say, love. But if your suspicions are right, that young man is your half-brother, whether your father admits it or not. Some might say it's time the truth was told but life is rarely that simple.' She stopped and wrapped the pastry in a damp tea towel. 'But whatever you do, take care. Your father won't like his secrets being exposed.'

44

Cordelia had asked Ben to meet her in the park rather than in the library. She didn't want to risk anyone overhearing their conversation, she knew how quickly personal news spread in Silvertown. Most of the park was given over to growing vegetables but it was still a pleasant place to be, a change from all the factories and damaged buildings. The government had allotted small patches of the park to those willing to grow their own vegetables: 'Dig for Victory', as the posters everywhere said. Every patch had been taken.

Cordelia and Ben sat on a bench, a pale sun sending shadows on the paths around them.

She'd rehearsed what to say to him many times since returning home from Stonehaven Hall, but now with him beside her she forgot all her carefully prepared words.

Ben turned to look at her. 'I'm guessing you've discovered something, Miss Carmichael, as you've asked to meet here rather than in the library. You look a bit stressed, if you don't mind me saying so.'

Her hands clasped tightly in her lap, Cordelia nodded. She knew what he said was true. Her sleepless nights showed when she looked in the mirror that morning and saw dark circles round her eyes.

'I know you'll be frustrated, but I don't have anything conclusive to tell you.' She paused and watched the disappointment cross his face.

'But you found out something?'

'I tried to look in my father's papers but couldn't locate anything on your sister. However, I spoke to Mrs Taylor. She's been the family cook for as long as I can remember.'

Hope lit up his face and she thought again that there was something about his features that was familiar.

'She isn't sure, but she thinks she remembers May. I think I do too, although I couldn't swear to it. She filled me full of stories about life in the East End. That might even be why I looked for a job around here.'

'But did the cook know anything for sure? Is May my mother? Do you and me have the same father?'

If only Cordelia could give him the definitive answer but that simply wasn't possible. 'I just don't know...'

'But it could have been one of the footmen or a gardener or something...'

She gave a strained smile. 'It could. But it seems my father had a bit of a reputation for liking the ladies.' She paused and took a deep breath. 'But there is no suggestion that he ever pushed himself on anyone.'

Ben gave a bitter laugh. 'So I might be the product of a wealthy man's dalliance with a maid. Will I ever know the truth? I don't even know if May is my mother or my sister for sure.'

An elderly couple walking past hand in hand nodded to

them then continued their slow way. The man was carrying a cabbage they had just pulled up from their small allotment.

Cordelia looked at the elderly couple. Would she and Robert look like them one day? Elderly, bent over but happy with each other? Since he'd been back from Africa, things had been going well between them, and she was finally allowing herself to feel hope for the future. She had done the right thing accepting his proposal.

Ben and Cordelia waited until the couple had gone past before continuing their conversation.

'There is one thing that might help me know for certain,' Ben said with a sigh.

'What's that?'

Guilt almost overcame him as he considered what he was about to suggest. 'She keeps a tin box under her bed. Once when Mum was ill, I stayed with May for a few days. One evening when she thought I was asleep I heard her crying.'

He remembered it so well. He'd only been about ten years old, and he'd been in that liminal state between awake and asleep. Confused, he sat up, wondering what the sound was. Then he realised it was May crying – not hard to hear as the walls were so thin people often said they were held up with wallpaper.

Tiptoeing, he crept along to her room and peered through a crack where the door wasn't quite closed. She was sitting on the bed with the tin on the bedcover. Spread around her were papers. She held one in her hand.

He had no idea what the paper was, but it was obvious even to him that the document upset her. He stood for a minute, uncertain. Should he go in and try to comfort her? Would she be cross with him? But then, just as he thought he really must decide, May got out her hankie and blew her nose. With a sigh she folded the paper, kissed it and put it in the tin with the others.

Shaken, he crept back to his bed. Next morning, it was as if the whole thing had been a dream. May was back to herself and didn't mention it at all.

Then Cordelia said something, bringing his attention back to their conversation.

'You mentioned May's tin,' she said. 'Do you plan to look inside it? How could you do that?'

He ran his fingers through his hair. 'She goes to a Women's Institute meeting every Wednesday evening. Never misses it. I could sneak in next Wednesday. She always leaves the key in the same place, so I won't have any trouble getting in.'

'I suppose you're hoping to find your birth certificate there.'

He nodded. 'It's a long shot, but I can't think of anything else to try.' He bit his lips. 'I feel bad looking through her private papers.' He shifted and sat more upright. 'I'm going to do it though. Shall I come into the library and tell you what I find? You've been so kind helping me.'

'Before you go, there are some things to consider if you haven't already. If May is your mother, it's unlikely that your father's name will be on your birth certificate. That's what usually happens. That bit is left blank.'

His face fell. 'I suppose I should have thought of that. Mind you, I've never seen a birth certificate so I wouldn't know what was on one.'

'The other thing to think about is, if you find May is definitely your mother and you still suspect we are half-brother and -sister, what do you want to do with that information?'

She watched as a myriad of emotions flew across his face like scenes from a silent film, each frame telling its own story. 'Umm, what do I want to do? It's well... it's tricky, isn't it? Do I tell her I know she's my mum? I've no idea how she would react. Do I do anything about approaching your father if he might also be my father?' He looked down at his hands, clasped so tightly together his knuckles were white. 'I don't think I can decide on any of that just now. I'll need to take one step at a time.'

45

The next Thursday, Ben came into the library a few minutes before closing time. Cordelia was checking out some books for a timid-looking elderly man who liked crime books, the more gruesome the better.

Ben waited for her to be free. 'Have you got a minute, Miss Carmichael?' he asked. 'I can see you're busy.'

Cordelia was surprised to find she had butterflies in her stomach at the thought of what news he might have. Knowing that Robert would keep secrets to himself, she had told him what was happening.

'It's like one of those Victorian novels,' he said when he'd heard the whole story. 'But what worries me is how this is affecting you. It's such a lot for you to take in. You already have another brother, Jasper. How would he react if he discovers he has a half-brother? And come to that, how will Ben react when he finds out the truth either way?' He reached out and touched her hand. 'And how do you feel about discovering your father wasn't always faithful to your mother? That's a lot to take on board.'

His questions merely reflected what had been going through her mind incessantly. She didn't know if illegitimate children could claim against their father's estate. What if Ben decided to try to do that? It would cause major upheaval in the family. Her father would be so furious she wouldn't want to be anywhere near Stonehaven Hall when he found out.

Discussing the issue with Robert helped to calm her worry, although it brought her no nearer having any answers. Yet here was Ben, obviously keen to discuss the issue further.

Ensuring the reader's books were all dealt with, Cordelia nodded to Jane to take over for the last few minutes of the day.

'Come into my office,' she said to Ben, leading the way. Through the window they heard children playing cowboys and Indians. 'Bang, bang! You're dead!' one of them shouted. The laughter outside was carefree, a marked contrast to the atmosphere in the office.

Ben followed her in but seemed reluctant to settle. First standing, then half-sitting against the window ledge, his hands worked at something in his pocket.

'Do sit,' Cordelia said, gesturing to the chair opposite. She noticed an unusual amount of tension in his stance. His eyes darted to her face then back again.

'I've been thinking of you all week,' he said, his voice unusually quiet. 'I've been turning what you said over in my mind, wondering what to do.'

Cordelia decided to sit quietly and let him tell her whatever it was at his own time and pace.

He rubbed his forehead with his hand. 'So much has changed since I first came into the library asking for your advice about finding my father. You've always been so kind even though it must have been difficult for you.' He reached into his pocket and took out a small bundle wrapped in newspaper. His hands trembled a little as he unwrapped it. 'These are more letters. They were hidden in my mother... grandmother's loft.' He began to spread them across her desk. There were five in all. 'They're addressed to May...' He swallowed hard. 'It's obvious from them that she is my mother... I don't know why they were hidden in my grandmother's loft. I've got the tenancy now and wanted to see what was up there.'

Intrigued, Cordelia leaned forward, her eyes drawn to the faded handwriting on the envelopes. Something in Ben's tone made her hesitate.

'There's more,' he said. His fingers found the other envelopes, although he seemed reluctant to touch them. He drew in a breath. 'It's... it's... the signature. It took me a while to work it out and most of the time it was just a first name but...'

Cordelia realised her shoulders were tense with fear as she listened to him struggling to tell her something important.

'The letters... they... they're signed by someone called Edward. Edward Carmichael.' His eyes finally met hers. 'That's not... your father... is it?'

His revelation, although not entirely surprising, seemed to hang in the air between them.

She did recognise the name. It hit her like a physical force. The portrait on the staircase at Stonehaven Hall, seeing the handsome, smiling man from her hiding place on the landing... him talking to her on those occasions when she was allowed to join the adults.

Edward. Her father's brother. Her uncle. Then she remembered the time when the house had been in mourning. Edward had died in a tragic accident. Her parents had been heartbroken, and the entire household wore black and spoke in hushed tones for weeks.

As she explained to Ben what had happened to Edward, her

mind was racing ahead, piecing things together. May had been so young then, barely more than a girl. From her memories of her uncle, Cordelia could understand why she had fallen in love with him. It was a story as old as humanity.

Did either of her parents know about Edward and May, about the baby on the way? What would they have done if they did? She thought about the times Edward had been mentioned since she had been an adult. He'd been dead some time by then so was rarely talked about. But she couldn't remember any signs that her parents were aware of his relationship with May.

Ben began speaking again. 'It's clear from these letters that it was a real love affair, not a man from upstairs taking advantage of a maid. I feel so much better for her – it must still have been dreadful when she found out she was in the family way. From these letters he was planning to marry her, despite their differences. That hope would have been shattered when he died. No wonder she kept me a secret. People are so cruel to girls who get in the family way out of wedlock.'

Cordelia looked at his thoughtful face. He'd been through so much and still had a lot to come to terms with. 'Have you decided what to do next?' she asked. 'You must have a million questions going through your head. Will you tell your mother what you've found out?'

Even as she asked the question, Cordelia imagined how that would go. May must have felt deep shame to keep Ben's identity hidden all these years, especially as she obviously cared for him deeply. From what Cordelia had heard, many women took this type of secret to their grave.

Ben shuffled the letters into a neat pile without really looking at them. 'I've spent sleepless nights wondering what to do. Not just about letting May... Mum know that I know about Edward, but so that she and I can have an honest relationship.'

He stood up and went to the window, resting his head against the glass. 'In the end I've decided not to say anything – not at the moment. I might change my mind, but the last thing I want to do is embarrass her. She's always been so good to me. And because I found these letters, I decided not to look through Mum's tin as I'd planned.'

He turned and she could see he was waiting for her reaction.

'I think that's a very considerate response. And if an opportunity to say something comes up in the future it's still an option. But there's something else. You and I are cousins, I'm sure you've worked that out. Have you thought about whether you'd want to make yourself known to my family?'

He took a deep breath and sighed. 'I've turned that over a million times in my head too when I realised this Edward must be part of your family. But I won't do anything. Apart from these letters, there is no proof that Edward was my father.' He hesitated. 'I don't know your parents, but some people faced with this situation would be very unpleasant – even saying that May could have had more than one boyfriend. I won't... risk bringing stress and shame to May – to my mother. She's suffered enough.'

Cordelia understood his caution but wanted him to know that she would support him in any way she could. 'Whatever you decide, you should remember that you have a cousin now who wants to help in any way possible.'

The clock on her desk ticked softly as Ben absorbed her words. Outside her office, she could hear Jane saying goodbye to the last reader, the familiar sounds of the library closing for the day. The sound of chairs being put in their correct places, the till being opened and closed, the door being locked.

'That means a lot,' he said. 'To think I only came in here for a bit of advice and now I find a new relative I never knew about. One I'll see every time I come into the library.' He looked down at his hands. 'Each time I think about the letters, I think about my mother – May – how young she was to deal with losing the love of her life and being in the family way too. Carrying all those secrets for years...' He trailed off. 'But with my mum... grandmother... they gave me a happy childhood. I'd do anything to protect her memory too.'

Cordelia smiled at him, impressed by his maturity and consideration for May. 'I respect your decision, Ben. But I was wondering if I could help in a small way. I could probably find some photos of Edward, your father, and write down little family stories about him. That would help you understand where you come from more.'

His face lit up like a child's on Christmas morning, full of wonder and delight. 'That would be wonderful if you can.'

'We have a photograph album at home. There's a picture of him standing next to my father, who is, after all, your uncle. I think you'll be surprised how much you look like your father.'

His smile widened even further. 'I'd love to see that. All my life I've wondered who I look like – not May – my colouring is very different.' He picked up the letters and wrapped them back in their newspaper package. 'Thank you, Miss Carmichael. For all your help.'

She grinned. 'I think you can call me Cordelia, don't you? We are cousins, after all.'

As she watched him leave, Cordelia thought about families. How often they had secrets, and how often those secrets caused rifts between people. She wouldn't let that happen. Even if Ben never took things further, he would know about his other family.

46

The library's main reading room had been transformed for the opening of the exhibition of Evelyn and Captain John Findlay's story. Rows of chairs faced the simple podium, while the display itself stood to one side, covered by a quilt donated by the ladies of the quilting circle. Behind it was Evelyn's comb, gleaming and surrounded by carefully chosen documents: her birth and death certificates, the soldier's letters and the faded newspaper clipping.

The Prof had found more – another two newspaper cuttings about events Evelyn had been involved in and a photograph of each of them. Separate, as they had been in life and death. He had also provided items from the period – books, a hat, a pair of lace gloves, a newspaper and an embroidered handkerchief. Bunting hung from the bookshelves and the scent of wildflowers and twigs collected by Joyce and Linda adorned the circulation desk.

Closed for the afternoon to allow the librarians and the Prof to prepare, the doors were once again opened, and guests began to arrive.

'Cor,' Mavis said, trying to count them. 'I 'ope we've got enough refreshments for this lot. I wonder 'ow many are interested or just fancy some freebies.'

Jane nudged her. 'You're such a cynic! Either way, it's great there are so many here.'

There was a mixture of library regulars, volunteers from the history society and newcomers curious about what was going on. All were greeted with a smile and warm welcome.

When it seemed as if no more people were arriving, the Prof opened the ceremony, getting attention by tapping a spoon on a cup. 'I'm so delighted to see so many of you this evening. History isn't just about dates and facts, as you may have been taught at school – it's about people. In this case, two people whose story was cut short.' His rich voice was warm yet carried authority. 'Evelyn and her lover lived in a different world from that we inhabit today, yet their story reminds us that love is universal and timeless. As history society members and librarians, we are thrilled to be the custodians of such an important and tragic story, ensuring these two lovers are never forgotten.'

He stepped aside and Cordelia took his place. 'Thank you, Prof.' She turned to the audience. 'Without the help of the Prof, as he likes to be called, and other volunteers from the history society, this exhibition would not be possible. They have worked tirelessly to gather all the fascinating items you will shortly see.' She paused briefly as more people arrived. 'You may not know how this all began. We found an old wooden chest that had been uncovered when work was done to repair the library after part of it was bombed. We librarians love a mystery, and we are thrilled to have found out so much about this one with the help of the history society volunteers.

'You can probably hear the water boiler bubbling away behind me, a sure sign that tea is about to be served along with refreshments provided by the kind members of the Women's Institute. Now, Prof, would you like to uncover the display, please?'

With a sense of pride, the Prof stepped towards the side of the room. It was in a glass cabinet covered with the blue and red quilt. Determined to make the audience wait a little longer, he continued. 'Every story begins with something.' His voice was steady and carried throughout the whole room. 'This story began long ago, but our involvement began with the librarians here finding an old chest, tucked away and forgotten. But within it, we found a universal story of love and longing, of service and sacrifice. Our two fated lovers, Evelyn and her Captain, were unknown to us once, but as we pieced together their story, we felt as if we knew them well. We felt sad for them. Their story is a reminder of what it means to be human.'

He paused and looked around at the waiting audience.

'Today, we unveil objects that reflect the lives of the two lovers across time. Let us all honour their story, not only for what it tells us about them, but for what it reminds us about ourselves.'

With a slow, deliberate motion, he removed the covering. The audience was silent for a moment as the display came into view. Then the Prof stepped aside.

'History is here now. Let us learn for the future. Enjoy the exhibition and your refreshments.'

Mavis and Jane were ready with cups and saucers on trays, along with donated biscuits. As the audience helped themselves, each of the staff enjoyed telling the part they had played in finding the objects and organising the exhibition. But they both made sure to include everyone, including the Prof who had done such amazing research.

He watched people looking at the exhibition with a sense of

pride. So often his volunteering at the history society was unnoticed, undervalued, invisible. Here he could see people were interested and overhear their comments. 'What a beautiful comb!' 'How sad they were never together.' 'She was so beautiful.' 'My grandmother remembers her. She said she was a lovely woman.'

When it was time to close the exhibition for the day and several people had already drifted off, the Prof spoke again. 'Thank you all for coming today to share with us this story of love and loss. The exhibition will be here for several more weeks so do come and look again. Tell your friends and family about it. And if you have any questions the librarians here will help. I will too. When I'm not at the history society I am often here. My last words: the past lives on in our memories – in your homes and in places like this wonderful library.'

47

Afternoon sunlight slanted on the small hospital garden and vegetable plot, highlighting the vegetables and the ivy on the shrapnel-wounded walls. Billy, an elderly volunteer, had just finished looking after the vegetable plot, leaving behind a fresh smell of turned earth. The scent mingled with the smell of antiseptic from inside the hospital.

Cordelia paused at the gateway to the garden. Robert was already there and seeing him filled her heart with joy again. Since he'd returned from duty in Africa, after so much time apart, every glimpse of him seemed like a gift. However, the army demanded his attention and the library hers.

'I'm sorry I'm a bit late,' Cordelia said, hurrying to join him. 'Another road was blocked by a fallen building.'

He was already rising, putting his book down and gathering her in a loving embrace. She breathed in his familiar scent, his woody cologne, the faint scent of antiseptic and that indescribable smell that was simply his alone.

'I've got a flask of coffee, here,' he said, leading her to the old wooden bench. 'Lucky the weather is kind enough to sit outside.'

She reached over and kissed his cheek, it still held some of the tan from his time in the field hospital. Day by day he was looking more like the man she had fallen in love with. The gauntness and wary look he'd had when he returned would soon be things of the past if everything continued as it was. How on earth had she managed without him all those months? She'd been busy with work, volunteering to fill boxes for soldiers and endless queueing for food. But even though she had enjoyed much of her life, there was always a hollow feeling inside. It was as if something had been ripped out of her body, leaving a gaping Robert-sized space.

'Here,' he said, pointing to two tin mugs and the flask. 'I sneaked an iced bun from the canteen.'

She watched him pour the rich brown liquid into the mugs, blinking when she noticed the smell of real coffee, not the awful acorn brew they'd all had to suffer. 'Real coffee!' she gasped as she took the mug from him. 'Wherever did you get that?' Her delight in his simple gift made him smile, the expression transforming his face into the one she remembered from before he went away.

He tapped the side of his nose. 'It's a secret, don't tell anyone or everyone will be wanting a cup.' He took a sip and groaned with pleasure. 'I'll give the game away – I bought it in Egypt. I only got a tiny amount and I've been saving it for a special day.'

A sparrow landed nearby, pecking for crumbs left by someone earlier in the day.

They sat happily sharing news since they had last met and eating the bun, leaving a few crumbs for the sparrow, who was immediately joined by half a dozen more.

'What I haven't told you is that the post is confirmed. The one I told you about, training medical officers in desert medicine.' He paused, turning the mug over in his hands. 'It's good work, important work, but I wish it was nearer.'

She reached across and squeezed his hand. 'It doesn't sound so bad; we can visit each other by train.'

He reached into his pocket and pulled out a small, red, slightly battered velvet box. 'I found this in a souk, one of those warren-like shops in the nearest town to our field hospital. The man said it was a hundred years old but who knows?' He patted the box and looked into her eyes. 'When I proposed at the cottage, I had forgotten to bring this ring.'

He opened the box, revealing a silver ring lying in a purple silk lining. Delicate Arabic scrollwork, so small it was barely visible, was on its surface.

'It's not much – you deserve so much more...'

'Robert, it's just beautiful. So unusual. It's very thoughtful.'

He gently took her hand and placed the ring in her palm. 'Hear me out, my love, before you decide which finger to put it on.' He took a deep breath.

A breeze stirred the ivy on the wall, bringing with it the sound of an approaching ambulance and the murmurs of everyday hospital life. They heard none of it.

'I love you,' he said simply. 'I've loved you since that first day I came into the library to enquire about using a room. I was struck not just by your beauty but by the warmth and integrity that shone from your face... I couldn't believe it when you accepted my proposal, and I am sorry I didn't have a ring to give you then. I'm hoping this will serve as an engagement ring until we find a proper one you love.'

She put her hands either side of his face, tenderly looking into his eyes.

His eyes locked on hers. 'Are you still sure you want to spend your life with me? I'm not much of a catch... your parents will expect you to marry someone with a title at least...'

Ignoring people inside the building who would be able to see them through the windows, she silenced him with a passionate kiss. It was far from their first, but they both felt their future unfold in that brief space between heartbeats.

'I don't have much to offer,' he began, but Cordelia stopped him by placing her finger to his lips.

She put the ring on the third finger of her left hand. 'You are all I need. All I want.'

He lifted her hand and kissed it. The ring caught the light, seeming to glint magically. 'We can choose a more traditional engagement ring soon, but this suits you perfectly. It's as if it was waiting all those years just for this moment.'

Cordelia turned her hand over, admiring the Arabic scroll-work which seemed to dance in the light. 'Do you know what this writing means?'

He nodded. 'The shopkeeper said it's an ancient blessing for love that lasts forever.' His voice grew thoughtful. 'He told me these rings were traditionally given when two people chose each other despite many obstacles – in our case distance, war, family expectations.' His fingers intertwined with her. 'It seems appropriate, doesn't it?'

A cluster of sparrows returned, emboldened by their stillness, still hoping for crumbs from their shared bun. The garden's relative peace wrapped round them like a cocoon, the outside world's sounds fading away.

Robert held her hand tighter. 'Even in my worst moments in the desert, writing to you felt like finding my way home.'

'Then if you agree,' Cordelia said, resting her head on his shoulder, 'let's not waste time. We can tell my parents soon and plan a small wedding in the village church. What do you think?'

The hospital bell chimed the hour and Robert started. 'I must go. I have to relieve my colleague, but let's meet this evening and begin making some plans.'

48

'Here I am a doctor, and I feel like a little boy at the thought of meeting your parents again, especially your father.'

Because they didn't want to wait long to get married, they were on their way to see Cordelia's parents. Not to ask their permission but to hopefully get their blessing and discuss getting married in the village church.

'I can hardly ask your father for permission to marry you, can I?' Robert's grin showed what he thought of that idea. 'Those days are past, surely.'

Secretly Cordelia thought her father might expect it, but they would deal with that when it happened. If it did.

The taxi wheels crunched on the gravel drive as Stonehaven Hall came into view. Robert's hand tightened on Cordelia's as the impressive grey edifice showed more clearly through the trees.

He shook his head. 'It must have been a terrible adjustment for your parents when a huge part of their home was requisitioned. How on earth did they cope?'

'Father was furious, still is, to be honest. He even tried to persuade Churchill to block the whole idea. He's... well, he's used to getting his own way.'

'And your mother?'

Cordelia thought back to those first few visits after the hall was requisitioned. 'At first she seemed as if she didn't know what to do with herself. She was used to running a big house, dealing with staff, holding dinner parties, and so on.'

As she spoke, she spotted her mother going into the door the family now used.

'That's her now. She began volunteering in the hospital, reading to the troops, that type of thing. It's been a big eye-opener for her. To be honest, we get along a lot better now she understands more how people NLU live.'

He frowned. 'What does NLU mean?'

She was almost embarrassed to say. 'Not like us. They've always categorised people into PLU – people like us – and those who are NLU.'

He shuddered. 'Gosh, that makes them sound like NLM – not like me!'

'Don't worry, Mother is a changed woman these days. She already likes you and you would never see much of Father. He'll probably give you a bit of a grilling though even though he's softer since his heart attack.' They walked round to the side door, and Cordelia stopped and kissed Robert gently on the lips. 'It'll be fine. They love you. Everyone does.'

Robert's laugh was slightly strained. 'After facing desert warfare, surely I can handle aristocratic parents again, or can I? This visit is different, after all. I'm a prospective son-in-law, not just a boyfriend any more. And I'll never be able to keep you in the style you're accustomed to.'

She laughed. 'I haven't lived here for years. I've lived in college, then in two flats in Silvertown. I'm sure you'll manage that level. In any case, I don't see myself ever being a kept woman!'

The maid of all work, Maisie, let them in and took them through to Lady Carmichael's sitting room. It was cosier than many other rooms in the hall, which were mostly too big to be comfortable.

Lady Carmichael greeted Cordelia and Robert with a wide smile and a kiss on each cheek. 'I'm so glad you could both come.'

Outside they could hear the soldiers singing 'It's a Long Way to Tipperary'.

'I do love hearing their choir,' she said. 'It is so good for their lungs and I'm sure it's good for morale too. The thing I enjoy most about church is the hymns, but enough of that, come in and have some tea.'

The maid appeared with tea and scones. The laden tray emphasised the difference in lifestyles between Robert and this family. Dainty cups and saucers on a starched white cloth, scones with jam and cream, and matching crockery. A mile away from his usual mug and soggy biscuit in a saucer, if he could find one.

Lady Carmichael looked at Robert. 'I didn't like to say so last time we met but if she's chosen you for your looks, it was a wise choice.'

'Mother!' Cordelia's face was red at her mother's words, so unlike her.

Lady Carmichael continued speaking as she poured the tea. 'Before I met your father, I was very friendly with an exceptionally handsome man. My mother warned me off him and she was right. In the end he married one of my friends and led her a terrible life.' She looked at Robert. 'Are you a trustworthy man?'

Robert almost spat out his tea in shock at such a direct question. Then he took a deep breath, wiped his lips with the linen napkin and looked Lady Carmichael in the eye. 'I've loved Cordelia since the day I met her. We communicated as often as possible while I was away, and I cannot imagine being unkind or unfaithful to her.'

She nodded. 'Cordelia has told me you are being posted away from London. Are you expecting her to leave her job and follow you?'

Cordelia could stand this grilling no longer. 'Allow me to answer, Mother, after all it's me you're talking about. We have discussed this. I plan to stay where I am for the foreseeable future. Robert's posting is not too far away, we'll be able to see each other often. And it seems as if the end of the war is in sight. That's when we can make proper plans.'

The door opened and Lord Carmichael entered, leaning on a walking stick and frowning.

Robert paled as he faced the none-too-welcome greeting. He stood as a sign of respect. 'I'm pleased to meet you again, sir. Will you join us for tea?'

Lord Carmichael frowned. 'Hmm. It's usually my wife who invites me, not a guest.' As her father settled himself, Cordelia saw that he had spotted her ring. His eyes opened wide in amazement. 'Does that... ring there mean you have committed yourself to each other without consulting me?'

Cordelia went over to him, perched on the arm of his chair and kissed his cheek, a rare physical gesture between them. 'Daddy, this is 1943, not 1800. Men don't need to ask a girl's father's permission to marry her these days. We are not chattels to be passed from one man to another.'

Her father's expression remained stern, though his eyes softened slightly at his daughter's kiss and he patted her knee. 'The world may be changing, my dear, but courtesy remains constant.

And you...' His gaze turned to Robert. 'As a military man you should understand the importance of proper protocol. We had hoped she would find someone with a title and the promise of a handsome inheritance. Do you have either?'

'I'm afraid I don't. I appreciate your view, sir,' Robert said, his voice steady despite tension showing in his face. 'This war has taught us that life is too precious and too uncertain to delay things unnecessarily. Cordelia has lived through the Blitz, and I have treated endless men in the desert, many of whom died or had their lives changed forever. I can promise you I will love and take care of your daughter always.'

Cordelia went back to her seat. 'I understand you wanting to protect me, Father, but I'm a woman with my own mind, my own career, and now my own choice of husband.'

'But a wartime marriage.' Lord Carmichael went on shaking his head. 'Our neighbour's daughter married last year. She was widowed within six months.'

There was a long pause, then Lady Carmichael put down her cup and spoke. 'May I remind you, dear, of a certain young officer who proposed to me in 1917. My parents had exactly the same objections as you now.' She turned to Cordelia and Robert. 'We married two weeks later, against everyone's advice. Sometimes, especially in times of war, the heart simply knows best.'

49

'Gosh, I didn't realise they'd finished it. It's very impressive, isn't it?'

Cordelia and Jane stood outside the new BBC building in Portland Place. It was very distinctive, a curved shape with smooth clean lines and large windows covered in blast tape, a reminder of wartime regulations. A large, bold sign saying BBC was prominently displayed, reminding people how important the organisation was.

Jane's face was so pale, Cordelia worried she might pass out any minute. She linked her arm through her friend's. 'Slow breaths, Jane. In for the count of five, out for the count of seven. Take your time, we're a bit early.'

She pressed Jane's arm tight to her side and demonstrated the breathing technique until she saw her friend was calming.

'I suppose... we'd better go in.' Jane was still looking shaky but, holding Cordelia's arm, took a step forward.

'Remember, they approached *you*. That talent scout thought you'd be perfect. And you are!'

People rushed past them, their voices rising and falling like the tide, each absorbed in their own world, oblivious to the two women nervously about to go in. One of them faced an audition that might change her life forever. A man pushing a large trolley huffed and puffed as he forced his way to a side door. Two young women were smoking and talking as they walked towards the main entrance.

Cordelia gently tugged Jane towards the door with determination. The reception area buzzed with energy, a busy hub where the sounds of ringing telephones and lively conversations competed to be heard. Staff hurried past, their footsteps echoing on the polished floors. In one area, a small group of people sat, all looking frightened.

Jane pulled her handbag further onto her shoulder. 'Do you think they're here for the test too?'

As they waited for their turn, they looked at the photos on the wall.

'I don't know who he is.' Jane was looking at a very formal and important man.

'I think that one over there is John Leith. He was in charge of the BBC. I believe he's doing war work now. But look, there's Tommy Handley, and goodness, David Niven, Joyce Grenfell – I love her monologues...'

Jane took over naming the famous people. 'Margaret Rutherford, Laurence Olivier... I didn't know they were on the wireless.'

'I expect they just do the occasional programme. Some others are regulars.' Cordelia felt a thrill being in the same building that so many famous people had also been in, people who cheered up the war-weary population.

'Wouldn't it be wonderful if I met one of them?' Jane said, her eyes wide with possibilities. 'Not that I'd know what to say. My mind would go blank for sure.'

They moved forward, closer to the reception area. The

receptionist sat at a sleek, polished desk, exuding an air of calm authority like the captain of a ship. She wore a tailored navy suit with a crisp white blouse. They complemented her elegant appearance, looking stylish and professional. She could have been a model or actress herself. Her dark hair was cut in a bob, parted at the side, with a rigid wave.

They noticed how confident she looked as she dealt with the public. 'I'm a great believer in copying how someone moves if they impress me,' Cordelia whispered to Jane. 'Look how she holds herself. I bet if you did that when you meet Mr... what's his name?'

'Fisher. Patrick Fisher.'

'Mr Fisher, he'd never know you feel nervous, and you'd soon feel confident too.'

Then it was their turn. 'How may I help you?' The receptionist's voice was as cut-glass as the BBC news announcers' voices.

'I'm here to see Mr Fisher,' Jane said, and Cordelia noticed she held herself upright, shoulders back. 'Patrick Fisher.'

The receptionist looked at a list in front of her. 'Your name, please?'

'I'm Mrs Wilkins. Jane Wilkins.'

The receptionist ran her fingers down the list in front of her. 'Ah, yes, he's expecting you. You're a little early.' She indicated some seats to one side. 'Wait over there and someone will come to get you.'

They sat where they'd been told and watched people come and go. Jane looked down at her dress and shoes. 'They're all terribly smart. I'm glad I found this dress at the jumble sale to alter. It's a good make at least.'

'It suits you very well. That blue matches your eyes, and the slim skirt shows off your figure.'

The front doors opened and there was a commotion as a group of people walked through, all surrounding one man.

'It's Tommy Handley!' Jane gasped, her eyes widening in disbelief. 'Wait 'til I tell Mavis I've seen him, he's her favourite. She'll be so jealous!'

The buzz in the room intensified as the group made their way through the area, leaving a trail of whispers and star-struck glances in their wake. Jane watched, star-struck herself, as the popular personality disappeared down a corridor to the left, his infectious laughter echoing behind him.

At first they didn't notice the young woman standing in front of them.

'Mrs Wilkins?' she said, getting their attention. 'I'm Margaret Thorpe. Mr Fisher's assistant. Welcome to the BBC. Follow me, please.'

50

They followed Mr Fisher's assistant through several corridors, convinced they'd never find their way out again. Behind each door they heard typewriters, voices and once or twice singing and music being played.

'I'm terrified!' Jane whispered, clutching on to Cordelia's sleeve.

'Remember what our cook told me...' Cordelia replied with a grin.

Jane sniggered. 'Oh, yes, they've all got...'

'Holes in their bums the same as us,' Cordelia whispered, hoping Miss Thorpe couldn't near her. But the comment had broken Jane's terror, and her shoulders relaxed as she took more confident steps.

Miss Thorpe opened a door into a moderately sized office, functional rather than lavish. The walls were painted a pale cream, with a few framed posters of popular BBC programmes on one wall. A large wooden desk dominated the room, its surface covered with papers and a large control panel. There was an ashtray on the table, with a pipe resting on its side.

Above it was an internal window that almost reached from one side of the room to the other. The room smelt of tobacco and papers.

'Mr Fisher,' Miss Thorpe said, trying to catch his attention as he had his head down studying a list of figures. 'Mr Fisher! Mrs Wilkins is here for her audition.'

He jumped up suddenly. 'Oh, I'm so sorry.' He turned to Jane and Cordelia. 'Which of you lovely ladies is auditioning today?' He was in his forties with a bald head and an air of confidence.

Jane seemed to be frozen to the spot so Cordelia nudged her, hoping Mr Fisher wouldn't notice.

'It's me. I'm Jane Wilkins.'

'Ah, yes. You are the singer our scout recommended. I've been looking forward to your audition. We need some additional singers.' He looked at Cordelia as if appraising her. 'And you are?'

'I'm just a friend of Jane's. Miss Carmichael.'

He raised an eyebrow and gave a creepy smile. 'Pity.' He pulled down the corners of his mouth in mock unhappiness. 'Can you sing? Dance? Anything?'

She wanted to give him a rude answer. *Unless you're about to offer me a starring role alongside Vera Lynn, perhaps we could concentrate on Jane's audition.*

But she couldn't do it. If she did it might ruin Jane's chances of acceptance. Instead, she just gave a half smile and muttered, ''Fraid not,' then she turned to Jane, who was still looking through the window into the recording studio the other side.

It was a moderately sized room with walls covered in panels that Cordelia assumed were some sort of soundproofing. A large microphone on a stand was in the centre of the room. She'd seen them on a film once and heard they were called Apple and Biscuit microphones. To one side was a table covered with a control panel not unlike the one in front of her on the desk.

She slipped her hand into Jane's. 'It's no more than you did at the ENSA show. You'll be fine. Remember how you wowed them then.'

'We're good to go!' a disembodied voice said through a speaker, making Jane and Cordelia jump.

Mr Fisher took it in his stride. He pressed a button on the control panel and replied, 'We'll make our way through now.' He picked up some sheet music. 'You ready, Jane? We will only ask you to sing half of your chosen song. That is enough for us to make a judgement so don't think we're being rude if we stop you before the end.' He gave Cordelia another creepy look. 'You can wait for her here.'

Jane had chosen 'As Time Goes By', the same song she'd sung for the ENSA concert. She knew it off by heart and felt confident with it. But she was far from confident in that room in front of that massive microphone. Her mouth had gone dry, and she longed for a drink of water.

Mr Fisher appeared not to notice her nervousness. Perhaps he had overseen so many auditions he just wanted to get another one out of the way without delay.

'Come over here,' he said, indicating the mic. 'Let me show you how it works. It's very simple. Hand me your sheet music.'

He put it on a stand in front of the microphone and for the first time she noticed an elderly man sitting at a piano against one wall. He gave her a friendly grin. 'I'm Dickie, your pianist.' His smile was warm and encouraging. 'I'll lead you in. I'm sure you know when to start. But we can always do it again if necessary.'

'But not too many times,' Mr Fisher said. Then he looked at

Jane. 'Nothing to worry about, my dear. I've heard you are a true professional, just sing as you did when our scout heard you.'

Dickie was gently playing the tune she would shortly sing as she learned how to use the microphone. Then she insisted on briefly singing the vocal scales to warm up her voice. She missed the first couple of notes but by the second repeat had found her sound again.

'Right,' Mr Fisher said. 'It sounds as if you're ready to go. I'll go back to the control room. From there I'll speak so you'll know when to start. Dickie will give you the lead-in and he'll stop at a prearranged part of the song.'

It was no more than four minutes later when Mr Fisher's voice spoke over a speaker.

'Ready to go whenever you are!'

Dickie turned to Jane. 'Ready?'

Gulping and trying to imagine she was back with those soldiers at the ENSA concert, she nodded. 'Yes, when you are.'

It was over in a flash. She blinked when Dickie stopped playing, wondering what had happened. 'That's all we need,' he said, then he looked up at the big window to the office. 'That one okay?'

'It was fine, but let's have it once more to be sure,' the reply came.

Jane took a few deep breaths, ignoring the butterflies chasing each other in her stomach. She loved butterflies, she reminded herself.

Dickie was gently playing again. 'Ready?'

She nodded.

'Right. One, two, three.' He began to play, and she soon joined in.

'You must remember this...'

Again, she was startled when he stopped playing, it had happened so quickly.

'Thank you, Dickie,' Mr Fisher's voice said over the loud-speaker. 'Now, let's do the other number.'

Jane looked up in shock. Another number? He'd never said there were two.

'What number?' Her voice sounded as if she hadn't had anything to drink for a week.

'"Boogie Woogie Bugle Boy",' Mr Fisher said. 'I presume you know it.'

She nodded. Everybody knew it. It was one of the most popular songs at the moment. She had even sung it in the pub one evening.

'He always likes to spring another one on people at the auditions,' Dickie whispered. 'You'll be fine.'

He immediately began playing the first few notes and Jane's heart lifted. It was such a positive, cheerful song about friendship, patriotism and energy. It was almost impossible to hear it without tapping your toes.

'Ready?' Mr Fisher called. 'Let it rip!'

Dickie winked at Jane and she joined in. 'He was a famous trumpet man from out Chicago way...'

As she sang, her hips swayed in time with the music.

To her surprise, they let her sing the whole song, not stop it halfway like with the first one. There was silence for a few seconds then Dickie clapped loudly. 'That was a real blinder, girl!'

Mr Fisher's voice broke through her euphoria. 'Jane, come back to the office, please.'

It was a short distance but Jane struggled to keep calm as she walked, taking deep breaths as Cordelia had shown her. Had her singing been good enough? She didn't think she'd missed a note, but then she couldn't remember a single second of it. It could have been terrible for all she knew.

She tapped on the door as if she were going to a terrible fate. Would she ever feel more confident about herself and her abilities?

'Come in!'

She opened the door halfway.

'Come in, come in,' Mr Fisher said. 'That was good. Now I need to ask you some questions. Sit yourself down. It won't take long.'

Jane glanced over at Cordelia, wondering if she knew what the questions would be. Cordelia just shook her head and shrugged her shoulders, mouthing, 'Don't know.'

'Here,' Mr Fisher said, handing Jane a glass of water. 'I know you girls get nervous during auditions. Just a few questions.'

He went on to ask her about her background, whether she had had singing lessons, what singing she'd done in public – her mind went blank and Cordelia had to remind her – what her aspirations were and, lastly, what her husband would think. Would he agree to her working for the BBC?

It was all Cordelia could do to stop herself jumping down his throat. What had Jane's husband got to do with it? But she took a deep breath and reminded herself that some women wouldn't do anything their husbands disagreed with.

'If I'm accepted, what sort of programmes would I be involved in?' Jane asked.

'I expect you'll have heard of them all. Things like *Workers' Playtime*, *Variety Bandbox*, *Music While You Work*. They're all very popular.'

Finally, he put down his pen and smiled at her.

'That's all we need for now, Mrs Wilkins. We'll be in touch soon.'

Jane's jaw dropped open. 'You don't tell me now then?'

He looked at her pityingly. 'I'm afraid not. We audition several people on the same day, so we have to choose between them. But you'll hear soon.' He stood up and patted her on the shoulder. 'You did well, my dear.'

His assistant showed them out, making small talk as they walked. She'd clearly been instructed not to give anything away. But as she said goodbye, she whispered to Jane, 'You did a lot better than the last one!'

* * *

Two weeks later, Jane received a letter.

Dear Mrs Wilkins,

We are pleased to inform you that following your recent audition, you have been selected to join our roster of singers.

We believe your voice would be a valuable addition to our musical broadcasts. We would like to discuss your potential engagements and scheduling at your earliest convenience.

Please kindly telephone our office at the number above to arrange a meeting. Our switchboard is open Monday to Friday 9 a.m. to 5 p.m.

Yours sincerely,

Richard Fisher (Mr)

51

'Your dress is wonderful,' Cordelia said, stroking the pure white satin. 'Seeing it must bring back so many memories.'

They were in her mother's sitting room discussing wedding plans.

'I'm still disappointed we can't have a huge wedding, Cordelia,' her mother said. 'But at times of war so many traditions are changed or ignored.' She sighed. 'We'll just have to make the best of it. One excellent piece of news – your brother Jasper is coming down from Scotland, trains permitting.'

Cordelia's heart lifted. She hadn't seen Jasper for ages. He'd once been a reckless adventurer, skimming through the surface of life, gambling, drinking, never thinking of the future. But when he got in too much debt and the gangster debtors were after his blood it was Cordelia he turned to. She resolved the issue, and he reluctantly moved to Scotland to manage their elderly aunt's farm. To her amazement he loved it and would probably never leave.

'Oh, that's wonderful, I'm so looking forward to seeing him.'

'Now,' her mother said, moving the dress out of the way. 'The dressmaker will be here in an hour. I'm hoping you will wear the gown exactly as it is...'

This was going to be difficult. Cordelia had ideas for alterations to make the dress more up to date and more importantly her own. 'I really don't want to upset you, and the dress is beautiful but I've got some ideas...'

Her mother sat back in her chair and looked down at her hands, twisting her cotton handkerchief. 'Oh... I, well, I've been imagining you wearing it just as I did...'

Cordelia was torn. Should she give in to please her mother or have the dream dress she wanted?

She reached for her bag. 'Can I show you my ideas, Mother? It will still very much be your dress – just a few alterations. If you hate it, we can discuss it some more.'

The dress as it was featured a high neck and long, tight sleeves and a flowing train. Beads circled the neckline and cuffs. It was elegant and very much of its time.

Cordelia pulled a chair next to her mother and opened her notebook. 'See what you think, Mother.' The alterations were a scoop neckline with the beads moved to surround it. The train would be removed and some of the fabric used to make a belt with a bow at the back. A full-length layer of tulle would be attached to it. The changes still valued the dress as it was but brought it up to date.

Lady Carmichael studied the sketch and, touching the paper, looked up at her daughter. 'My goodness, Cordelia. It looks completely different. I'm not sure how I feel about it.'

Her heart sinking, Cordelia sat back down. 'Is it too much? Too many changes? My aim was to respect the beauty and history of your dress. You look so wonderful in your wedding photograph.'

They were interrupted by the dressmaker, Mrs Unwin, arriving.

'Do sit down,' Lady Carmichael said. 'We are just discussing whether or not to alter my wedding dress.'

Mrs Unwin handed her coat to Maisie and got out her notebook. She had already seen the dress as it was. 'Alterations are like magic spells, turning one thing into another. With a few snips and tucks here and there, it is possible to produce another masterpiece as good as the original.' The sparkle in her eyes showed how much she enjoyed her work.

She was brilliant at her job but never one to hold back her own opinions. She looked from mother to daughter.

'One good thing is you're about the same size so that's easier for me. I had to alter a dress recently that had belonged to a slim woman and a... shall we say larger... woman thought I could somehow make it fit her. I'm good but I can't do miracles! Now, where's the tea? I need regular refreshments to do my best work.'

She soon had Cordelia standing on a stool wearing the dress.

'You look like something from the cover of a *Vogue* magazine, sweetheart. Nineteen twenty edition, of course. But don't you fret, we'll soon have it exactly as you want. Now, where's my tools?' Opening her toolbox, she began laying out what she needed. Each item had a nickname. Her dressmaking chalk was Mr Chalky, her scissors were Mrs Snippy, and her pins Lord Prickly. As she worked, she talked to each of them. 'Now, where are you, Mrs Snippy? You're always trying to hide! Now then, Lord Prickly, don't stab me. I can't bleed on this wonderful dress!'

The door opened and instead of Maisie, it was Mrs Taylor, the cook, who brought in the next refreshments. 'I hope you don't mind me bringing this, Madam,' she said to Cordelia's mother. 'I'm dying to see what's happening to your lovely gown.'

Mrs Unwin downed tools quicker than a dog when it sees a squirrel. 'Thank goodness, my mouth's so dry even a cactus would feel sorry for me!'

Cordelia stepped off the stool and took off the dress, putting her silk wrap around herself as she showed Mrs Taylor her sketch.

'You'll look beautiful in that, Cordelia, just as your mother did when it was her turn. I hope you'll show it to me when it's done.'

She smiled at Mrs Taylor. 'I'll make sure you see me in it before I head off to church,' she promised. Staff attended weddings of anyone in the household whenever their duties permitted. Cordelia would ensure that Mrs Taylor did.

Lady Carmichael was studying the sketch of the dress again. 'I suppose a little modernisation wouldn't go amiss as long as we keep the essence of the original.'

'We will, I promise,' Cordelia said. 'It'll be a bridge between the past and the future. We'll use all the same beads and trimmings. I really hope you'll love it. It would mean a lot to me. I want you to be happy. And we have seeing Jasper to look forward to.'

They shared stories of mischief Jasper had got up to as a lad. Getting stuck up a tree, swapping all their shoes around so they had to hunt to find the pairs, eating all the cakes for afternoon tea before they even got as far as the cake tin, then being sick.

'He got a good telling off from me for that one,' Mrs Taylor said. 'There was a big dinner party that day and I had more than enough to do without making more cakes.' She paused and smiled. 'But he was such a lovable scamp, you couldn't keep a straight face sometimes.'

The mantle clock struck the hour and Mrs Unwin started. 'Come on then, Miss Cordelia, we need to get on. I've got another fitting later.'

As Mrs Taylor left, Cordelia donned the dress again.

'Remember, my dear,' Mrs Unwin said. 'This dress will be so stunning on you the fabric will blush.'

Mrs Unwin continued talking to her sewing tools and as she worked the atmosphere in the room shifted even more, filled with warmth and shared stories. Cordelia gradually felt assured that her mother would love the dress. Traditions were important, but there was always room for change when appropriate.

With every moment and every shared smile, she knew they were building something beautiful for her special day, one stitch at a time.

52

Jane huddled under her umbrella, looking at the building opposite. It was the headquarters of the BBC in Portland Place where she had come with Cordelia.

'Come on, girl,' she told herself. 'Remember the applause from the ENSA concert. They loved you.'

She was so busy giving herself a pep talk she almost walked in front of a car and had to jump out of the way, narrowly missing a deep puddle. She sighed with relief. She might only be on the radio, but she still didn't want to arrive with soaking wet shoes – her best ones at that. She would get paid for her appearance, but she had more important things to spend the money on than new shoes for herself. Linda had grown out of hers yet again, complaining they pinched her feet.

Pushing back her shoulders, she stepped inside, glad she had been there once before so she wasn't quite so overwhelmed this time. She approached the reception desk and was greeted with a warm, 'How can I help you?' by a receptionist with cherry-red lipstick and jet-black hair.

'I'm going to sing in *Workers' Playtime*. Can you tell me where to go, please?'

She secretly hoped the receptionist would look impressed, but she merely indicated where to go. Internally Jane shrugged. The woman must see much more important and famous people each day than a humble singer from the East End.

She was convinced she'd get lost as she walked down long corridors, all decorated with framed photos of people who had been on the BBC – George Formby, Rudyard Kipling, Benjamin Britten, Edith Sitwell, Noël Coward, Gracie Fields, Eric Coates, Winston Churchill, Vera Lynn and Peter Ustinov among them. She gaped as she looked at their well-known faces, feeling a complete fraud. Who was she to think she should be on the BBC too? She was just Jane Wilkins, unqualified librarian, wife and mother who lived in Silvertown. Nothing special about her.

Then she remembered the applause she'd always had. Perhaps, she told herself, she had one special thing – her voice.

Finally, she found the right room and knocked tentatively on the door. It was opened promptly by a young woman who smiled.

'You must be Mrs Wilkins – can I call you Jane? Come on in. I'm Millie – we're on first-name terms here. I hope I can call you Jane. I know you've heard *Workers' Playtime* many times so you'll understand that we would expect you to travel to factories to perform. They could be anywhere in the country.'

Jane nodded. 'I'm a librarian but I'm sure I can change my days off to make that work.' Millie's face dropped a little at that news, but she didn't say why.

They could see the next room through an internal window and an announcer was finishing telling the nation about the weather. As he finished and the BBC jingle played, he swapped seats with a man Jane recognised as John Meadows, the man who often introduced *Workers' Playtime*.

'He'll just do a bit of chat, then he'll introduce you. You're one of two singers today, the other one will be here later. Come with me. It's the usual format today – he'll read letters from listeners and one of the songs he's asked you to sing is a request, then we've got some light jazz – the band are in the waiting area. Then there's a comedy sketch, and very excitingly he'll be interviewing a special guest, Gracie Fields.'

Jane's heart leapt. Gracie Fields. She was going to be on the same show as Gracie Fields. 'Will I get a chance to meet her?' Her voice showed her excitement.

'Sadly not,' Millie replied. 'We've been told she's on a tight schedule today, so John is the only one who'll get a chance to speak to her.'

She led the disappointed Jane into the studio, a simple yet functional room, adorned with microphones and soundproof panels. A large clock on the wall silently reminded the presenters of their schedule. The programme had started and a comedian in another studio was telling one joke after another.

John Meadows shook her hand. 'You must be Jane, pleased to see you. You're on in about twenty minutes. You know both numbers, I presume?'

'By heart,' she replied, thinking how bored her landlady and daughter were with hearing her practise. He turned back to the microphone and read another listener's letter. This time it was a woman pining for her husband who was fighting abroad. She didn't know what had happened to him. Her story made Jane think of Mavis, who was still waiting to hear from Joe.

The presenter turned to her. 'Right, Jane, you're after this next piece of music. You know how to use the mic, don't you?

You'll be in the smaller studio next door. You'd better get in there now.'

She went into the smaller studio, relieved to see the same pianist she'd met before. '"Don't Sit Under the Apple Tree" first?' he asked by way of confirmation. She nodded. 'Then "It's a Lovely Day Tomorrow". You'll hear the countdown soon and John will introduce both numbers so don't start singing the second one until he's spoken after the first. He'll probably read out some more letters in between.'

As had happened before, her time singing was over so quickly she couldn't believe it was all done. As soon as she'd finished the second one, she heard John telling the listeners that they could look forward to hearing a lot more from this wonderful new singer. She imagined the applause she might have got if she'd been in a hall somewhere and hoped her singing had at least brought a few minutes' pleasure to those hard-working factory girls.

'You did well,' the pianist said. 'I can tell from what John just said that he's pleased. You'll be back!'

Jane thanked him and went back to Millie.

'That was great,' Millie said. 'I know this is your first time, but John and I had a discussion before you arrived. One of our regular singers is very ill, not likely to return and we are looking to fill her slots. John gave me a thumbs up while you were singing your second number. That was a sign for me to ask you if you'd be willing.'

Stunned, Jane was speechless for a while, then asked, 'How many sessions are we talking about?'

'Two a week most weeks. It'll mean travelling, of course, when we are visiting factories, but we'll pay your travel costs.' She saw Jane's hesitation. 'It's excellent exposure for you. If you want a career singing, you couldn't ask for a better way to be noticed. Who knows what it could lead to?'

Although she could think of a wealth of problems if she accepted, Jane immediately knew she would. She just needed to speak to George and discuss with Cordelia if she could go part-time. She knew Tom would be glad of the extra hours so that should be a good solution.

Her life had certainly turned around and she was determined to make the most of every opportunity. Life for the East End librarian was definitely looking up.

53

The morning sun streamed through the bathroom window, illuminating the delicate steam that rose from the bath. The walls were a soft cream colour and in one corner a pile of luxurious Egyptian towels were neatly stacked. Cordelia sank into the warm water, the fragrant oils swirling around her, calming her guilt at having more than the regulation five inches of water. As she closed her eyes, she could hear distant sounds of laughter and chatter from the household. Her mother must have put on the gramophone, and she could just make out the strains of Chopin's Nocturnes.

Jasper had arrived from Scotland the previous day and she thought how changed he was since the day he left under a very threatening cloud. Now his weather-beaten face was calmer, his eyes no longer haunted, his smile genuine. Instead of his usual brotherly teasing he was friendly, congratulating her on her forthcoming wedding.

'I haven't met Robert yet, but I hope he knows how lucky he is.'

She couldn't have been happier for him and for their relationship. Nor could her parents, if their reaction to his arrival was anything to go by.

She had asked Mavis and Jane to be her maids of honour. 'What, me, at my age? I'm a bit over the hill for that, girl,' Mavis had protested, but it was easy to see she was thrilled. The three women had had a wonderful time choosing dresses in several London shops. The choice was small because of clothing rationing, but they still giggled at some they were offered that were more suitable for a twelve-year-old. 'Too many frills!' 'It makes me look huge!' 'I look pigeon-chested in this!' They finally settled on simple pale-blue cotton – fresh and special-looking.

When the bathwater cooled, Cordelia pulled the plug and stepped out onto the thick cream bath mat. She stood in front of the long bevelled mirror, looking at herself. Like most people in wartime she was slim, and she had long legs Mavis often envied.

'I'll be a married woman this time tomorrow,' she thought, studying herself and thrilled at the thought. Although many would disapprove, she was relieved that she and Robert hadn't waited until their wedding night to become intimate with each other's bodies. She could only imagine how nerve-racking her wedding night would be after the stress of the day otherwise.

'Are you decent?' Mavis called, knocking on the door. 'Can I come in?'

Wrapping her towelling robe around herself, Cordelia let her in. 'Keeping me to schedule, are you?'

'I'll tell you what,' Mavis said, looking at her glowing eyes, 'you ain't even dressed nor got make-up on yet and you could already knock the socks off anyone else there.'

Full of fondness for her brave and hard-working friend,

Cordelia hugged her, then stepped back. 'You've got a gleam in your eye too. Has something happened? Something good?'

Mavis nodded and her cheeks coloured. She was buzzing with her news. 'The best thing of all. I 'ope you won't think I'm trying to steal your thunder telling you now...'

'I know you'd never do that. You're too thoughtful. What is it? What's happened?'

Reaching out for her friend's hand, Mavis stumbled over her words. 'It's Joe. You know 'e's in a prisoner-of-war camp. I never found out which one, but yesterday I 'ad a letter from 'im! 'E didn't say much, I suppose their letters are read by the bloody guards, but 'e's alive and that's the main thing! Me and Joyce went out for fish and chips to celebrate last night.'

Cordelia grabbed both her hands, and they twirled round the room, laughing at the wonderful news. 'I'm so, so glad for you,' Cordelia said when they stopped. 'You're such a lovely couple and Joyce will get her dad back one day.'

The grandfather clock chiming on the landing got their attention.

'Come on then, boss,' Mavis said. 'Time to get ready. You know that Jane's gone on ahead. She's a bit nervous about singing during the ceremony and wanted to try her voice in the church. She'll be back soon.'

'What about Linda and Joyce? Do they like their brides-maids' dresses?'

Mavis laughed. 'You know Joyce. She'd rather be outside playing and doesn't think much to pretty dresses, but she'll be okay. Linda keeps pretending she's a singing star like her mum. Jane will help them get ready when she arrives.'

They went to Cordelia's bedroom where she had a box of bobby pins and other things they would need for Mavis to do her hair. Cordelia was taken aback when Mavis had suggested it, but her friend just chuckled.

'Not many skills I don't 'ave, love. Let's do a practice run.'

And they had. Cordelia had been so thrilled with the result that Mavis got the job.

As they worked, they heard Jane arrive. She and the girls popped their heads in the door. 'We're going to another room to get the girls ready,' she said. 'Back shortly so Mavis and I can get changed.'

Then Mrs Unwin arrived with her sewing toolbox. 'Time for the magic,' she said with a self-satisfied grin. 'Always come to make sure the dress fits before my brides walk down the aisle, don't I?' She had the dress with her, safe inside a massive white cotton bag. She took it out and hung it on the wardrobe door. 'It's a masterpiece if I do say so myself. And I do!'

The three women stood and admired the dress, almost at a loss for words at its beauty. It seemed to send a warm glow throughout the room.

'You have excelled yourself, Mrs Unwin. I'm thrilled.' Cordelia couldn't take her eyes off the dress and imagined Robert seeing it for the first time. 'We'll be a few more minutes doing my hair and make-up. Do you want to get yourself some tea? Mrs Taylor is sure to have made some delicious biscuits to go with it.'

When she'd gone, Mavis expertly twisted Cordelia's hair into an elegant style, securing it with delicate pins that would be hidden by the veil. 'I know you want to do your own make-up, so I'll get on with doing mine if that's okay.'

From the next room they could hear the girls giggling and Jane telling them to stand still while she got them ready.

Soon they all appeared, the girls wrapped in the luxurious towels they had used when they shared a bath. Their mothers had wisely decided not to let them put on their bridesmaids' dresses until the last minute, despite cries of, 'Oh, Mum, let me wear it now!'

When she was ready, Mavis called to Cordelia to come back to the bedroom.

Taking great care not to disturb the new hairstyle, she helped Cordelia into her dress. 'I'll join Jane and the girls,' she said. 'I can't wait to see us all done up to the nines!'

As the dress slid over her slim hips, Cordelia felt a wave of happiness wash over her. The fabric hugged her in all the right places, elegant and breathtaking. Looking in the mirror, she saw not just herself but a ghost of her mother in the dress all those years before.

'You look pretty as a picture,' Mrs Unwin said, making very minor adjustments to the way the skirt hung. 'Fits like a blooming glove. Told you I did magic. My middle name should be Merlin. You'll take everyone's breath away.'

There was a tap on the door and Lady Carmichael entered the room. She stood and stared at her daughter, wide-eyed. 'You look so beautiful, Cordelia. I couldn't be prouder. You were right about the alterations to the dress. It's still recognisable as my old one, but very up to date.'

She reached into her bag and pulled out a pearl necklace.

'You're supposed to have something borrowed. This belonged to my mother, it's a family heirloom. Now it's yours if you want to wear it. Perhaps one day you'll have a daughter to pass it on to on her wedding day.'

Cordelia struggled to hold back tears as she took it from her mother. 'It's beautiful, Mother, thank you so much. It will be the perfect necklace for this dress. I couldn't have asked for more.'

As they spoke, Mrs Unwin pinned Cordelia's veil, taking care not to disturb her new hairstyle. 'There,' she said to herself. 'That's just perfect now.'

'The car's here!' Cordelia's father's voice called her mother to leave for the church.

She stepped forward and fixed the necklace around Cordelia's neck, then quietly went towards the door. 'See you in church,' she whispered, also struggling to hold back tears.

54

The final touches of her wedding preparations complete, Cordelia stood at the entrance to her childhood home, the gentle sun illuminating her lovely dress which flowed like liquid silk against her skin. Her heart raced with a mixture of excitement and nerves as her father, Lord Carmichael, adjusted his cufflinks.

The horse and carriage waited, both adorned with white ribbon that fluttered in the gentle breeze. The carriage itself was elegant, polished to a high shine, reflecting the beauty of the day.

Lord Carmichael cleared his throat, an unusual sign of nervousness which he would never admit. 'Ready, my dear?' he asked his daughter, his voice warm.

'Yes, Father,' Cordelia replied, holding out her hand for him.

They walked together to the carriage, and he helped hold the bottom of her dress out of the way to keep it clean as she stepped inside.

He climbed in beside her, closing the carriage door with a gentle thud. 'Ready, sir, miss?' the driver called out.

'Ready!' Cordelia and her father replied in unison.

As they rolled past the front of the house, several soldiers who were convalescing in the main part of the house cheered and clapped, several calling, 'Good luck!'

The carriage travelled down the winding country lanes flanked by hedgerows and birds singing in the trees.

'It's a perfect day for your wedding,' her father said, breaking the brief silence between them. 'It reminds me of the day your mother and I married. She looked as lovely as you do today, although I remember she was much more nervous. Her father wanted her to marry the son of one of his friends. They'd had it planned since the pair were children. He seemed to forget they had their own minds.'

Cordelia recalled her mother mentioning that. 'She told me the unfortunate woman he married had a hard time. I'm confident Robert won't be like that. I've never felt safer with anyone than I do with him.'

'Hmm,' her father continued. 'It took me a while to get used to him, but I agree you've made a good choice. Your mother's so proud of you, you know. We both are.' He turned to look at her. 'I know we haven't always agreed about things, and I've occasionally been a bit too forceful when we've disagreed. I shouldn't have done that...'

She touched his hand. 'You don't...'

'No, let me finish. I should have realised that the world has moved on. Women, even women in our circle, want to choose their own lives... I couldn't accept that you wanted to work in such a rough area for a long time. Your mother, though, after she'd been working with the wounded soldiers for a while, well, she made me see my views were too narrow. That I should see people for what they do, their actions, rather than their accent or where they come from.'

Cordelia reached across and took his hand. Now was not the time to mention areas they still disagreed on. His views were beginning to change and the last thing she wanted was to make him defensive. In any case, she knew that his hard work and indeed business acumen was what ensured that the family had kept their home when many others, people like them, had had to sell theirs. Mostly she was relieved he had survived the heart attack and seemed to get a little stronger every day.

'I've always admired you, Father, even when I've disagreed with some of your views or actions. I'm proud to be your daughter.'

The carriage rolled on, the rhythmic sound of the horses' hooves blending with the soft rustle of the wind in the trees. Cordelia glanced at her father, who seemed lost in thought, yet his face was relaxed.

'Not far now,' he said, a catch in his voice. 'Do you remember all the times we've been to this church? You were christened there, though you won't remember that, of course...'

'And we came to midnight Mass every Christmas Eve... and I went to Sunday school, which I hated. It was so boring.'

He chuckled. 'Your grandparents made me go to Sunday school too. It was boring then. Perhaps we shouldn't have made you go. But you did make friends there so perhaps it had its good side. And now, now, you are about to get married, stepping into a new life, a new adventure.'

Cordelia nodded, her heart full of happiness. Almost there. The horses were beginning to slow down, the clip-clop of their hooves changing pattern.

'We're here,' her father said, his voice firm and clear. 'In a few minutes I'll be a proud father walking you down the aisle. Giving you to another man.'

The carriage stopped and the driver opened Lord Carmichael's door.

'Wait,' he said to his daughter. 'Let me help you out.'

Helped by his steady hand, Cordelia stepped down from the carriage, her veil rippling in the breeze. She paused, taking a moment to gather herself. The pathway to the heavy wooden doors, open now, stood before her like a portal to her new life.

'Ready?' her father asked, holding out his arm. 'You look stunning, even more beautiful than normal.' A few villagers lined the pathway, smiling at the father and daughter, wishing them well. As they neared the church, the pathway widened, bathed in sunlight. It felt as if the very earth was welcoming her to a new life, each step a gentle nudge towards her destiny.

They stepped into the porch and paused. It was cool in there and Cordelia could just smell the rich scent of aged timber, mingled with the sweet, warm scent of beeswax from the altar candles. The familiar smell calmed the butterflies in her stomach.

Her breath caught in her throat as she looked through the inner doorway. The congregation sat either side. The four bridesmaids – two mothers and their own daughters – stood ready, holding their posies of flowers made by one of the convalescing soldiers who had been a florist.

There, at the front, was Robert, his handsome face turned toward her. Time seemed to stand still as they gazed at each other, and a wave of love and warmth washed over her. He looked dashing in his uniform, so smart Cordelia was sure every woman in the church would be admiring him.

'Shall we go in?' her father said. 'He's waiting for you. Your doctor.'

The reality of the moment reassured her. She was ready to step into this new chapter in her life, hand in hand with the man she loved. The man she trusted above all else. The man she would love for the rest of her days.

With one glance at her father, who smiled and squeezed her arm, she took a deep breath and stepped forward, ready to embrace that future.

55

ONE YEAR LATER

The library was empty, all borrowers gone for the day. Returned books waited quietly on the trolley, paperwork done. On such a lovely summer day, the door had been open so the normal library smell of books and polish was fainter than usual. The August sun shone low shadows through the taped windows.

Outside the newsboy shouted, 'Paris liberated! Read all about it!' The mood in the country was increasingly optimistic. The end of the war might be in sight.

The three librarians were doing a final tidy of the day. Mavis was inspecting more returned books to place ready on the returns trolley. 'Strike a light!' she said in disgust. 'Someone's only used 'alf a rasher of bacon as a bookmark. Wish I could waste food like that! Some people've got more money than sense.'

Jane was wiping the children's table and picking up paper aeroplanes left behind from the afternoon session. She felt a moment of sadness, knowing this would be the last time.

And Cordelia checked her desk was empty for the final time too. She stood at the door and looked over the library. It looked the same as ever – battered, past its best, but full of knowledge and hope. A place that offered help and support to so many Silvertown residents. She wiped a tear from her eye and pulled back her shoulders. This was a time for celebration, not sadness.

'Come on, girls. What's not done can wait!'

The three librarians sat behind the circulation desk, tired but content after a busy day. They'd been working together for so long they were firm friends and knew each other's hopes and dreams, triumphs and disappointments.

'Well, it's the end of a blooming era,' Mavis said. 'And I'm not talking about the damn war. Us! End of us! It's enough to make a grown woman blub.'

They clinked their glasses. Stout for Mavis as usual, cider for Cordelia and Jane.

'They say that endings are just new beginnings,' Cordelia said. 'What is it T. S. Eliot said? The end is where we start from. Something like that.'

Jane took a sip of her drink. 'I was thinking back over all we've achieved. Part of the library was bombed...'

'And we had to make do with the school hall,' Mavis said, remembering how cold and impersonal it was. 'But we soon got up and going again when the repairs were done.' She looked around proudly. 'Good as new, that's what people say. And we've increased the number of readers so Cordelia's boss is happy.'

'He's your boss from Monday,' Cordelia said with a smile. 'You're the new library head. You'll have the pleasure of all the paperwork and meetings with the boss, not to mention sorting out problems two new librarians can't deal with.' She grinned. 'Not that I'm worried about you. Any woman who can sort out greedy landlords and get rents reduced for half of Silvertown is going to find managing this library a walk in the park.'

A familiar banging on the door startled them. 'It's blooming

Bert!' Mavis said with a grimace. 'I'd know that sound anywhere. Oy,' she shouted. 'We're closed, you daft sod!'

The banging continued. 'Go on,' Cordelia said. 'See what he wants. He's a pain but it must be important.'

'All right! All right! I'm coming!' Mavis shouted, reluctantly getting up and walking towards the door. The banging continued as she drew back the two big metal bolts and turned the old key in the lock. It protested as usual. Bert almost knocked on her face in surprise as the door opened.

'At last!' He nearly fell into the building. 'I ain't coming in so you can wipe that frown off your mug.'

Mavis remembered she'd better start acting more like a manager. Politer. More patient. It'd be tough.

'Nice to see you, you old scallywag. 'Ow can we help?'

He'd had one hand behind his back and produced a bag holding three cauliflowers. 'I heard two of you were leaving, and you're being made manager.' He looked at her as if for confirmation. 'These are leaving gifts for them two and a sweetener for you so's you look after me in future.'

Cauliflowers. Not an obvious leaving gift. 'Um, thank you...' she started.

'I know they're not a normal sorta present, but you can pick flowers off the bomb sites any old day this time of year. Thought this would be more useful.'

Jane and Cordelia had approached the door and were, by now, standing beside Mavis. 'Bert, that's so considerate,' Jane said, taking one of the cauliflowers. 'I'll miss you, but I'll remember you when I'm in Broadcasting House singing on the wireless.'

She stepped forward and planted a kiss on his cheek. His cheeks bloomed bright red and so did his ears.

'*Sing Something Simple*, will it be?'

'And some other programmes like *Workers' Playtime*. I'll be travelling all over the place, visiting factories. It'll be full-time from next Monday.'

He scratched his head. 'Blimey. I'll soon be saying, "I used to know 'er, I did." No one'll believe me.' He looked over at Cordelia. "Ere's your cauliflower, boss lady. Make something nice for your old man. I 'eard you was moving away. That right?'

Taking the gift, she tucked it under her arm. 'Yes. My husband has a posting at a base near a little country town. We'll probably end up there permanently if he can get a post there after the war.'

She thought back to all the conversations she and Robert had had about moving away from Silvertown, a place she'd grown to love. It might be poor and smelly but she loved the mixture of people, the different ethnic groups, wonderful food types and of course the library customers.

Taking her lead from Jane, she kissed Bert on his cheek, trying not to notice the smell of cigarettes that made her want to heave. 'Do you know, Bert, we'd be lost without you coming in regular as clockwork to read the papers. Keep coming, won't you?'

He rubbed her kiss off his cheek and nodded. 'Course. Where else would I go? Anyway, one of them new librarians is a proper bobby-dazzler. Might take me mind off the racing results.'

Mavis raised an eyebrow. 'That'll be Miss Andrews. You'd be wasting your time there; she's got a bloke already.'

He tilted his head, expecting a kiss from her too. Her eyes opened wide in horror. 'You expecting a smacker from me? I'll give you one but don't go getting ideas! Thank you for the cauliflower, Bert. It's a very thoughtful gift.'

She grinned and kissed his cheek so lightly he probably

didn't feel it. But she managed not to wipe her mouth afterwards.

'Right, I'm off,' Bert said. 'See you Monday, Mavis, and you two...' He looked at Jane and Cordelia. 'Good luck for the future.'

He spun on his heel and was gone.

The three friends smiled at each other as they carried their cauliflowers back to the desk. 'They don't make many like him,' Jane said.

'Just as well,' Mavis muttered. She looked at her friends. 'Never mind 'im. I've got a bit of good news.' She paused for dramatic effect. 'I 'ad another letter from Joe yesterday! At last. It's been so long since I 'eard from 'im, I was really worried. 'E's still alive even if 'e's not 'appy! The letter was censored, of course, but it wasn't 'ard to read between the lines. Still, 'e's made some mates there and that 'elps. I'm not sure the parcels I've been sending 'ave all got to 'im, but 'e's got some, so that's something.'

'That's wonderful!' Cordelia said and gave her a big hug. 'The best news I could hope for on my last day. It's been such a worry for you. And of course, our other wonderful news is our world-famous singer starting her new job on Monday.'

Jane's smile was wide and happy.

Cordelia stood up and fetched two small parcels she'd tucked away earlier. 'These are little keepsakes for my two wonderful librarians. I've loved every minute of working with you. And Tom too. It's a pity he couldn't be here today, but I'll drop something round to his place before I head for pastures new. I am going to miss you both so much.'

Jane began opening her present.

'No, don't open them,' Cordelia said. 'It'll be a surprise when you get home. Something to remember me by.' She watched as they put the gifts in their bags. 'I've got some news, too.' She paused and waited for them to look up at her. 'I think Mavis has already guessed. She's dropped hints but never asked me outright.'

Mavis clapped her hands and bobbed up and down on her chair. 'You're in the club! I thought you'd put on a bit of weight. I can always tell. When's it due? I'll get knitting.'

Instinctively Cordelia put her hands to her stomach. 'Not for another four or five months. I'll have to learn to knit.'

'That's wonderful! I'll be busy sewing,' Jane said, hugging her tight. 'Let us know as soon as it's born so I know what to make. I'm going to be doing a lot of sitting on trains in my new job. Give me something to do to pass the time.'

As the day drew to a close, the three friends gathered their belongings and locked the library doors for the last time as a team. But outside they paused, reluctant to separate, the late August sun still warming their faces. They looked around at the familiar scene – people of different races and religions, smoke from the factories, the trolley bus trundling by, hooters from the docks, and children running past chasing each other.

They'd weathered some dreadful times together, the Blitz, the loss of friends and loved places, yet stuck together, always giving each other support and friendship. Now they prepared to embark on their separate lives, knowing that even apart their friendships would endure.

With a final hug and a shared laugh, they turned towards their futures, taking with them the strength and resilience their lives had given them – and the stories they had shared of life in the old library that had become their sanctuary.

* * *

MORE FROM PATRICIA McBRIDE

The next book from Patricia McBride is available to order now here:
https://mybook.to/BrandNewMcBrideBackAd

ACKNOWLEDGEMENTS

I would like to give huge thanks to Emily Yau, my editor. I am always so impressed with her fabulous attention to detail (never my strong point). Her help and kind support have ensured this book, and indeed the series, is what it is.

Thanks too to Ross Dickinson, who has provided excellent proofreading of this whole series.

My husband, Rick Leggatt, is always a great support and my number one fan. His willingness to talk through plot ideas and encourage me have been invaluable.

Thanks also to Maggie Scott, my friend who is so skilled at spotting my mistakes before I dare to send the manuscript to Emily. And thanks too, to Fran Johnstone, my friend and writing buddy, without whose encouragement I might never have written fiction at all. And Jacqui Kemp who reads all the books. Once or twice, I've told her what I'm planning for a character to do and she puts me right. 'No, you can't make her do that. It's out of character!' She's always right.

If you'd like to be kept up to date with my books, you can sign up to my author page on Amazon – https://www.amazon.co.uk/stores/Patricia-McBride/author/B001KDXEV8?ref=dbs_a_mng_rwt_scns_share&isDramIntegrated=true&shoppingPortalEnabled=true

ABOUT THE AUTHOR

Patricia McBride is the author of several fiction and non-fiction books as well as numerous articles. She loves undertaking the research for her books, helped by stories told to her by her Cockney mother and grandparents who lived in the East End. Patricia lives in Cambridge with her husband.

Sign up to Patricia McBride's mailing list for news, competitions and updates on future books.

Visit Patricia's website: www.patriciamcbrideauthor.com

Follow Patricia on social media here:

facebook.com/patriciamcbrideauthor
instagram.com/tricia.mcbride.writer

ALSO BY PATRICIA MCBRIDE

The Lily Baker Series

The Button Girls

The Picture House Girls

The Telephone Girls

The Air Raid Girls

The Blackout Girls

The Bletchley Park Girls

Christmas Wishes for the Bletchley Park Girls

The Library Girls of the East End Series

The Library Girls of the East End

Hard Times for the East End Library Girls

A Christmas Gift for the East End Library Girls

A Better Tomorrow for the East End Library Girls

Wedding Bells for the East End Library Girls

Sixpence Stories

Introducing Sixpence Stories!

Discover page-turning historical novels from your favourite authors, meet new friends and be transported back in time.

Join our book club
Facebook group

https://bit.ly/SixpenceGroup

Sign up to our
newsletter

https://bit.ly/SixpenceNews

Boldwood

Boldwood Books is an award-winning fiction publishing company seeking out the best stories from around the world.

Find out more at www.boldwoodbooks.com

Join our reader community for brilliant books, competitions and offers!

Follow us
@BoldwoodBooks
@TheBoldBookClub

Sign up to our weekly deals newsletter

https://bit.ly/BoldwoodBNewsletter

9 781836 333029

www.ingramcontent.com/pod-product-compliance
Ingram Content Group UK Ltd.
Pitfield, Milton Keynes, MK11 3LW, UK
UKHW040658210825
7506UKWH00018B/217

9 781836 333029